SPLURCH ACADEMY

FOR DISRUPTIVE BOYS

THE RAT BRAIN FIASCO

Grosset & Dunlap
An Imprint of Penguin Group (USA) Inc.

D0190129

GROSSET & DUNLAP
Published by the Penguin Group
Penguin Group (USA) Inc., 375 Hudson Street,
New York, New York 10014, USA
Penguin Group (Canada), 90 Eglinton Avenue East, Suite 700,
Toronto, Ontario M4P 2Y3, Canada
(a division of Pearson Penguin Canada Inc.)
Penguin Books Ltd., 80 Strand, London WC2R 0RL, England
Penguin Group Ireland, 25 St. Stephen's Green, Dublin 2, Ireland
(a division of Penguin Books Ltd.)
Penguin Group (Australia), 250 Camberwell Road, Camberwell,
Victoria 3124, Australia
(a division of Pearson Australia Group Pty. Ltd.)
Penguin Books India Pvt. Ltd., 11 Community Centre,
Panchsheel Park, New Delhi—110 017, India
Penguin Group (NZ), 67 Apollo Drive, Rosedale,
North Shore 0632, New Zealand
(a division of Pearson New Zealand Ltd.)
Penguin Books (South Africa) (Pty.) Ltd., 24 Sturdee Avenue,
Rosebank, Johannesburg 2196, South Africa

Penguin Books Ltd., Registered Offices:
80 Strand, London WC2R 0RL, England

If you purchased this book without a cover, you should
be aware that this book is stolen property. It was reported as
"unsold and destroyed" to the publisher, and neither the author nor
the publisher has received any payment for this "stripped book."

The scanning, uploading, and distribution of this book via the Internet
or via any other means without the permission of the publisher is illegal
and punishable by law. Please purchase only authorized electronic editions
and do not participate in or encourage electronic piracy of copyrighted
materials. Your support of the authors' rights is appreciated.

Copyright © 2010 by Julie Berry and Sally Gardner. All rights reserved.
Published by Grosset & Dunlap, a division of Penguin Young
Readers Group, 345 Hudson Street, New York, New York 10014.
GROSSET & DUNLAP is a trademark of Penguin Group (USA) Inc.
Printed in the U.S.A.

Typeset in Imprint.

Library of Congress Control Number: 2009053456

ISBN 978-0-448-45359-0   10 9 8 7 6 5 4 3 2

SPLURCH ACADEMY

FOR DISRUPTIVE BOYS

THE RAT BRAIN FIASCO

by Julie Gardner Berry and Sally Faye Gardner

Grosset & Dunlap
An Imprint of Penguin Group (USA) Inc.

To the original disruptive boys.
I love you dearly. You're still in trouble.
—J.G.B.

To my nephews, Keith, Johnny, Kiff, Seth,
Joseph, Wes, Daniel, Adam, and David.
—S.F.G.

A Word of Warning
to All Disruptive Boys

The story you are about to read is true.

If parents or teachers try to tell you otherwise, don't believe them. They're part of the conspiracy, trying to make you believe in chocolate chip cookies and happy endings, while secretly they plot your doom.

They definitely don't want you knowing about places like Splurch Academy for Disruptive Boys.

It's possible they've already begun filling out your application.

Cody Mack had never heard of Splurch Academy. He had no idea he was in danger, just from a few disruptive stunts here and there.

And look what happened to him.

Wait. You don't know yet what happened to him. But you will.

This book is here to warn you, to save you from a fate like Cody's. I won't say, "Stop being disruptive forever," because I might as well tell a hound not to bark, but I will say, "You might want to tone it down a notch," or just, "Keep a very close eye on your parents," and maybe also, "Look through their papers to see if they've been in contact with Dr. Archibald Farley, the headmaster."

You don't yet know who Dr. Archibald Farley is, or why you should fear him.

It's far safer to meet Dr. Farley in the pages of this book than to face him in real life.

Read and be warned. Read and be wise. Read and know what really happens to disruptive boys once they've crossed that line.

I suspect you still don't believe me.

In that case, all I can say is farewell.

And good luck.

CHAPTER ONE
THE MEETING

Cody Mack swung his legs back and forth as he sat in the plastic chair outside Principal Small's conference room. What was *taking* so long? Usually when his parents were called in, which seemed to be every other day, it was a short meeting, with words like "lock" and "room" and "had it this time." But from the voices coming through the keyhole, this meeting needed longer words, and lots of them. "Breakthrough brain research." "Remedial neuro-therapies." "Patented techniques." And it wasn't just his parents and the

1

principal. There was another voice, a deep one. What on earth were they talking about?

He slid off the chair and pressed his ear to the keyhole.

Just then, the door opened and out came Ms. Robusto, Principal Small's secretary.

"Mr. Mack," she sniveled. "Would you be so kind as to come in?"

Cody followed her. Around the table were his parents, Principal Small, and a tall, old, freaky-looking man who Cody had never seen before.

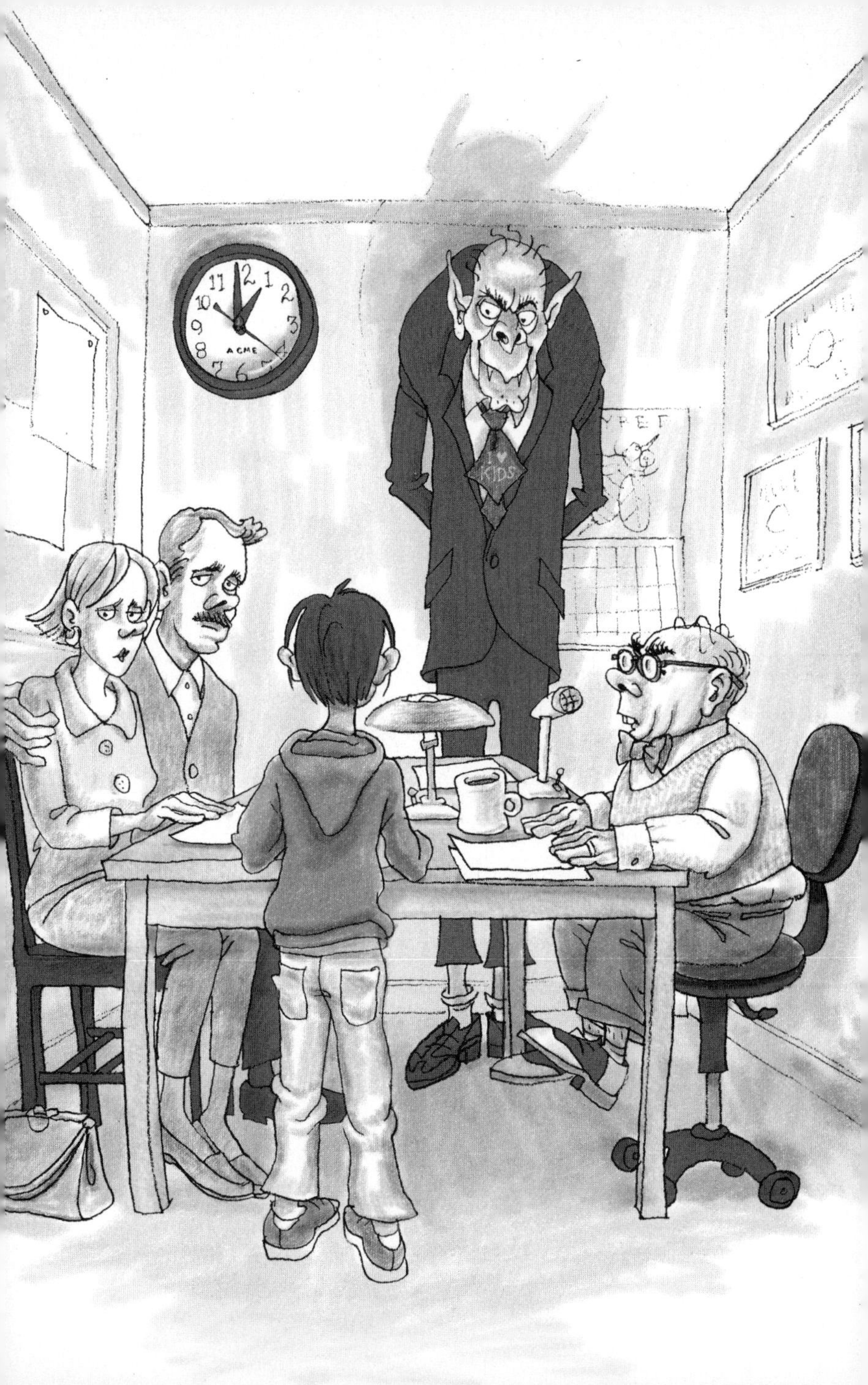
ACME
I ♥ KIDS

"Sit down, Cody," Principal Small said. "We've brought in an educational expert to help us solve the problem of *you*."

Cody blinked. "The problem of what?"

"The problem of YOU."

Principal Small rose to his feet, which didn't really make him any taller. "You see, Cody, in baseball, after three strikes, you're out. Not in public school. No matter how often your behavior disrupts *everything*, and makes it *impossible* for other students to learn, and forces my best teachers to *demand* early retirement, we are required to keep on teaching you."

Whew, Cody thought.

"This time, you have pushed us too far. Reports on your bad behavior have filled two whole binders. We've had enough!"

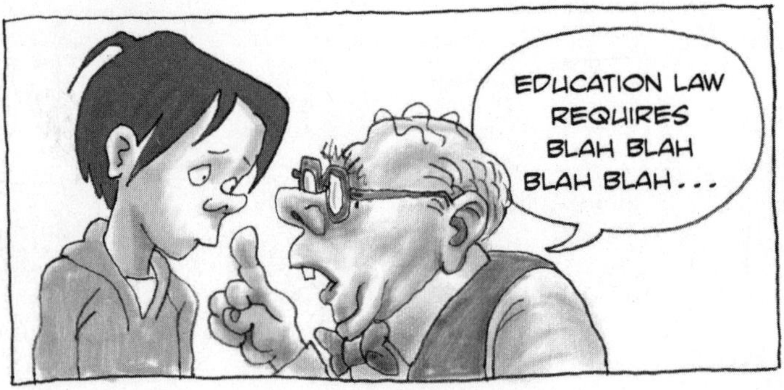
EDUCATION LAW REQUIRES BLAH BLAH BLAH BLAH . . .

Cody tuned out Principal Small's lecture. It was always the same. His throat felt full of cotton. His shirt collar itched at his neck. *I haven't been that bad lately, have I?* he thought. *Well, there was that rotten egg thing. Big deal.*

And then there was the fire.

Yep, come to think of it, definitely the fire.

That had been a shame, that thing about the fire in the teacher's lounge.

But other than that, Cody couldn't see any reason why Principal Small should be this upset.

Then, out of the corner of his eye, Cody saw the freaky old man licking his lips and grinning. Cody could swear he was wearing pointy false teeth, like something you might find in a costume store.

"Well?" Principal Small roared, startling Cody out of his thoughts. "Answer me!"

"Huh?" Cody asked. "Could you please repeat the question?"

"Aaargh! Do you see what I mean, Dr. Farley?" the principal said. "The boy never listens! He's impossible!"

So that was the freaky geezer's name. Dr. Farley.

"No, no, no," Dr. Farley said, flashing a pointy white smile. "He's like the dozens of other boys that I teach every day. Bright, gifted, clever. Talent and intelligence searching for an outlet."

Huh? Cody had never heard a teacher say things like that. Not about him, anyway.

"And do you really think you can help him?" Cody's mother said, her hands clasped together.

"Absolutely, dear lady," Dr. Farley assured her. "You'll be overjoyed with the results when we're through helping your Cody."

"Help me *what*?" Cody asked.

Cody's dad spoke up. "You see, son,"

he said, "Dr. Farley is a world-famous specialist in . . . well . . . in naughty kids like you. And your school has decided to send you to his special school, where you can get the best possible education."

Mrs. Mack dabbed her eyes with a tissue. "You'll really do that for our Cody?"

"In a heartbeat!" Principal Small said. "And, best of all, he can start immediately." Principal Small grabbed Dr. Farley's jacket lapels. "How about tomorrow?"

"Hold on there a second," Cody gasped. "Tomorrow?"

WHY WAIT? I CAN DRIVE CODY BACK WITH ME THIS AFTERNOON.

"Wa-wait a minute! This afternoon? You're joking, right?"

The adults all shook their heads.

Cody's stomach turned like he was in an elevator and falling fast. "But it's almost the end of the school day. Time to go home, anyway. How come Mom doesn't just drive me there in the morning?"

Dr. Farley adjusted his necktie. "You misunderstand, Master Mack. Splurch Academy for Disruptive Boys is a boarding school. You will not be going home in the afternoons. You will live at the academy with all the other students."

Cody clapped his hands over his ears. "I can't hear you, la-la-la-la . . ."

Dr. Farley laughed. Even with his ears covered, Cody could hear him say, "Ah, young Cody, you might not believe me now, but I can promise you that at Splurch Academy, you'll feel right at home."

Ms. Robusto cut in. "We'll need a signed consent form from the parents, of course."

Dr. Farley handed some papers and a feather pen to Cody's parents.

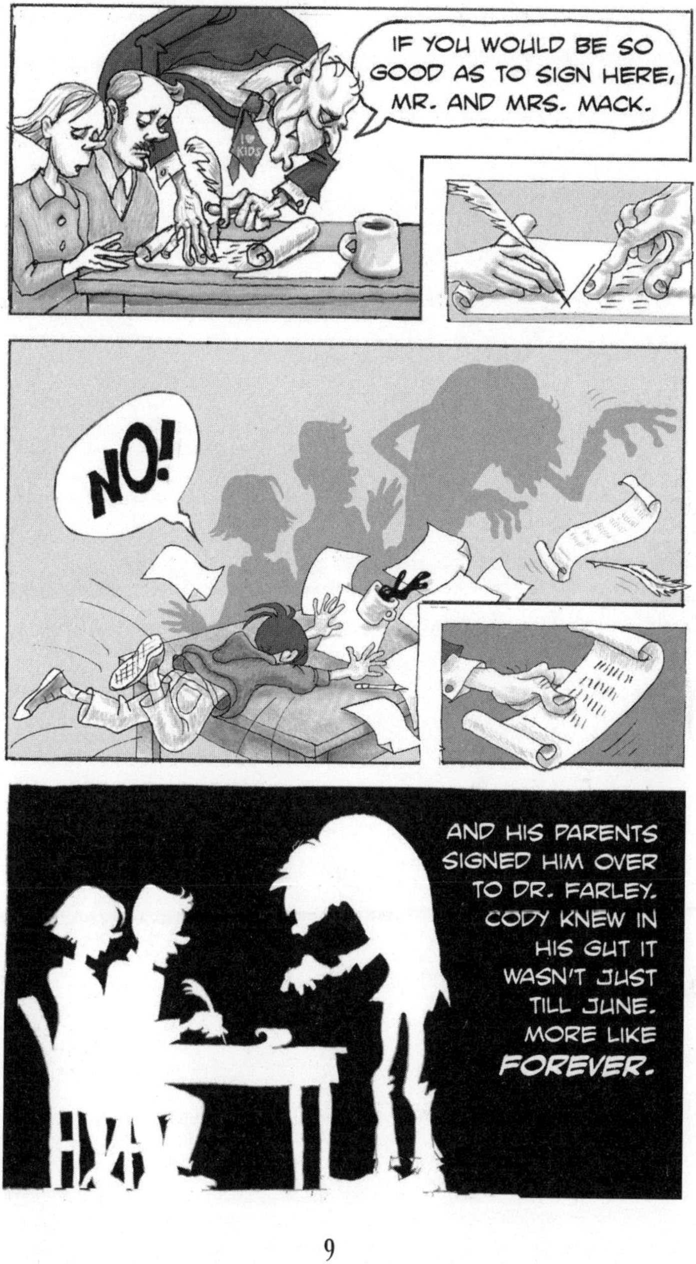
IF YOU WOULD BE SO GOOD AS TO SIGN HERE, MR. AND MRS. MACK.
NO!
AND HIS PARENTS SIGNED HIM OVER TO DR. FARLEY. CODY KNEW IN HIS GUT IT WASN'T JUST TILL JUNE. MORE LIKE FOREVER.

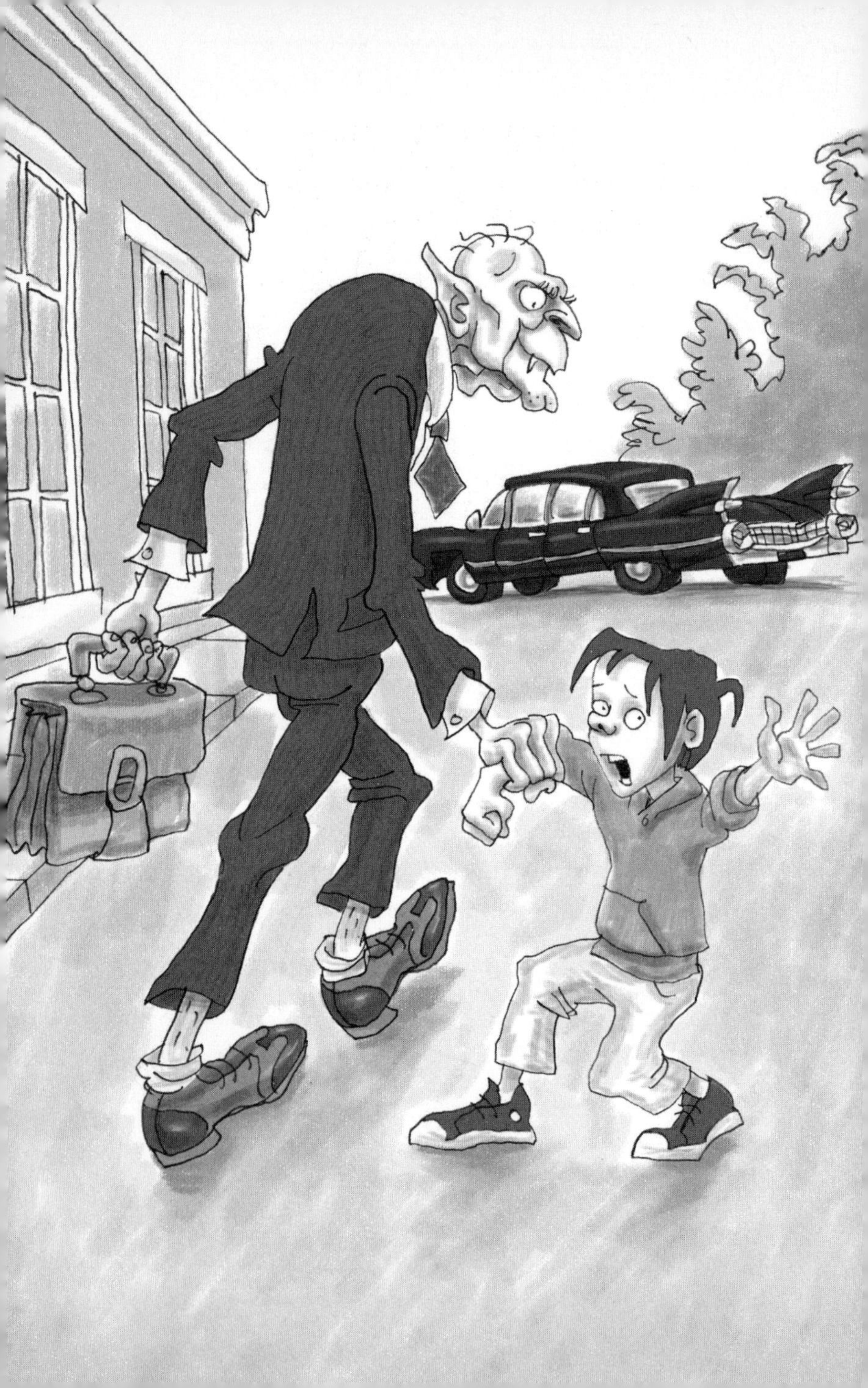

CHAPTER TWO

THE ARRIVAL

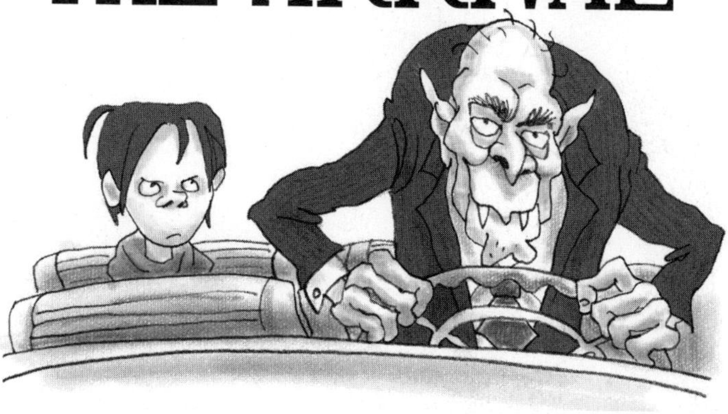

Cody slumped in the backseat of Dr. Farley's car, feeling bluer than an exploded ballpoint pen. His parents had farmed him out to a boarding school run by some creep who never trimmed his nose hairs! It was more than any kid should suffer. Even if that kid did break into Principal Small's e-mail and send Ms. Robusto a phony love letter. Still. Nobody deserved *this*.

Cody slid over so he was behind Dr. Farley and stared at the hair sprouting out of his ears.

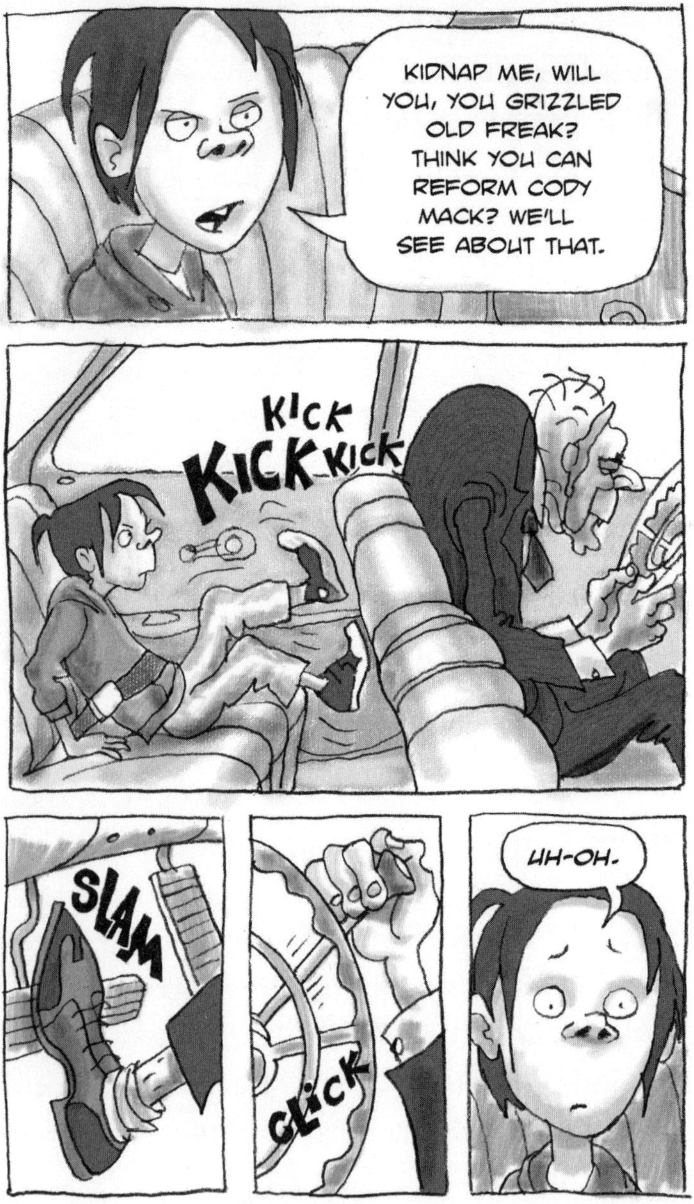
KIDNAP ME, WILL YOU, YOU GRIZZLED OLD FREAK? THINK YOU CAN REFORM CODY MACK? WE'LL SEE ABOUT THAT.
KICK
KICK KICK
SLAM
CLICK
UH-OH.

Cody's heart pounded in his chest. He didn't care. Let the old creep yell at him. It didn't matter. Cody Mack wasn't one to be afraid of some dumb principal. That was all a headmaster was.

Dr. Farley got out of the car and turned to open the rear door. His eyes glared and his teeth shone in the light.

Then again, maybe sometimes Cody Mack could be afraid of a principal. Just a little bit.

Cody scrambled to the other side.

Almost in the blink of an eye, Dr. Farley appeared at the other door.

Yikes!

Cody scooted back to where he was before, but Farley was already there waiting for him.

How did he *do* that?

Cody scooted back one more time, opened the door, and tumbled out. He took off running through the dark woods, sure that at any minute Dr. Farley would snatch him. For an old fizzle-fozzle, he was pretty quick.

But when Cody looked over his shoulder, there was no sign of anyone following him. Soon he heard Dr. Farley's car engine start and drive away.

Up ahead, through the trees, Cody saw a light. Was it a house? It must be. Whoever lived there would help a lost kid, wouldn't they? He doubled his speed.

But the light he saw wasn't coming from a house.

Cody's feet crunched to a stop in the fallen autumn leaves. Splurch Academy! The prison itself. He turned to run back toward the road.

But he hadn't gone two steps when he saw Dr. Farley appear from the shadows.

Cody crouched down low and tensed his legs. There had to be a trap.

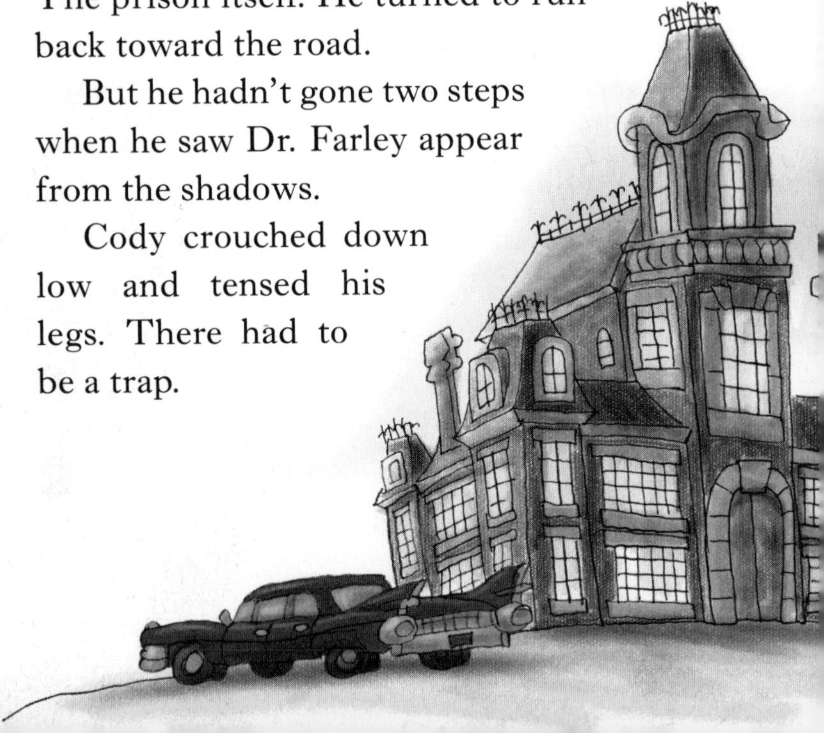

A night bird screeched and a wolf howled. Dr. Farley leaned against a tree trunk and folded his arms as if he had all the time in the world.

"Of course, if you ran all the way to the road, you might flag someone down who could help you," Farley said. "The funny thing is, boys who run away from my school never seem to make it as far as the road. Perhaps you could be the first."

Cody felt caught, like a moth in a lamp. He stared at Dr. Farley. How could he be so ugly? How was it even possible? And what was *with* those teeth of his? Were they getting bigger?

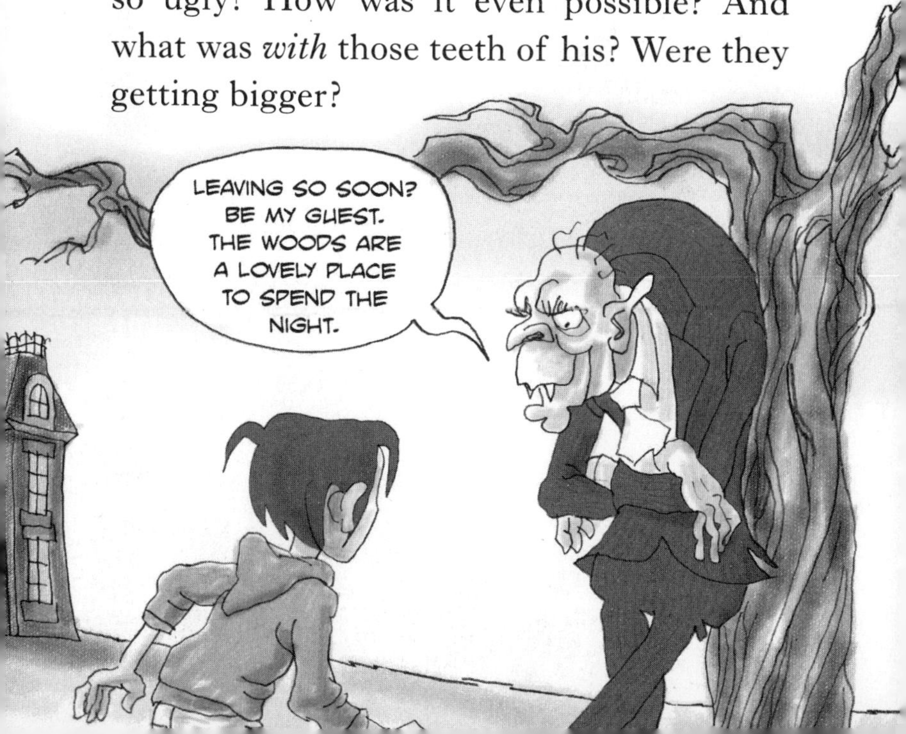
LEAVING SO SOON? BE MY GUEST. THE WOODS ARE A LOVELY PLACE TO SPEND THE NIGHT.

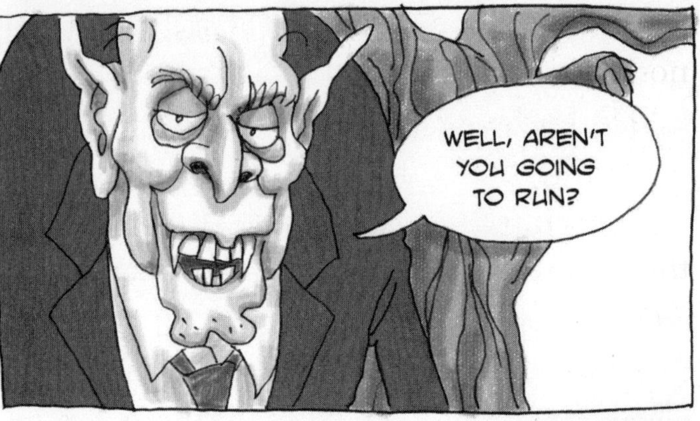
WELL, AREN'T YOU GOING TO RUN?

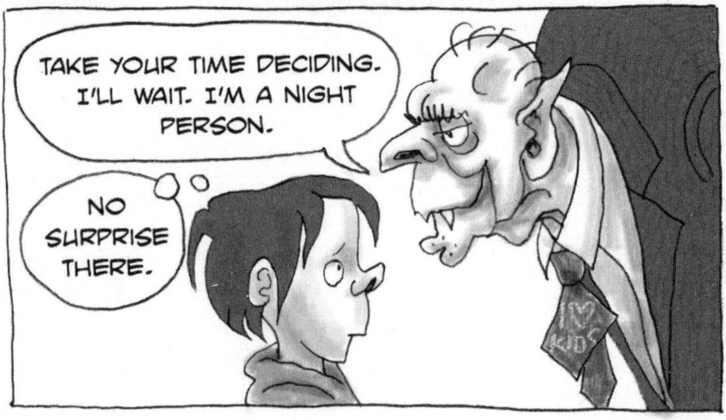
TAKE YOUR TIME DECIDING. I'LL WAIT. I'M A NIGHT PERSON.
NO SURPRISE THERE.

"I have a proposal for you, Cody," Dr. Farley said. "A deal. You come with me now, into Splurch Academy, behave yourself and obey the rules. That means no escaping, no devious pranks, no impertinence." Farley unfolded his arms and took a step closer to Cody. "Do everything right and I promise nothing bad will happen to you."

Cody gulped at this. "Whaddya mean, nothing bad?"

Dr. Farley shrugged. "You'll be safe."

"Safe from what?"

"From the things that go 'bump' in the night." There were those teeth again. *"And worse."*

Cody's heart pounded in his chest.

"If you don't cooperate, there are no guarantees," Farley said. "Accidents do happen. These woods are filled with ferocious beasts." He chuckled. "As for your behavior, the Farley Method is famous for fixing bad boys. Or rather, it soon will be."

Chills crawled all over Cody's skin. The Farley Method? What was that, weeklong visits to the torture chamber?

A cold wind blew across the dark lawns and spiraled up around the towers of Splurch Academy.

"I take it you've decided to stay," Dr. Farley said, giving Cody's shoulder a painful squeeze. "In that case, march inside. Your new classmates are dying to meet you."

CHAPTER THREE

THE HOMECOMING

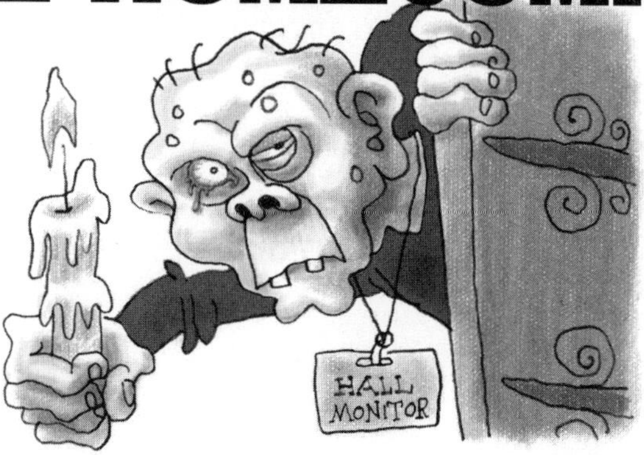
HALL
MONITOR

They reached the top of the steps. Dr. Farley pulled on a long rope, and Cody heard bells ring inside. Funeral bells.

Footsteps approached. Slowly, slowly the door creaked open. A bald, stooped man stood in the doorway holding a candle. The badge hanging around his neck read: **HALL MONITOR**.

"*Masssterrrr,*" he said.

"Good evening, Ivanov," Dr. Farley said, pushing past him and dragging Cody along the gloomy hallways. He yanked a door open and shoved Cody inside a small room.

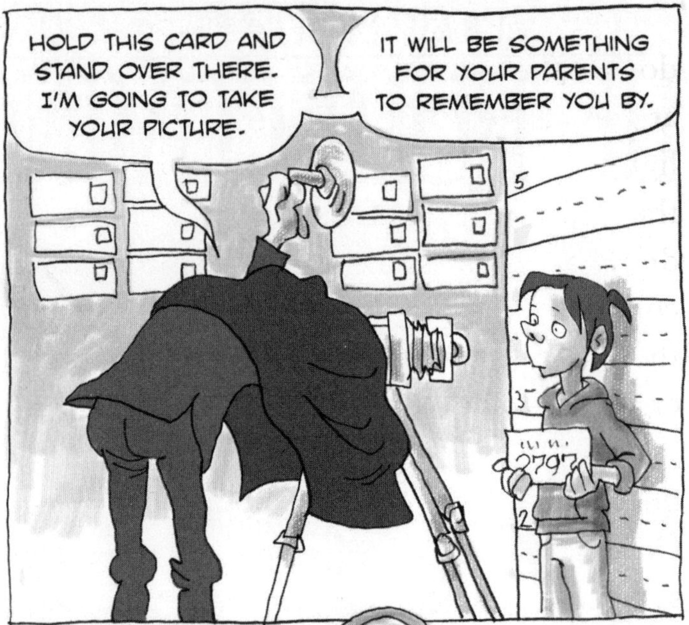
HOLD THIS CARD AND STAND OVER THERE. I'M GOING TO TAKE YOUR PICTURE.
IT WILL BE SOMETHING FOR YOUR PARENTS TO REMEMBER YOU BY.
2797

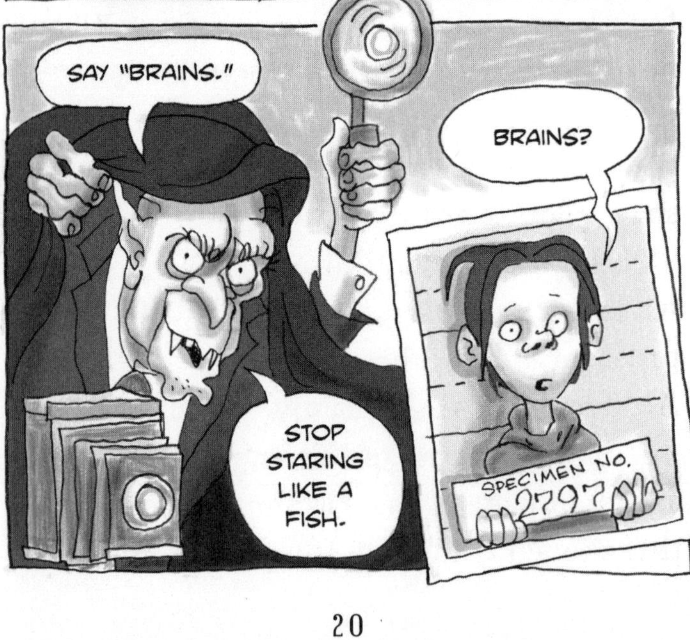
SAY "BRAINS."
BRAINS?
STOP STARING LIKE A FISH.
SPECIMEN NO. 2797

They left the camera room and trudged down the corridors. Flickering candles at the end of each hall provided the only light. Cody glimpsed cobwebs hanging on the doors of old, broken lockers and gross drinking fountains covered with strange-colored mold. A stick figure scratched into the paint on a locker showed kids with crosses for eyes. Dead kids. Dead meat.

Their footsteps echoed back and forth down the long halls. With every step, Cody's terror grew. How could his parents send him to this place? It was so unreal. It felt like it had to be a joke—like any minute now, someone's mom dressed in a pumpkin suit would pop up from behind a corner with a plate of cupcakes and candy corn and shout, "Surprise! Happy Halloween!"

But it wasn't Halloween, and everything was much too real for that. And Cody felt pretty certain that nowhere at Splurch Academy was there a mom.

Dr. Farley dragged Cody out the door and prodded him down the hall. Farley threw open a set of double doors.

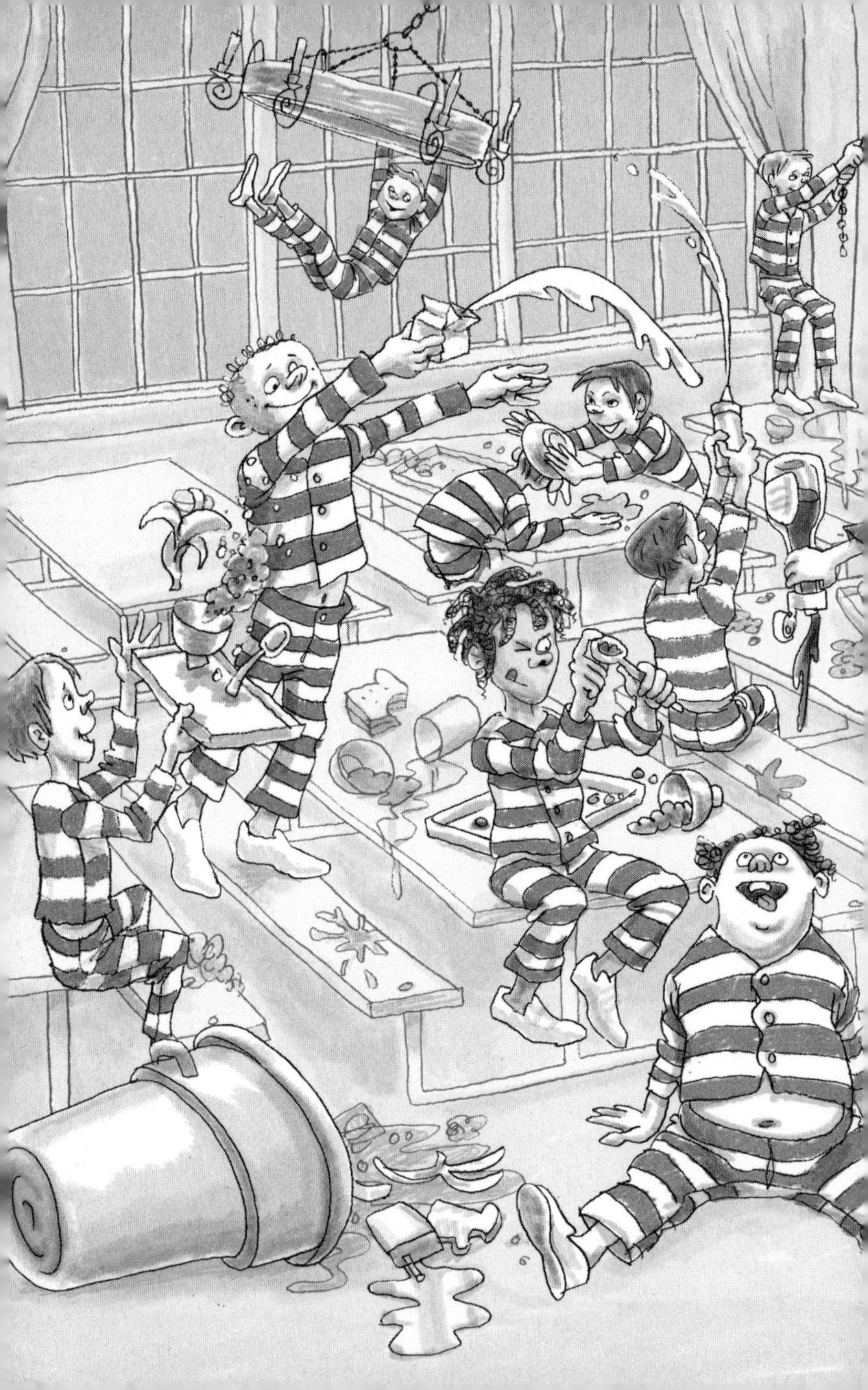

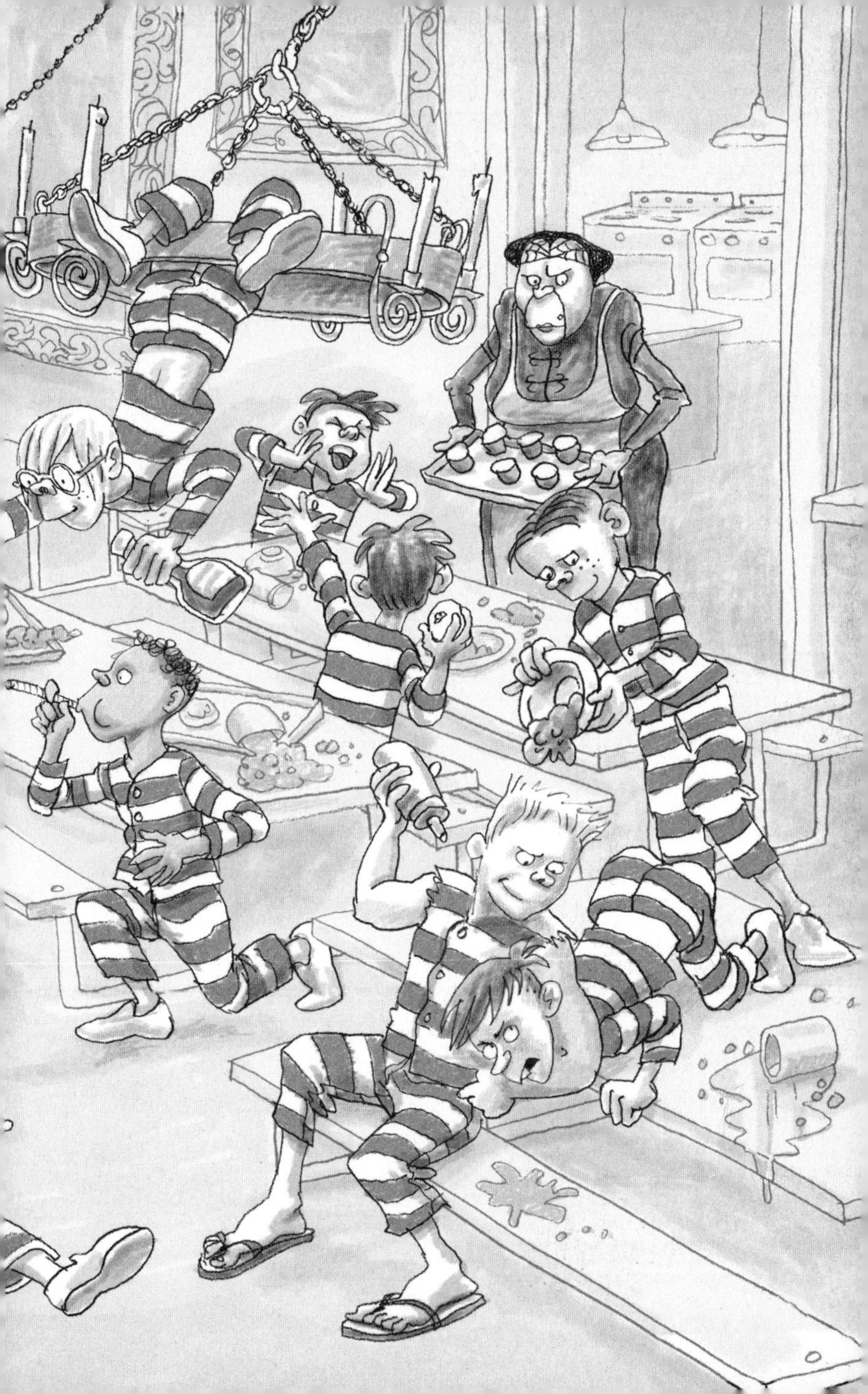

When Dr. Farley and Cody walked through the door, everyone froze. The hollering ceased. Then, as fast as you could say "brains," all the boys slunk back to their seats and sat, staring forward, hands folded in front of them.

These were his classmates?

Wearing *prison suits*?

Dr. Farley surveyed the room. "Tsk, tsk. Disappointing." He reached for a clipboard hanging on the wall and scribbled a few notes on it, frowning. He pointed at one boy and said, "Reginald! Name for me the capital of Turkey."

Reginald gulped. "Um, Stuffing?"

Dr. Farley's nostril twitched. "James, do you know the answer?"

James scratched his head. "Cranberry sauce?"

Dr. Farley scribbled something else on the clipboard. Then he turned to a sour-faced woman wearing an apron and a hairnet, pushing a sponge across the cafeteria counter. She looked like she'd lost a bad food fight.

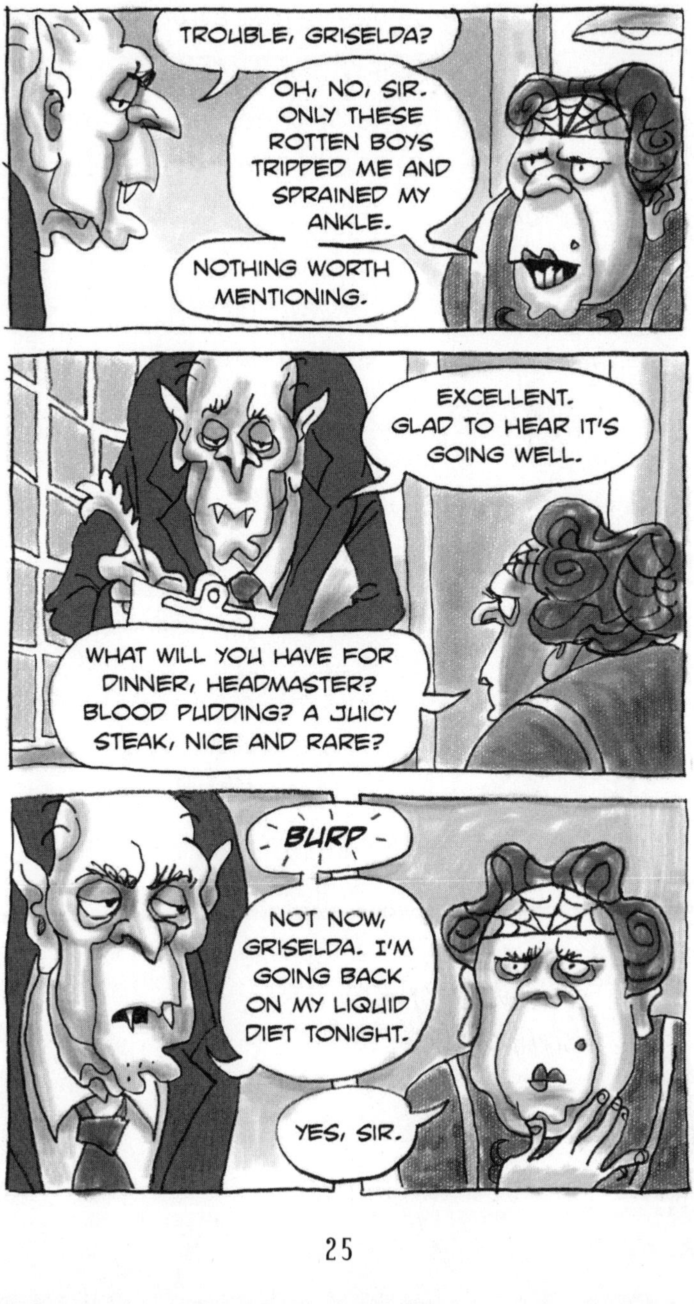
TROUBLE, GRISELDA?
OH, NO, SIR. ONLY THESE ROTTEN BOYS TRIPPED ME AND SPRAINED MY ANKLE.
NOTHING WORTH MENTIONING.
EXCELLENT. GLAD TO HEAR IT'S GOING WELL.
WHAT WILL YOU HAVE FOR DINNER, HEADMASTER? BLOOD PUDDING? A JUICY STEAK, NICE AND RARE?
BURP
NOT NOW, GRISELDA. I'M GOING BACK ON MY LIQUID DIET TONIGHT.
YES, SIR.

Cody looked at the other boys. They sat limp, staring at their food. Like zombies. Like prisoners. Some of them were watching him out of the corners of their eyes. Most of them were covered in food filth.

Oh no, Cody thought. *Cody Mack doesn't "do" prison. No way. I am not staying here in this loony bin and turning into one of them. I am outta here.*

He glanced back up at Farley, who was still talking to Griselda. Slowly, he tiptoed backward. Would the boys rat on him?

He scooted his way back farther.

Nobody said a word.

In fact, Cody could swear some of them were urging him on.

He took another soft step backward.

No tattlers.

Cody had to hand it to those Splurch kids. They were all right. He was almost sorry to ditch them. *Yeah, right!* He couldn't get out of there fast enough.

He thought back to what Farley had said about kids never making it as far as the road, but he was probably just bluffing.

He kept sneaking backward.

Pretty soon, he was through the cafeteria doors. He turned and sprinted for the outside exit.

A tiny bell tinkled.

He was almost to the door when a huge *WOOF* shattered his eardrums.

A big set of gleaming black eyes and a bigger set of gleaming teeth stood right in his path.

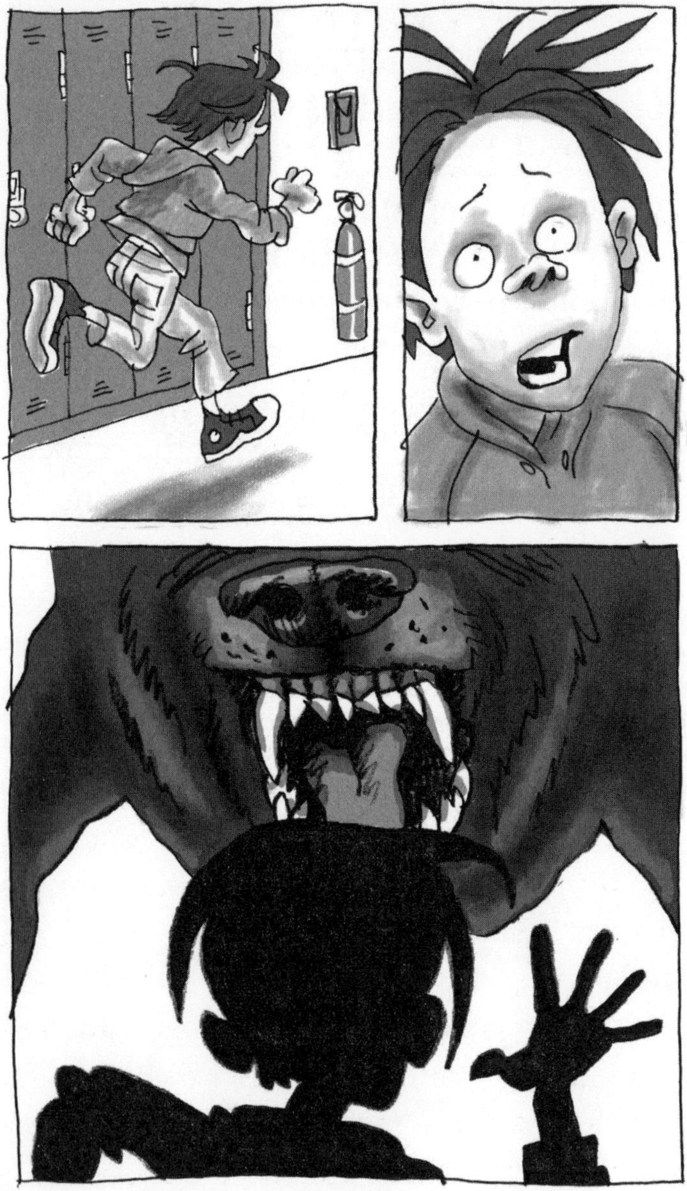

CHAPTER FOUR

THE NURSE

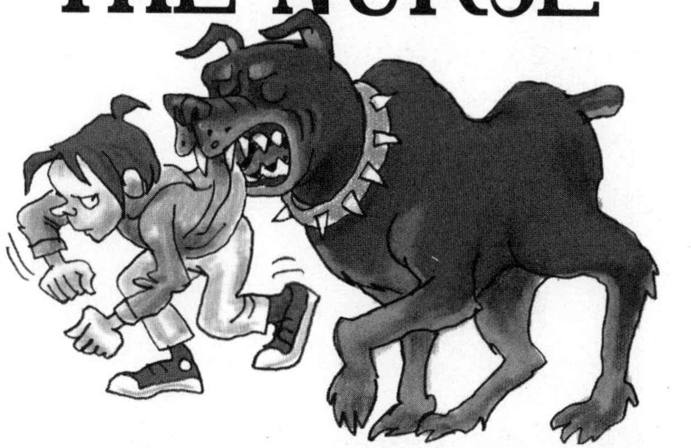

The dog's jaw opened, and out came a tiger-sized growl, along with a Niagara Falls–amount of dog drool. Cody tried to make a dash for it, but the dog sunk its teeth into the hood of Cody's sweatshirt.

Dr. Farley appeared in the doorway. He dropped a little brass bell back into his pocket. "Ah, Pavlov," he said, patting the dog on the head. "Good boy."

Pavlov dragged Cody back into the cafeteria. At the sight of him, several of the boys shook their heads. *Too late, better luck next time*, their expressions seemed to say.

But Dr. Farley's bloodshot eyes bored holes right through Cody.

"Nurse!" Farley barked.

In moments, a burly woman barged through the swinging door to the cafeteria.

Cody Mack did not like needles.

"Which one tonight, doctor?" she asked. "It's a shame how many of these boys need sleep serum to help them settle down."

"Yes. A shame." Dr. Farley nudged Cody with his shoe. "That one, Nurse Bilgewater. Showing quite unruly tendencies. Prone to escape."

"Well, we can't have that, now can we?" the nurse said. "On the other hand, if he were to go outside, who knows . . ."

She looked hopefully at Dr. Farley, but he shook his head firmly. Nurse Bilgewater sighed and turned her attention back to Cody.

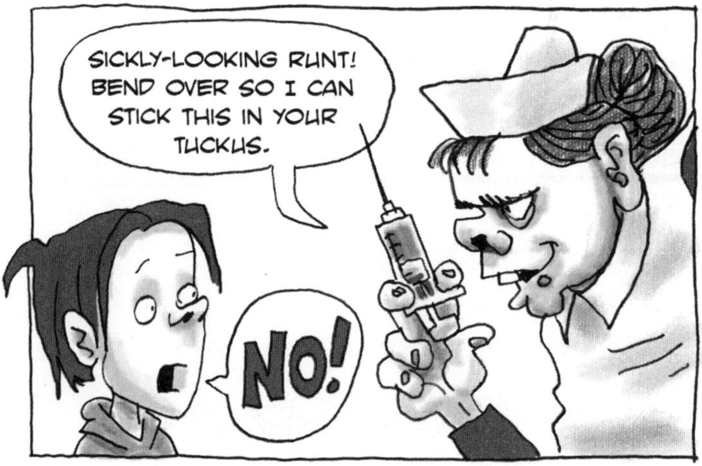
SICKLY-LOOKING RUNT! BEND OVER SO I CAN STICK THIS IN YOUR TUCKUS.
NO!

Nurse Bilgewater's double chins burbled. "No?" She elbowed Dr. Farley. "We've got a feisty one here, haven't we, Archibald?"

"Shall I hold him still for you?"

She shook her head. "No, thanks. I need to teach these little demons respect, right from the get-go. It's like training alligators. You don't get a second chance."

Nurse Bilgewater gripped him tight against her with her enormous arm. She smelled like the inside of Cody's grandpa's fishing tackle box—half dead worm, half rotting trout.

Cody felt the eyes of all the disruptive boys at Splurch Academy on him as Nurse Bilgewater brandished her syringe. He pushed and strained against her mighty grip, but she had the strength of a pro wrestler.

Dr. Farley watched with a lazy smile.

Nurse Bilgewater squirted another drip of sleep serum from her needle.

Cody *really* did not like needles.

This Nurse Stinkwater, or whoever she was, wasn't going to stick Cody Mack without a fight.

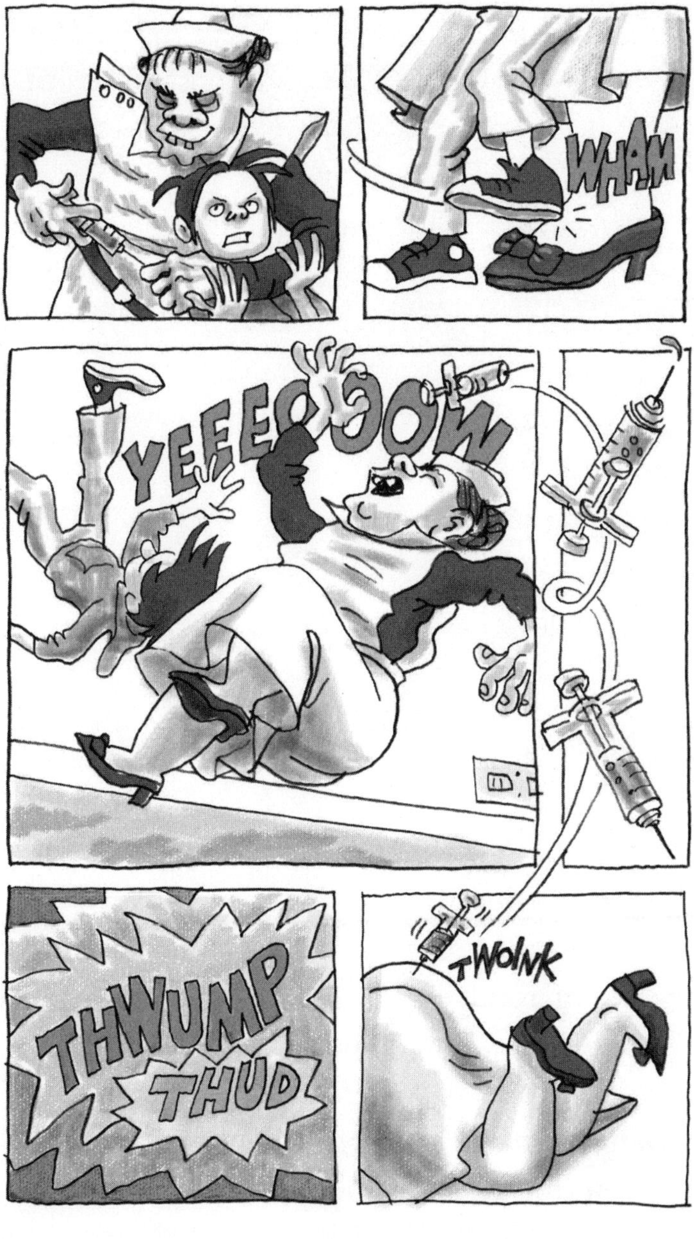
WHAM
YEEEOOOW
THWUMP
THUD
TWOINK

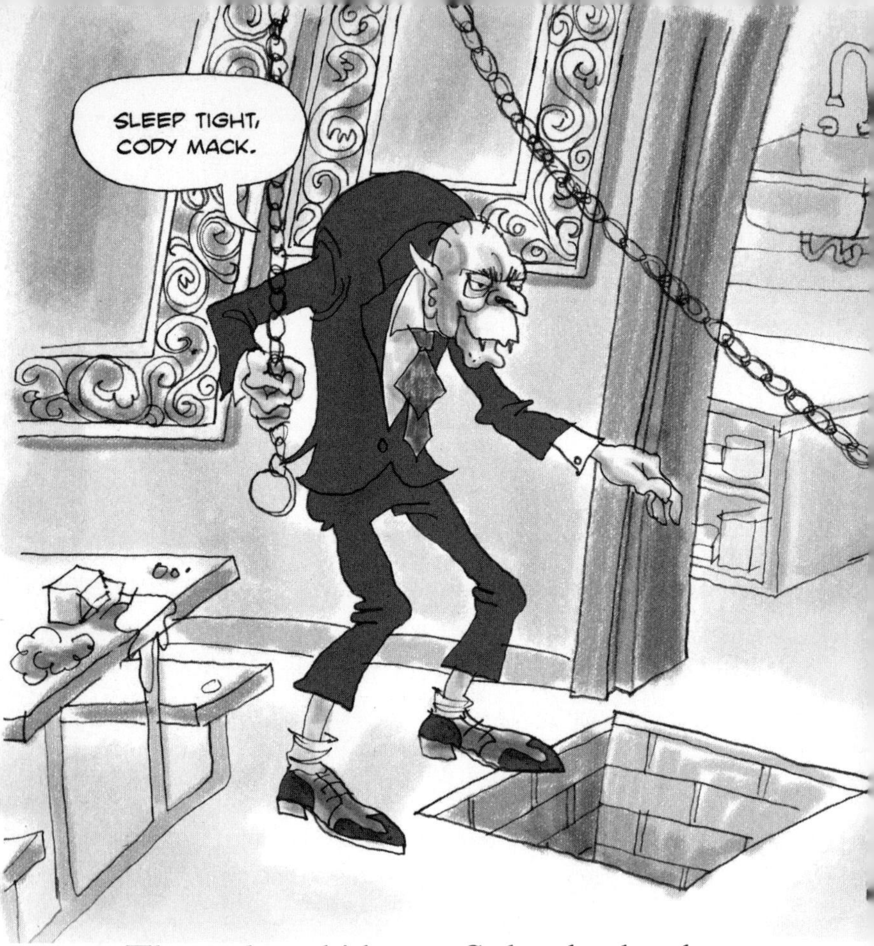
SLEEP TIGHT,
CODY MACK.

The other kids at Splurch Academy began to cheer.

Cody kept on running, skidding through plates of food.

Dr. Farley swooped in to grab him, but Cody leaped for the dangling chains of a chandelier and swung out of his reach.

For one glorious moment, Cody was free!

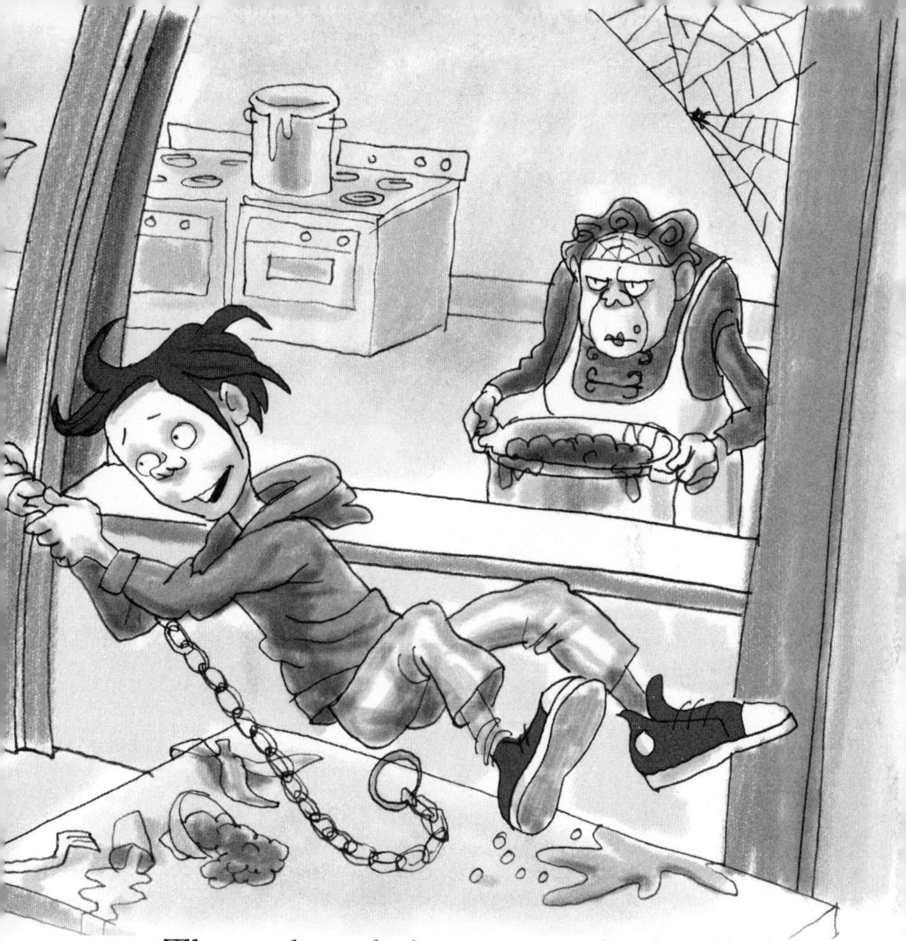

Then the chain swung back. Cody headed back toward Dr. Farley, who yanked on the other end of the chain.

Just then, a hole opened in the floor beneath Cody's feet.

Cody couldn't help it. He let go of the chains.

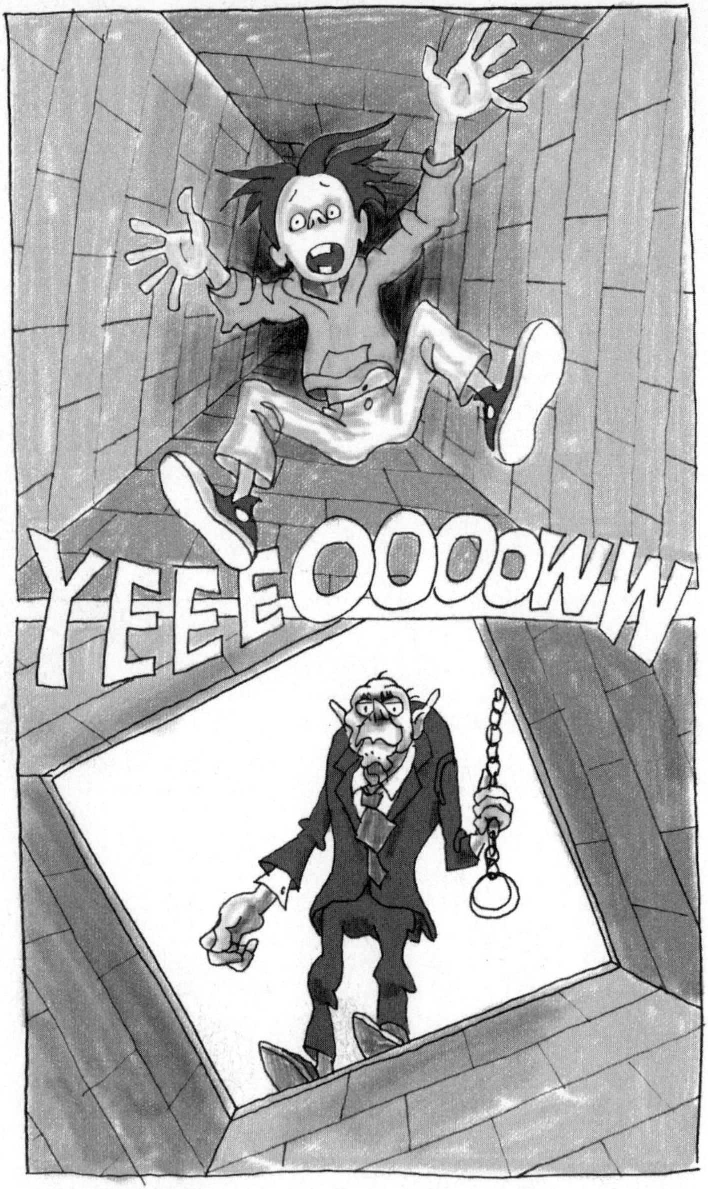
YEEEOOOOWW

CHAPTER FIVE

THE DUNGEON

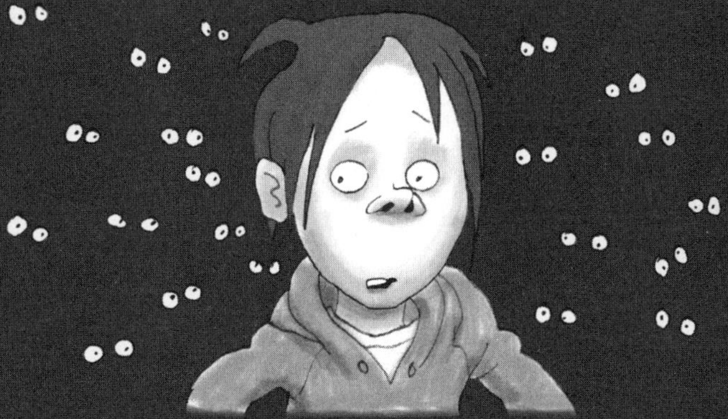

He fell, *thumpety-whack*, against the sides of a long, steep chute made of rough stone blocks. His clothes snagged, his hair caught, and his skin scraped against the endless slide.

Then he landed on his knees in a pile of something scratchy, damp, and *stinky*.

The first thing he noticed was pain, everywhere he got jostled.

Then, the dark.

Then, the *squeaks*.

The kind of squeaks made by things with scratchy claws. And beady eyes.

And big. Sharp. Teeth.

Lots of squeaks.

And wheezing, from the ancient furnace. Booming, from the radiator. Shooshing, through the water pipes. Creaking, from the floors overhead. And groaning, as the tons of stone that made up Splurch Academy pressed down into the ground.

Or was it ghosts?

"Okay," Cody said slowly to himself. "Let's just relax. I don't need to freak out. There's nothing to freak out about here. I'm cool. It's just an old basement, probably with a mouse in it somewhere. Who's afraid of mice? Not me!"

Slowly, Cody's eyes adjusted to the dark. The pale moon peeped through a small, grimy window, tucked away in a high corner near the ceiling. It gave just enough light for Cody to see that *the floor was moving*! Swarming past his legs, like a wave of dirty water, was a river of . . .

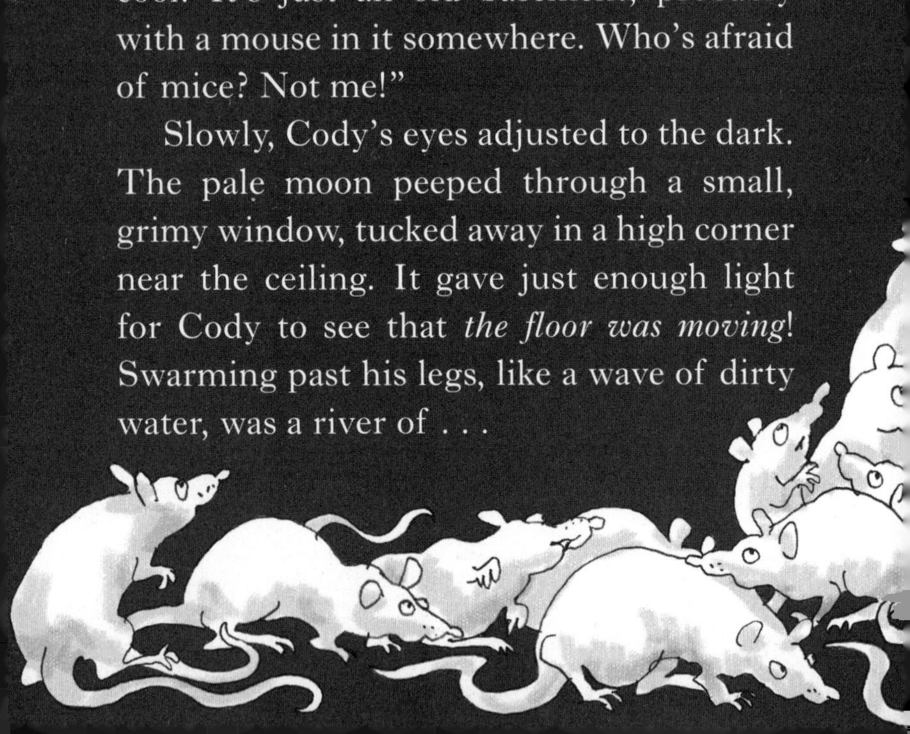

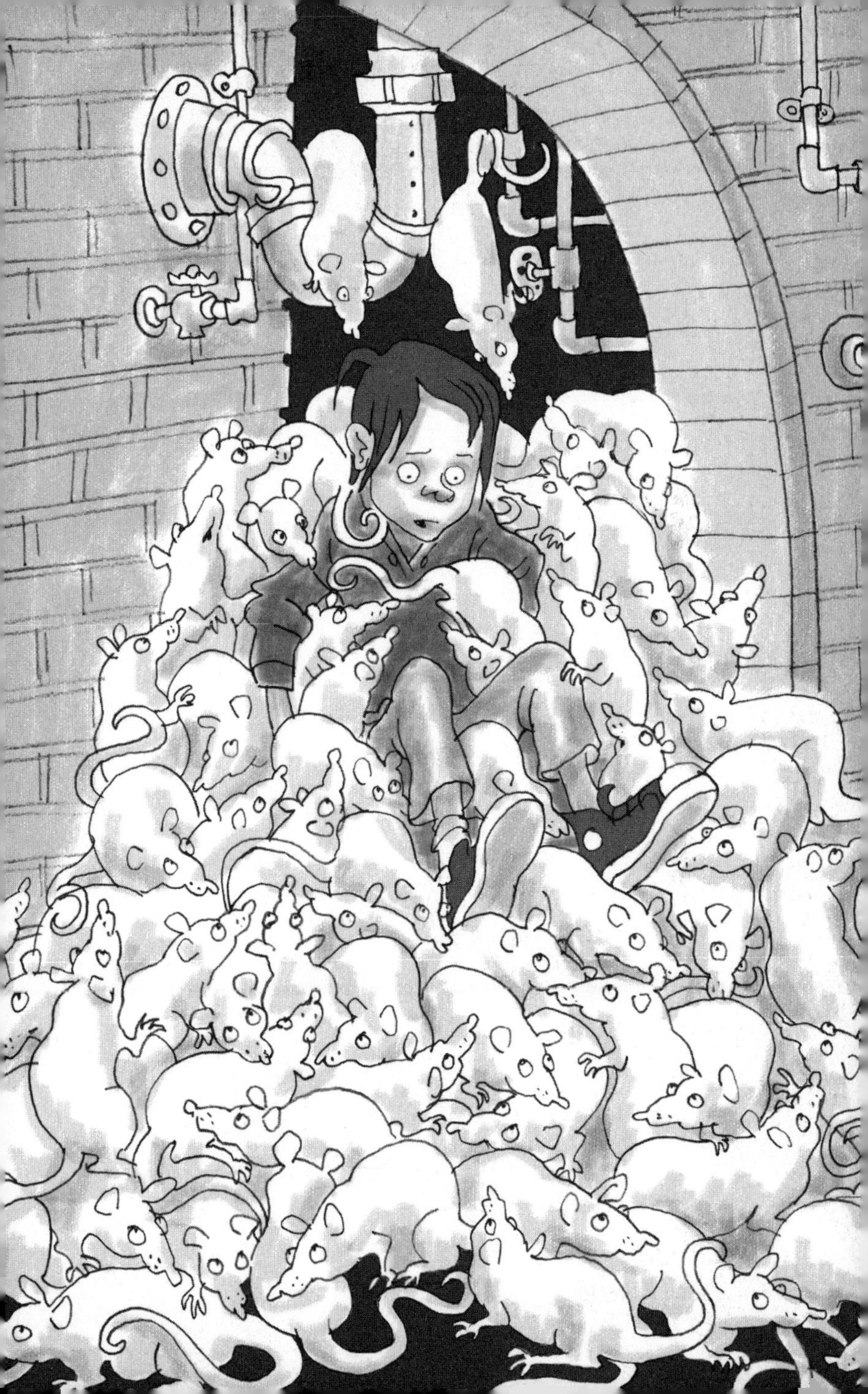

RATS!

Cody jumped up and clonked his head on some low-hanging pipes. They were slimy, dripping with who-knows-what, probably toxic sewage, but they were better than whiskery rat noses sniffing your ankles. So Cody climbed up on them.

And for a second, he could relax and think. After he finished sneezing all the cobwebs out of his nose.

Cody wasn't scared of rats, if there was only one of them, and it was living in a tank.

But these rats were different.

Cody'd never been scared of much. What was there to be scared of back at home? The worst teachers and parents could do was yell at you.

But this crazy place! Splurch Academy for Disruptive Boys . . . A haunted house nightmare run by lunatic freaks who didn't care what they did to poor, innocent, disruptive boys, who never did anything worse in their lives than set the elementary school on fire. And those freaks got away

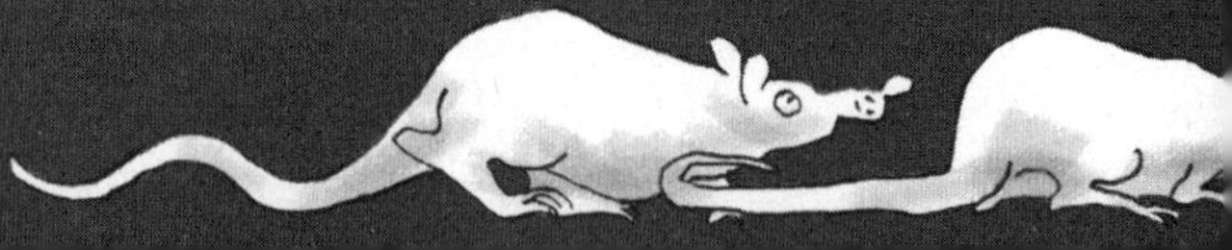

with it because there was no one watching, no one willing to stop them!

Well, that was about to change.

They *couldn't* send kids to schools swarming with rats, run by living skeletons and devil dogs and huge nurses waving hypodermic needles!

Not if Cody Mack had anything to say about it.

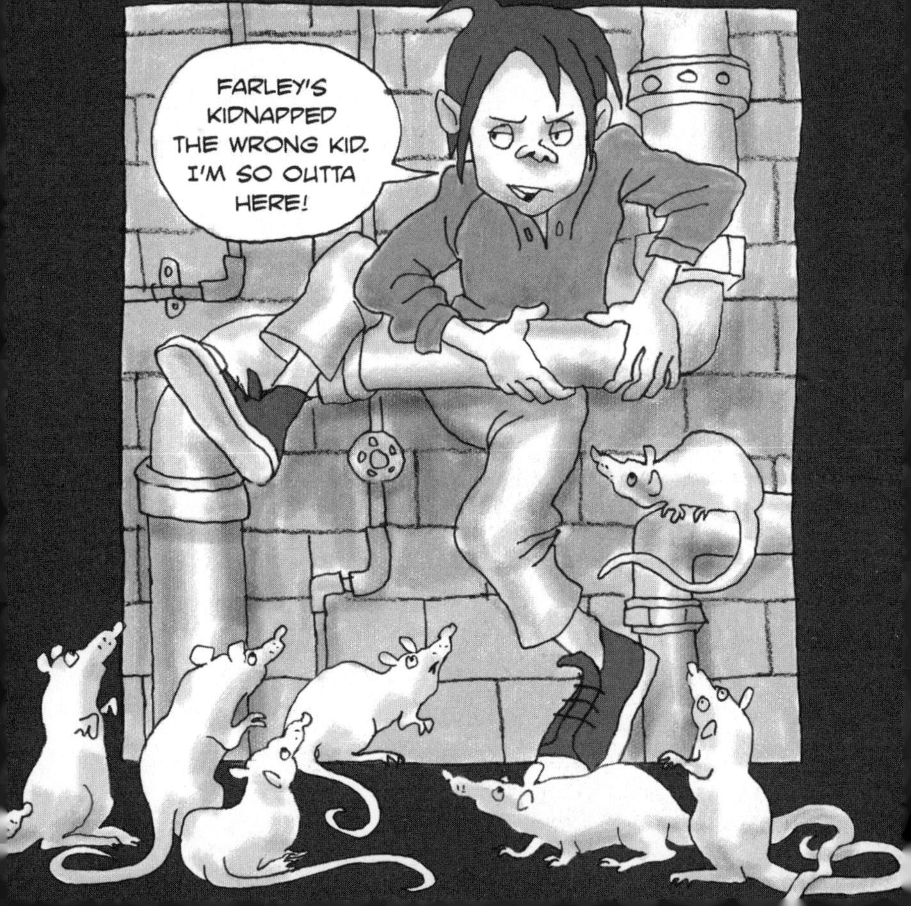
FARLEY'S KIDNAPPED THE WRONG KID. I'M SO OUTTA HERE!

That Archibald Farley was about to meet his match.

He looked toward the light.

He climbed toward the light.

A huge spider—probably a tarantula—crawled across his hands. Rats ran along the pipes like tightrope walkers. Centipedes reared up and waved fifty or sixty legs at him. At one point, he slipped and conked his head on a pipe above, and at another he fell and landed on a pipe below. *Ouch*.

He was covered in cobwebs by the time he finally reached the light.

Moonlight clouded the warped and stained window. Its sills were made of rotting wood, locked by rusting iron bars. Cody shoved it with the heel of his hand.

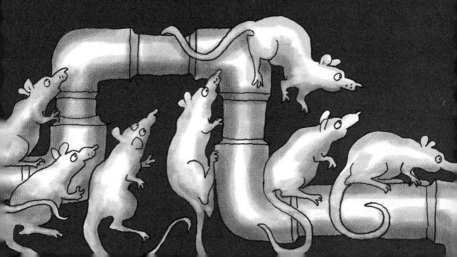

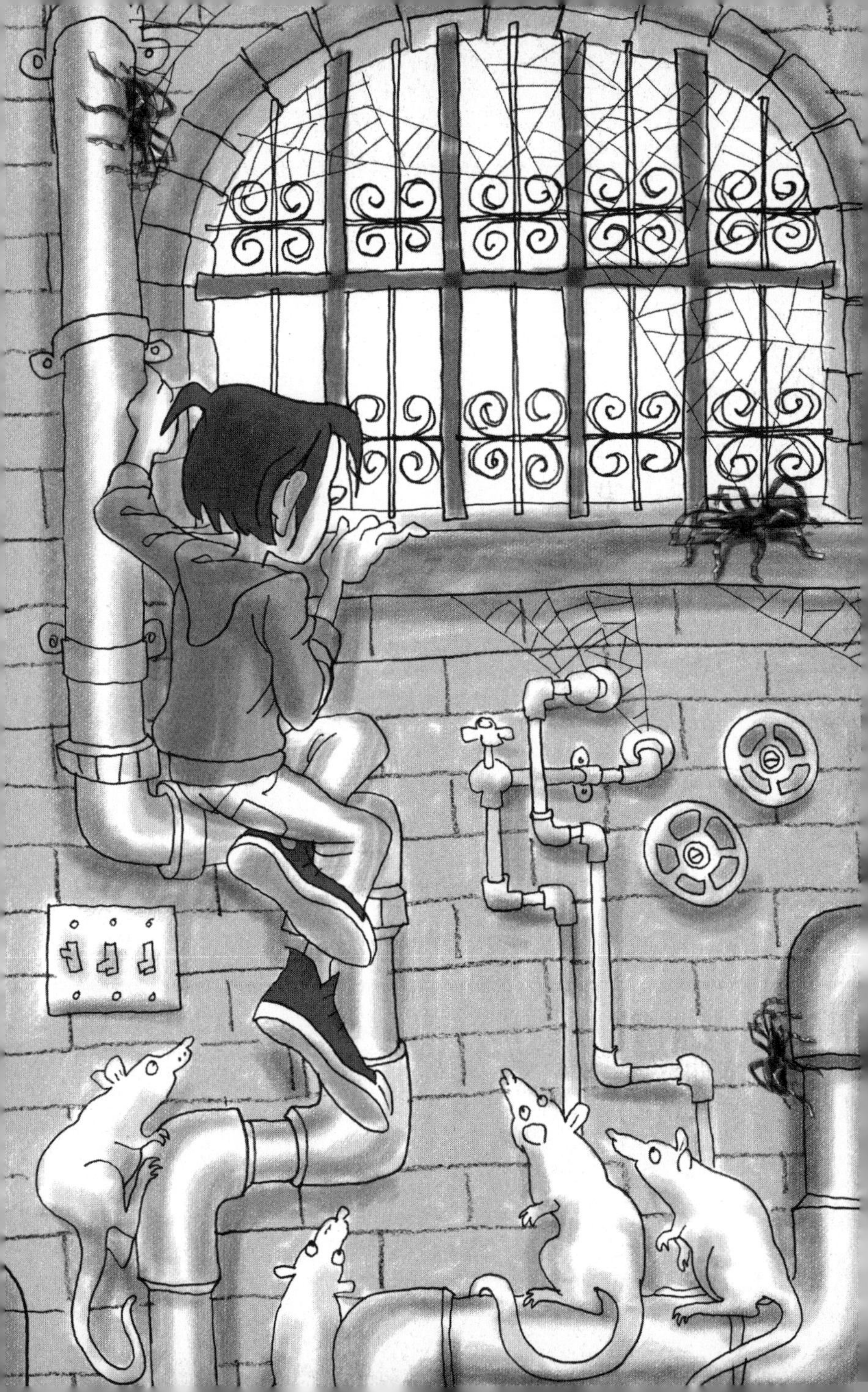

It didn't budge. He wiped at the grimy window with his sleeve to get a better look.

Something was moving out on the grounds. Several somethings.

Was that a dog? Pavlov, maybe, running loose? No. Pavlov was big, but this hound was even bigger.

Cody looked up at the moon, hovering over a bank of clouds. It was the same moon he saw out his bedroom window back home, yet here at Splurch Academy it seemed colder, more menacing. Just then something flew past the moon, blocking its entire shape with its large bat wings. Cody drew back. Something slithered past the window, parting the dark grasses with its long, thick body.

Cody rubbed his eyes.

Farley *wasn't* bluffing when he said there were ferocious beasts around here.

Or maybe Cody's eyes were just playing spooky tricks on him, because it was late and he was tired and hungry and far away from home.

CHAPTER SIX
THE CAFETERIA

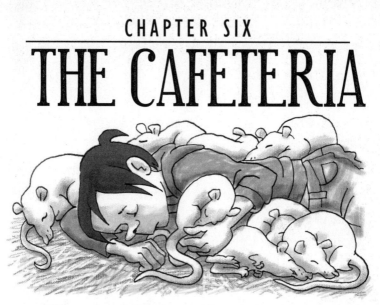

"New boy! Wake up!"

Cody flinched. Something was prodding him. In his dream, he was about to eat a stack of pancakes, with melted butter and syrup, bacon, and a bowl of Fruity Tooters.

Breakfast vanished. "Okay, okay," he said. "I'll get up!"

"New boy misssssed breakfasssst." Ivanov squinted at Cody. "Missssed morning classes, heh, heh. New boy gonna have detention!"

Ivanov's one good eye oozed with repulsive gunk.

"Hear noisesssss last night, new boy? Did ssssomething haunt your worrssst nightmareses?"

Cody gulped.

"Come on," Ivanov harrumphed. "Sstudentsss is eating their lunch."

Cody followed him through the dungeon. With a bit of morning sunlight leaking through the dirty window, Cody could see enough to notice dozens of strange, shoebox-sized cages stacked along the stone walls. He looked closer. There were rats inside some of them, playing with wheels and bells. Occasionally a piece of food fell down a chute for them. They got all excited whenever it fell. *Weird*.

Cody climbed the tall, rickety stairs leading out of the dungeon. He blinked in the bright light of day, then followed Ivanov down the halls to the cafeteria. He wondered if he smelled like rat poop after sleeping in the straw with them all night.

"Fifth grade, here," Ivanov said. He left Cody at a table and shuffled off.

There's no point getting friendly, Cody thought, *because the first chance I get, I'm gone.*

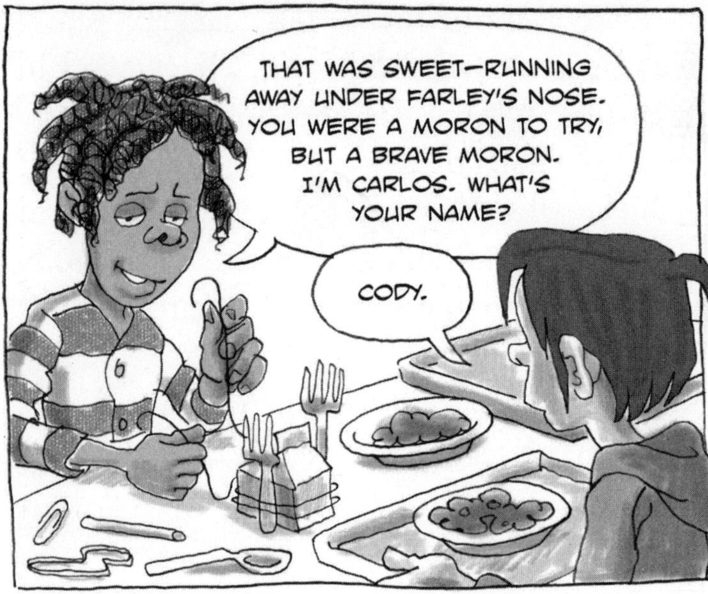
THAT WAS SWEET—RUNNING AWAY UNDER FARLEY'S NOSE. YOU WERE A MORON TO TRY, BUT A BRAVE MORON. I'M CARLOS. WHAT'S YOUR NAME?
CODY.

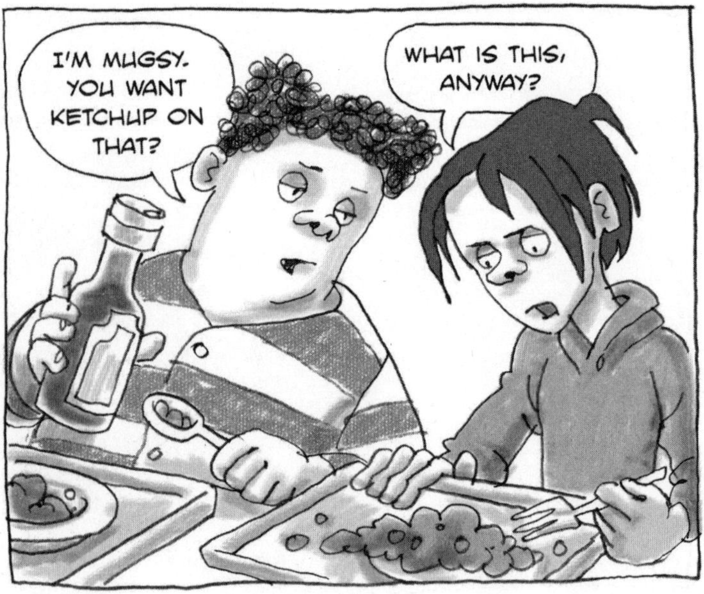
I'M MUGSY. YOU WANT KETCHUP ON THAT?
WHAT IS THIS, ANYWAY?

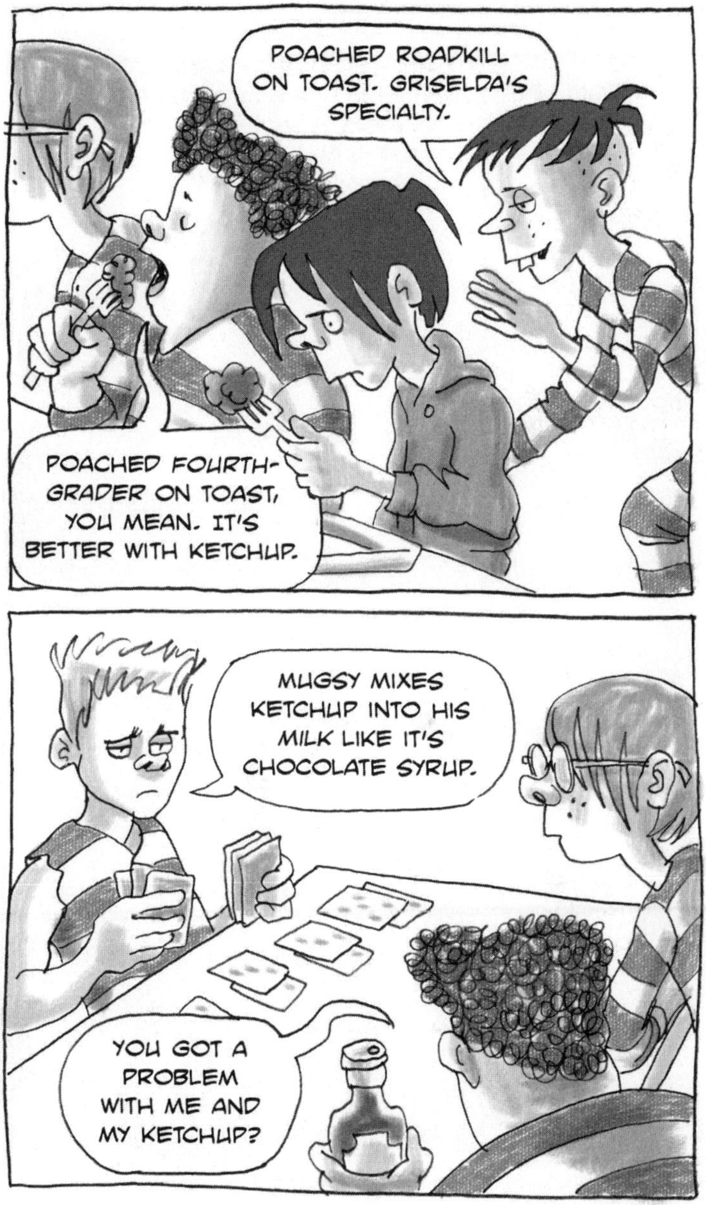
POACHED ROADKILL ON TOAST. GRISELDA'S SPECIALTY.
POACHED FOURTH-GRADER ON TOAST, YOU MEAN. IT'S BETTER WITH KETCHUP.
MUGSY MIXES KETCHUP INTO HIS MILK LIKE IT'S CHOCOLATE SYRUP.
YOU GOT A PROBLEM WITH ME AND MY KETCHUP?

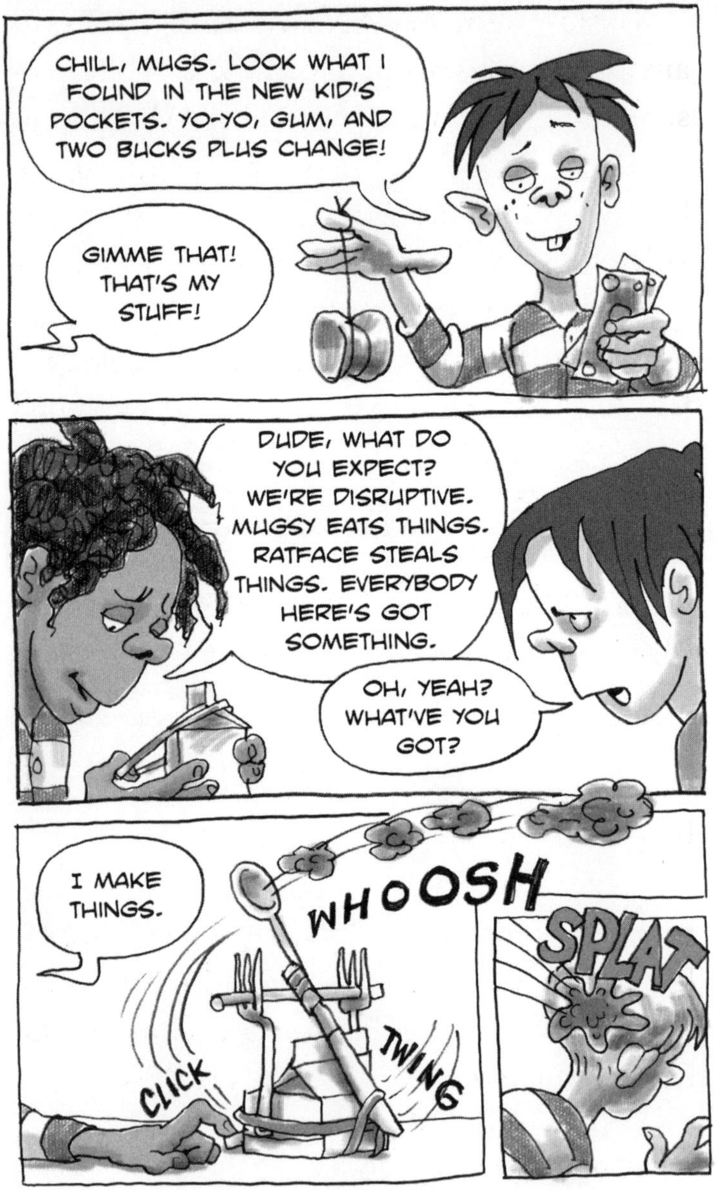
CHILL, MUGS. LOOK WHAT I FOUND IN THE NEW KID'S POCKETS. YO-YO, GUM, AND TWO BUCKS PLUS CHANGE!
GIMME THAT! THAT'S MY STUFF!
DUDE, WHAT DO YOU EXPECT? WE'RE DISRUPTIVE. MUGSY EATS THINGS. RATFACE STEALS THINGS. EVERYBODY HERE'S GOT SOMETHING.
OH, YEAH? WHAT'VE YOU GOT?
I MAKE THINGS.
WHOOSH
CLICK
TWING
SPLAT

Carlos went on. "Now, Sully, he won't answer a grown-up. Ever. Not if they're screaming in his ear. Acts deaf. Makes 'em cuckoo. Victor," Carlos pointed toward the kid playing solitaire. Carlos lowered his voice to a whisper. "Victor's a bad loser."

Cody nodded. Good to know.

"How come I was a moron to run away?" Cody asked. "Don't you ever try to escape?"

"Not since Billy Whistler," Sully said.

"So you *do* talk," Cody said, puzzled. "I thought Carlos said . . ."

"I only don't talk to grown-ups," Sully said. He shoved his glasses up his nose. "They're the enemy. You talk to them, you give them power."

Wacko, Cody thought. "So what happened to Billy Whistler?"

"Billy Whistler tried to escape one night," Sully said. "His parents got a letter, and flowers." He mimicked Farley's voice. *"Such a tragedy, how he drowned in the river, and his remains were never found."*

"What river?" Cody asked.

"Exactly," Sully said.

"You mean . . . "

They all nodded.

"But . . . but . . . didn't the parents call the police—get it investigated or something?"

"Funny thing about the police in this town," Sully said. "Whatever Farley says, goes. You'd think they were afraid of him."

"But then," Cody said, "how come you're not all scared to death?"

"Just keep your head down, go to class, go to bed at night, and nothing much happens to you," Carlos said. "Except for Dr. Farley's behavioral experiments."

The other boys shuddered like they'd just swallowed bad medicine.

"What about your parents?" Cody asked. "Don't they flip out when they learn what happens here?"

No one said anything.

"What about parents?" Cody insisted.

"Farley doesn't let us write to them. It's a year-round school. No vacations. If parents visit, we sit in Farley's office, and he supervises," Carlos said. "'Family contact disturbs our behavioral progress.'"

"Some parents don't come at all," Sully said.

Victor slapped down a solitaire card so hard, it made the other cards jump.

Sully lowered his voice. "Some parents were actually glad to get rid of their disruptive kid."

Everyone looked away from Victor.

Cody thought of his own parents. They wouldn't be happy to be rid of him, would they?

Would they?

"LUNCH IS OVER!" a female voice came screeching from the loudspeakers.

"REPORT TO CLASS IMMEDIATELY!"

Cody fell in beside Carlos. "If it's really that bad, how can you stand it?"

Carlos put a hand on Cody's shoulder. "Welcome to Splurch Academy, pal," he said. "The state makes Farley set everyone free when they turn eighteen. So the name of the game is: Survive."

CHAPTER SEVEN

THE CLASSROOM

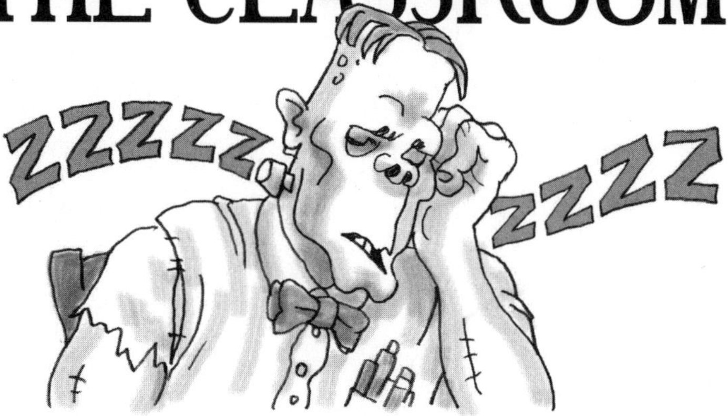
ZZZZZ
ZZZZ

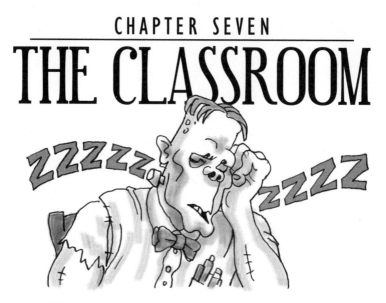

They reached the classroom. Cody's new teacher snoozed in his chair. A dusty placard on his desk read: **MR. FRONK**.

Cody slid into a desk behind Carlos. He waited for class to start, but nothing happened. Carlos made a paper airplane, looked around cautiously, then launched it into the air. The paper airplane glided straight for the teacher, landing softly in his combed-over hair. Mr. Fronk didn't budge.

Ivanov shuffled through the door, muttering. He went behind Mr. Fronk's chair, bent over, and plugged in an extension cord. The lights flickered. There was a loud buzzing sound, followed by a pop. Mr. Fronk's eyes flicked open.

Cody sniffed the air. Was that smoke he smelled?

"Ah. Thank you, Ivanov." The hall monitor, still grumbling, left the room.

Mr. Fronk stood and stretched. Then he noticed Cody.

"New boy." His voice was deep and rumbly. He slapped his massive hand on Cody's desk. "What was the title of the last book you read?"

"Revenge of the Soul-Sucking Grease Goblins?"

Mr. Fronk waved that away.

"Frivolous comic trash. What did you read before that?"

"Um . . . *Attack of the Soul-Sucking Grease Goblins?*"

Mr. Fronk snorted. "Figures. Another ignoramus. Is there never a disruptive boy who appreciates literature?"

Weirdo.

Mr. Fronk slapped Sully's desk.

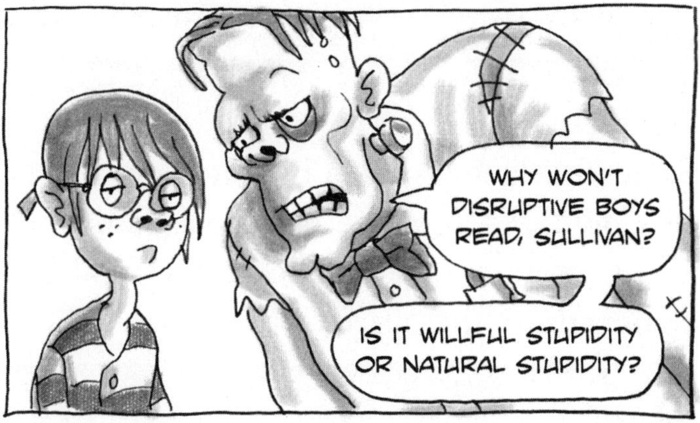
WHY WON'T DISRUPTIVE BOYS READ, SULLIVAN?
IS IT WILLFUL STUPIDITY OR NATURAL STUPIDITY?

Fronk gave up on Sully. He pulled out a polka-dotted handkerchief and wiped his forehead. "Your task for the afternoon, new boy, is to copy these sentences a hundred times. When that's done, you and all the other students will write an essay entitled 'Why I Love Splurch Academy.'"

"What?"

"You're joking!"

"You'd have to be dead in your grave to love this place!"

Fronk scowled at the class. "Who said that? Tell me!"

Everyone looked at their desks.

"*I* love Splurch Academy," Fronk said. "Are you saying, Mugsy, that I am dead?"

Mugsy turned pale. "Is that a trick question?"

"Get on with your work." Fronk sat, leaned back, and closed his eyes.

Copying sentences, eh? Cody had done that a million times before. He read the sentences on the board:

> ZZZZZZ
>
> 1. I'M A WASTE OF SPACE.
> 2. MY PARENTS ARE LUCKY TO BE RID OF ME.
> 3. MR. FRONK IS HANDSOME, CHARMING, AND NIMBLE ON THE DANCE FLOOR.

Nimble on the dance floor? The guy looked dead.

Inside his desk, Cody found stubby pencils and some paper. He tiptoed to the pencil sharpener on the windowsill.

Cody fed his pencil into the sharpener. Nothing happened.

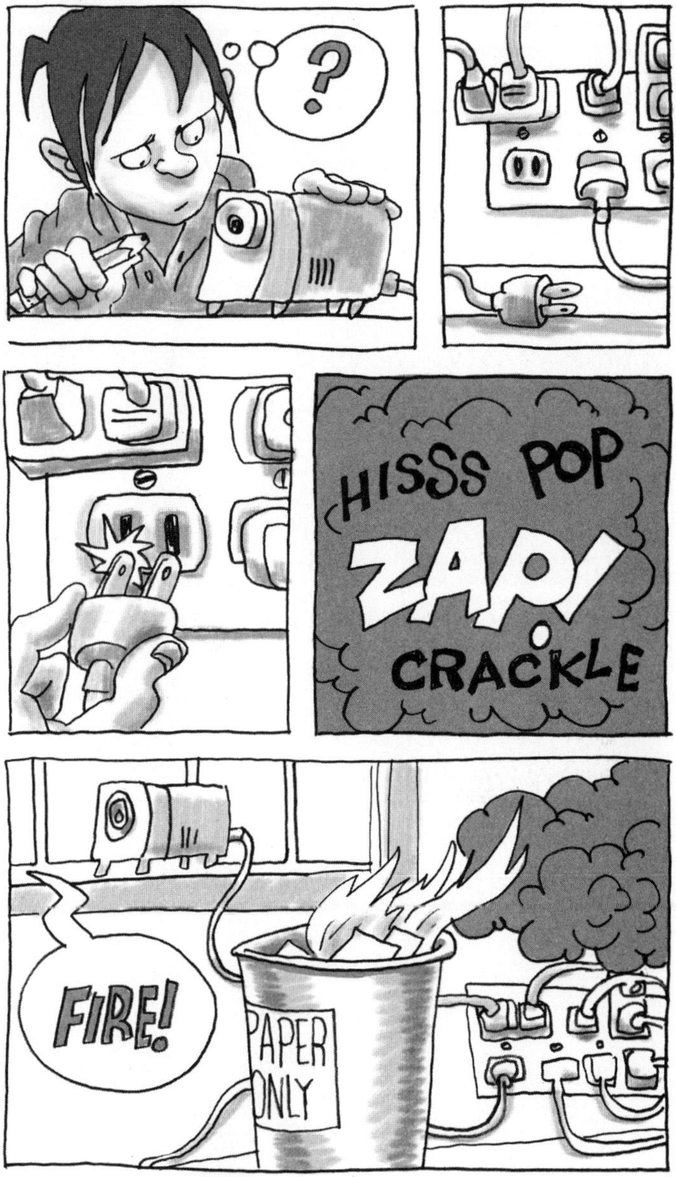
?
HISSS POP
ZAP!
CRACKLE
FIRE!
PAPER ONLY

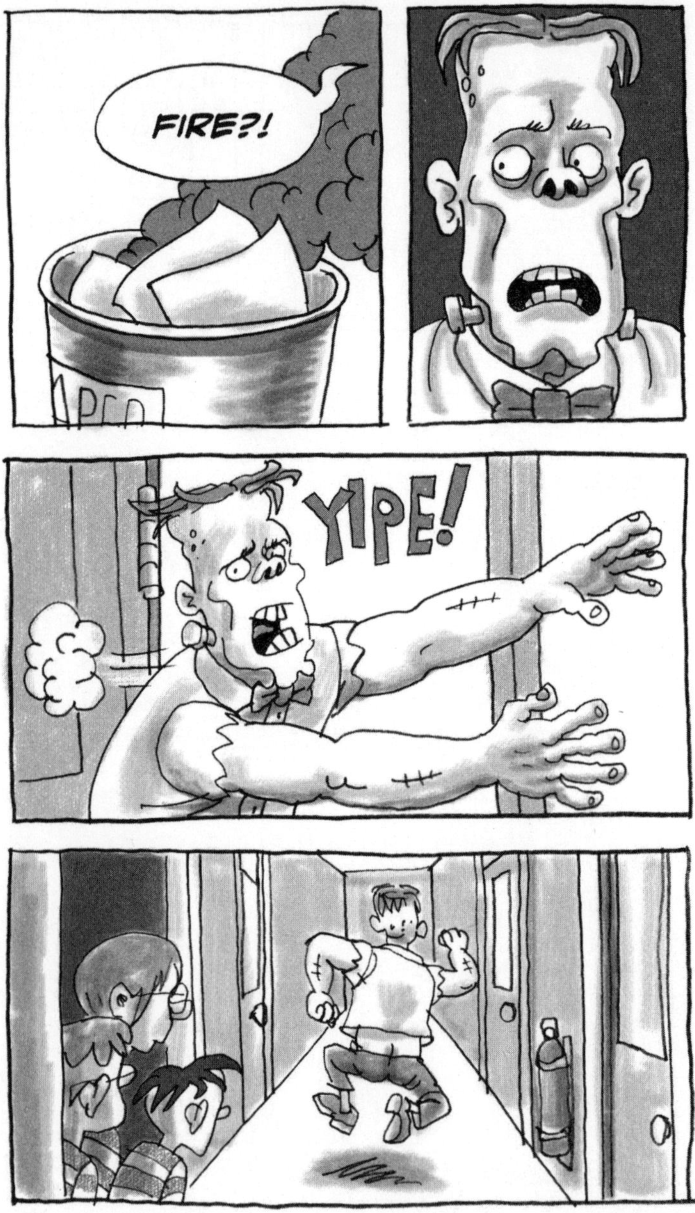
FIRE?!
YIPE!

The blaze in the trash can fizzled out. Cody yanked the pencil sharpener cord out from the wall, then jumped up on the window ledge.

No teacher watching . . . an empty lawn . . . and a straight shot to the highway . . . this was his chance! Did he dare take it?

Was he Cody Mack, or wasn't he?

"Well, adios, guys."

"Cody, what are you doing? Get down!" Carlos cried.

Teachers' voices echoed down the hall. Would the kids tattle?

That was a chance he had to take. Cody climbed out the window, jumped, landed on soft grass, and took off running.

Freedom! Sunshine, blue skies, and the highway. He'd flag a car down and use their phone to call his parents. When they heard what Splurch Academy was really like, they'd *beg* his forgiveness.

He raced across the grass, wishing he'd worked harder in gym. But he was close!

Uh-oh.

Footsteps. Pounding closer. Panting breaths. Glancing back, Cody saw a man running, his feet tearing up the grass. *No!*

Inches from freedom, the man tackled him. Cody was buried under a wiry form that smelled like dog and Dr. Pepper.

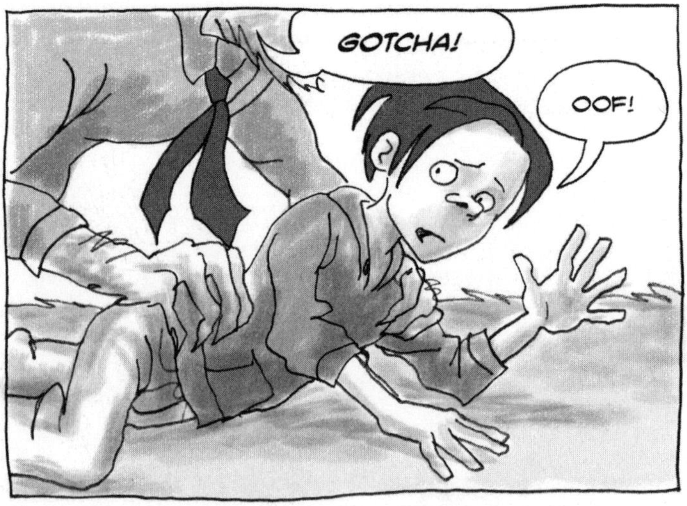
GOTCHA!
OOF!

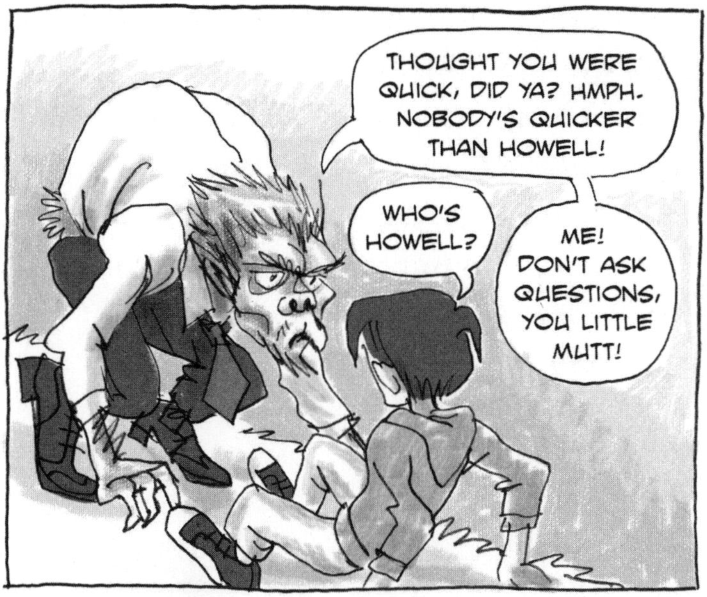
THOUGHT YOU WERE QUICK, DID YA? HMPH. NOBODY'S QUICKER THAN HOWELL!
WHO'S HOWELL?
ME! DON'T ASK QUESTIONS, YOU LITTLE MUTT!

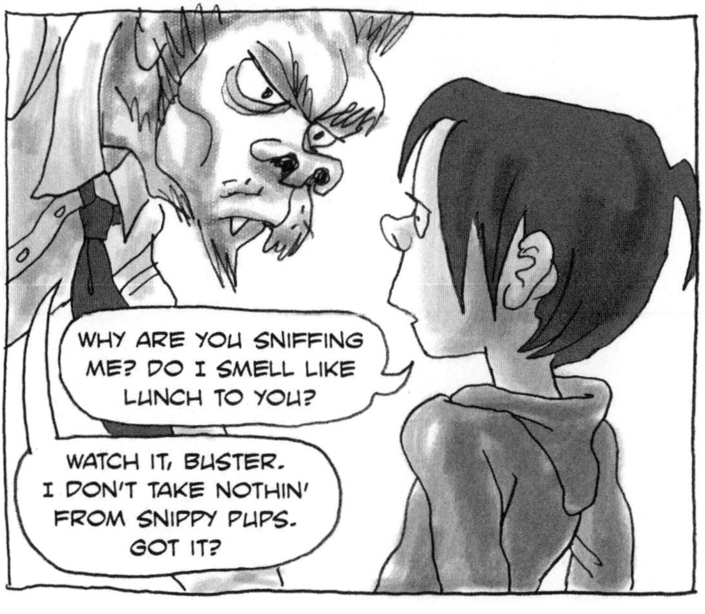
WHY ARE YOU SNIFFING ME? DO I SMELL LIKE LUNCH TO YOU?
WATCH IT, BUSTER. I DON'T TAKE NOTHIN' FROM SNIPPY PUPS. GOT IT?

"Get moving, mutt," Howell said. "It's back to the kennels for you."

Cody shuffled toward the academy. Headmaster Farley stood at the front door.

"Thank you, Mr. Howell, for showing our newest pupil around the grounds," Dr. Farley said. "And now, young Cody, you will come with me."

CHAPTER EIGHT

THE HEADMASTER'S OFFICE

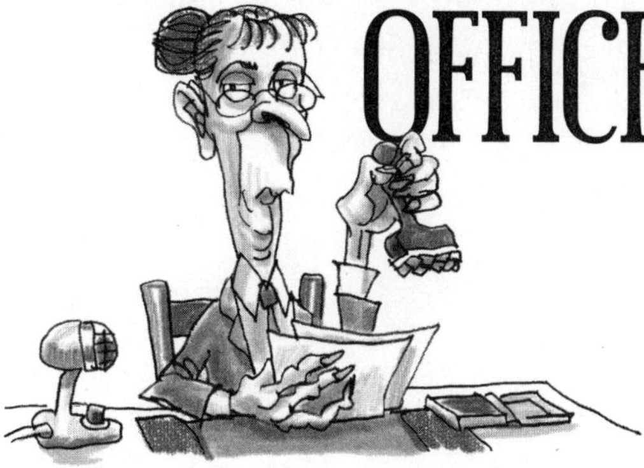

Cody followed Dr. Farley down the grimy corridors. Even at a distance, Farley smelled like mothballs. They passed through a door marked **OFFICE**.

"Miss Threadbare, meet Cody Mack. Master Mack, please meet my assistant, Miss Threadbare."

"How do you do?" Miss Threadbare asked. "Your clothing is amiss."

"A miss what?" Cody asked.

"Amiss," she screeched. "Wrong."

Farley disappeared through a door marked **HEADMASTER** in gold.

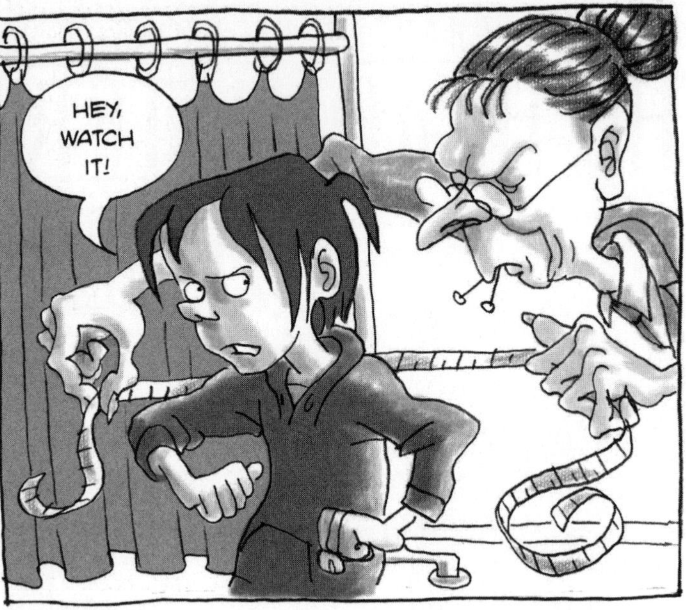
HEY, WATCH IT!

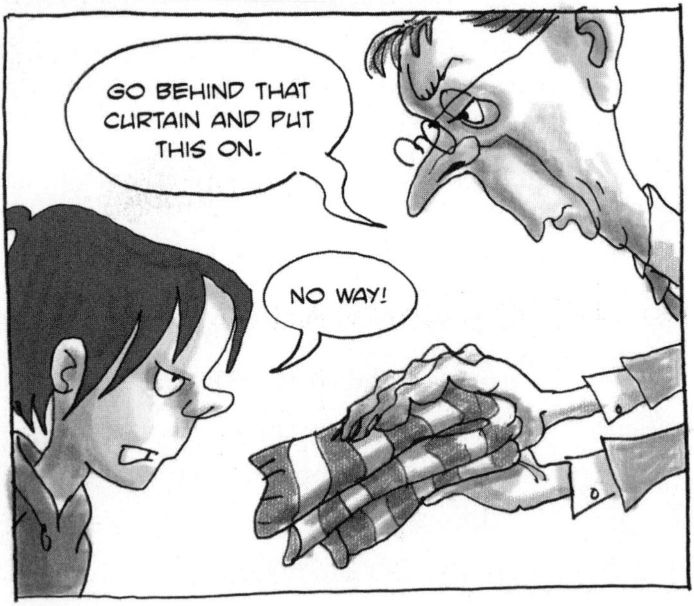
GO BEHIND THAT CURTAIN AND PUT THIS ON.
NO WAY!

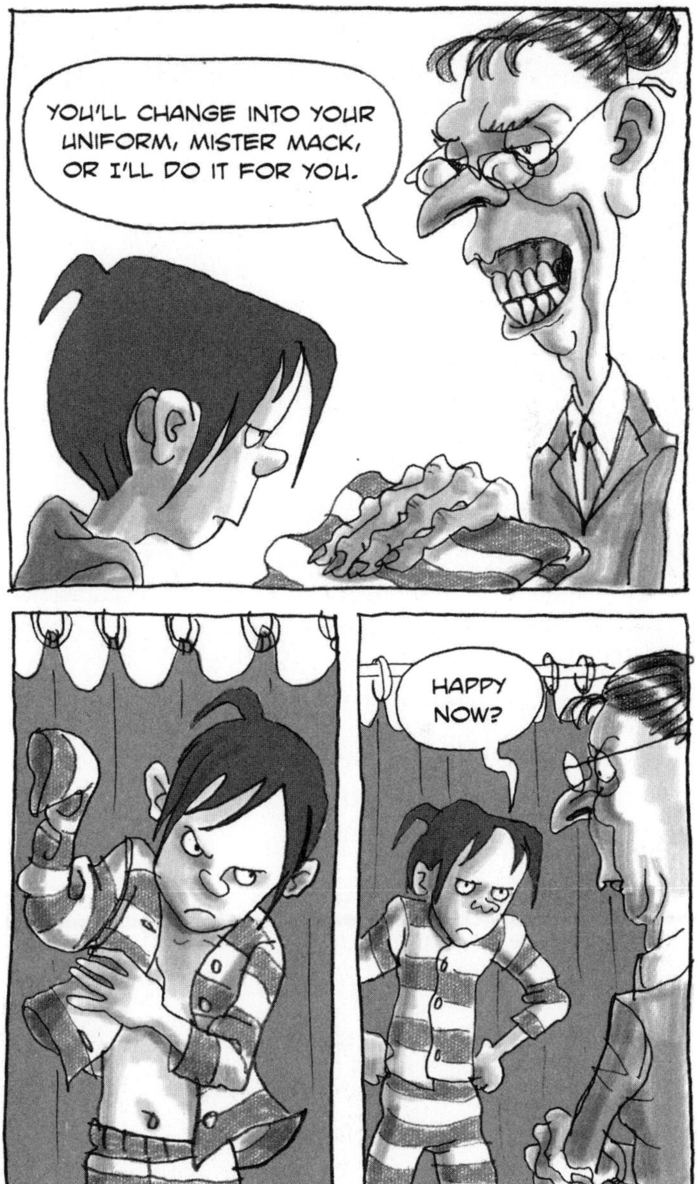
YOU'LL CHANGE INTO YOUR UNIFORM, MISTER MACK, OR I'LL DO IT FOR YOU.
HAPPY NOW?

"Every day's a happy day at Splurch Academy, where disruptive deviants reach daily toward their true potential," Miss Threadbare said. She banged a rubber stamper down on some papers on her desk. "Your paperwork is out of order. Here. Fill these out."

She handed Cody a stack of forms. He flipped through them. Name, age, date of birth, weight, blah, blah, blah. Wait a second. How rich are your parents? Are they lawyers? What's your blood type? Huh?

Farley's voice crackled over the office intercom. "Is he ready, Teresa?"

Miss Threadbare opened the door marked **HEADMASTER** and shooed Cody through. Cody gulped. He'd been to a lot of principal's offices in his time, but never one with a coffin-shaped desk.

There was barely any light. Heavy drapes were drawn shut, and only one small lamp shone over the headmaster's desk, next to an ancient framed photograph of a creepy old woman in a wheelchair.

"Sit down, young Cody," Farley said.

Cody sat.

"Nice job sitting down. Have a Swedish fish." Farley made a note on a clipboard. "Missing class . . . running away . . . you ought to have a week's detention, but as this is your first day, I thought, instead, we'd have a little chat."

Cody wasn't sure what a detention would be at Splurch Academy, but he doubted swapping it for a chat with Dr. Farley was a better deal.

A fly buzzed through the office, and landed on a plant sitting on Dr. Farley's windowsill.

The plant ate the fly.

"I trust your first evening here was comfortable?" Dr. Farley asked.

Cody popped the red candy fish into his mouth. "You know my night wasn't comfortable!" he said. "Your nurse attacked me with sleep serum and you threw me in a rat-infested dungeon. And I saw monster animals outside!"

And this candy is probably poisoned. He spat it out.

"Thank you for answering my question," Farley said. "Have another fish."

He pulled a gold watch and chain from his vest pocket, polished it, then dangled it in the air.

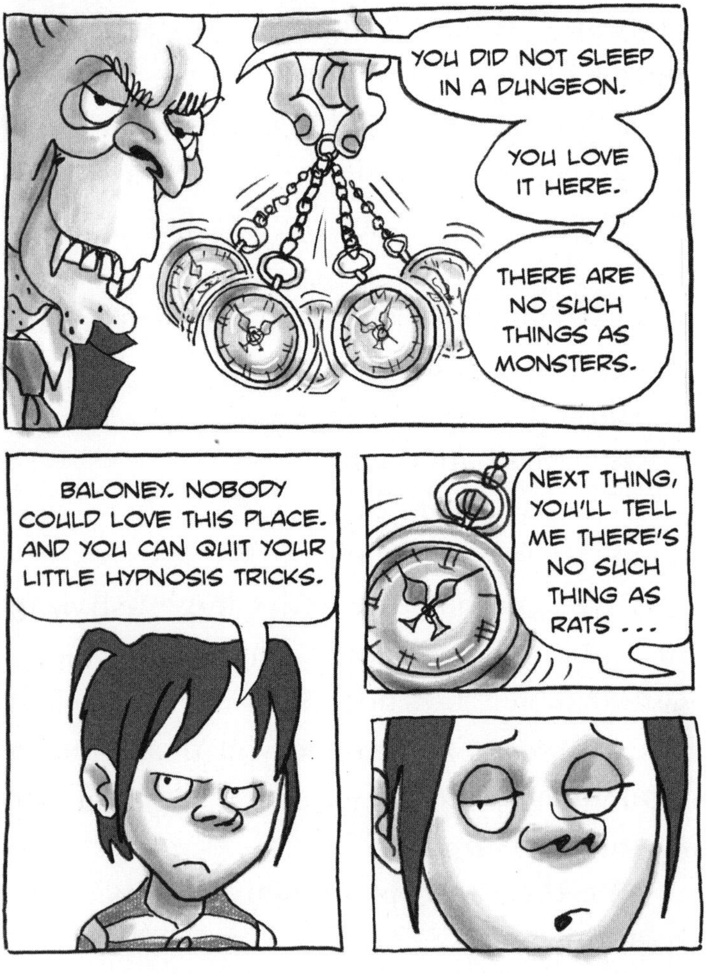
YOU DID NOT SLEEP IN A DUNGEON.
YOU LOVE IT HERE.
THERE ARE NO SUCH THINGS AS MONSTERS.
BALONEY. NOBODY COULD LOVE THIS PLACE. AND YOU CAN QUIT YOUR LITTLE HYPNOSIS TRICKS.
NEXT THING, YOU'LL TELL ME THERE'S NO SUCH THING AS RATS . . .

Dr. Farley chuckled softly. "Now, why would I say something so illogical? I have a pet rat myself. Let me introduce you to him." He pulled a silver pipe from his pocket, and blew a short tune.

A sleek, white rat with a long, pink tail and even pinker eyes jumped up on Farley's desk, its whiskers twitching as it studied Cody.

"This is Rasputin," Farley said, still using that gentle voice a dentist uses to tell you it won't hurt when he drills. "Would you like to see his tricks?"

Cody shrugged. "I dunno, he's not a ninja rat or anything, is he?"

Dr. Farley laughed. "Ninja rat! How droll. Capital humor! Bravo!"

The more Farley went on, the more annoyed Cody got. "Just show me the tricks, okay?"

"March, Rasputin," Farley said, and the rat high-stepped around the desk like a soldier.

"That's cool," Cody said.

"Play dead."

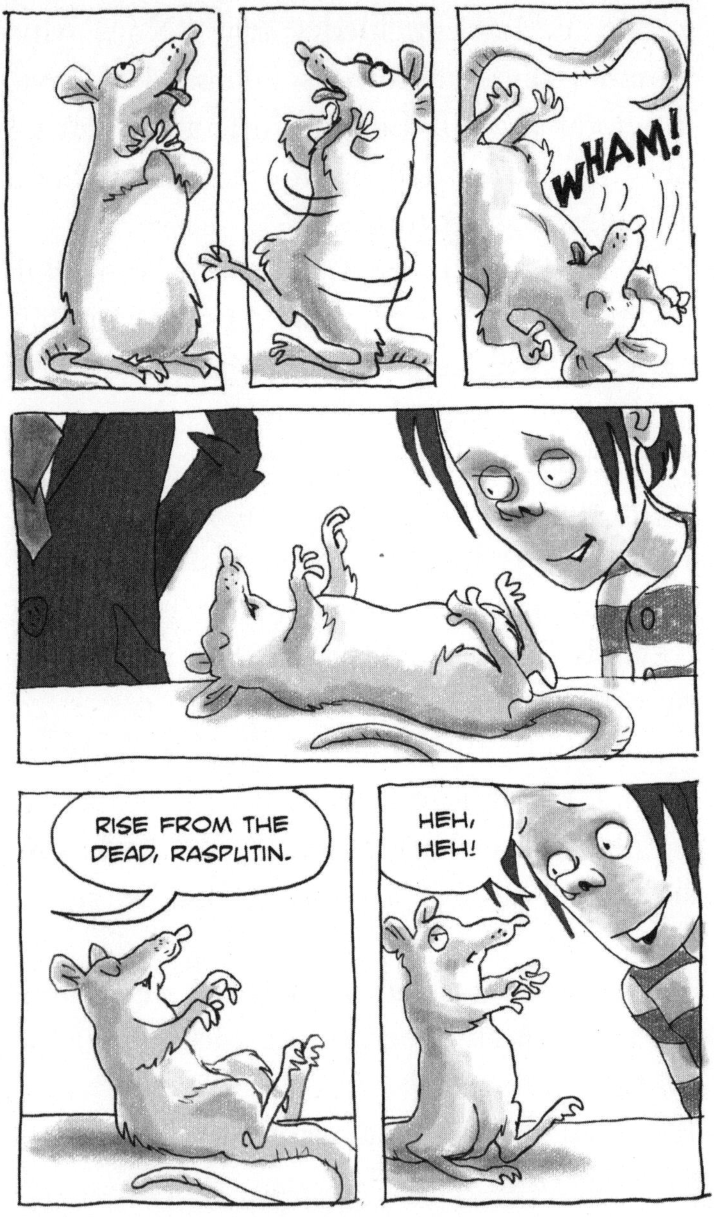
WHAM!
RISE FROM THE DEAD, RASPUTIN.
HEH, HEH!

"Good job watching my rat," Farley purred. "Have a Swedish fish."

Cody ignored the candy. "What's with all this fish and rat business?" he said. "What's the deal with this messed-up school?"

"Excellent question, Cody," Farley said. "Have a fish. It's not the school that's messed up, it's the boys' brains." The pendulum watch swung again. "I'm the world's top scholar of naughty boy neurology. I've invented devices that harness the power of deviant brains."

"Yippy for you," Cody said. "So what?"

"I discovered the part of the brain that makes boys naughty. It's no larger than Rasputin's brain. Isn't that right, you smart rat, you?" Farley tickled Rasputin's chin. "I call it the 'rebellium cortex.' Disruptive boys have large rebellium cortices, which is why they cause so much trouble."

"What'd you do, operate on kids to discover it?"

Dr. Farley swung his watch. "What a clever boy you are, Cody."

Cody shifted in his seat. Now that his

eyes had adjusted to the light, he could see diplomas on the walls. University of Tran . . . *Penn*sylvania. Doctor of Neurology. Doctor of Abnormal Psychology. Doctor of Brain Surgery.

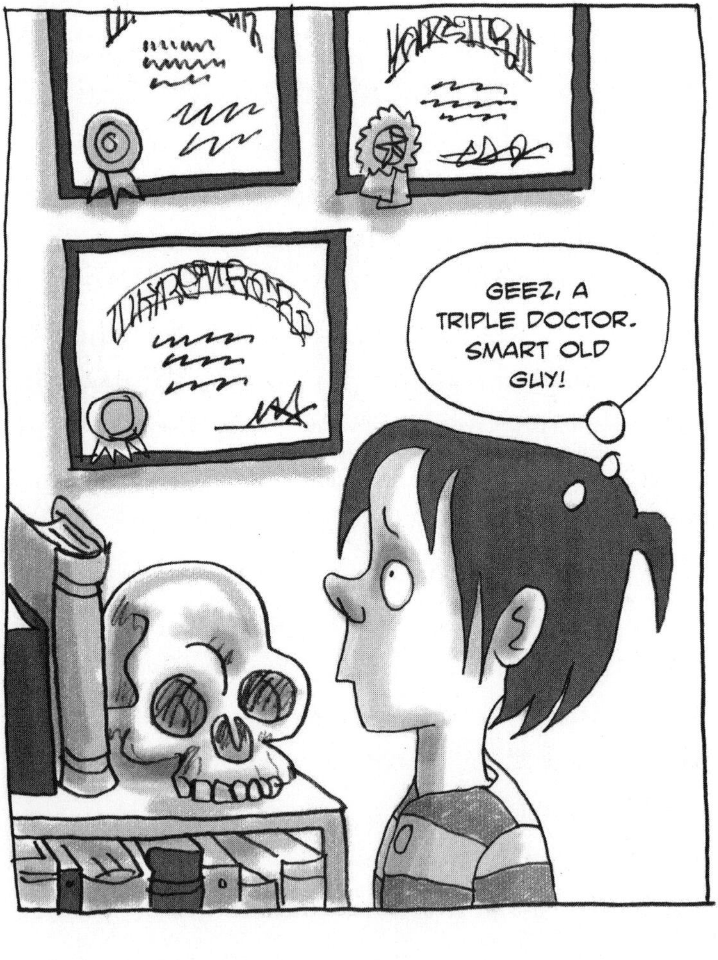
GEEZ, A TRIPLE DOCTOR. SMART OLD GUY!

"I'll let you in on a secret," Dr. Farley said. "Something special is coming to Splurch Academy. Soon. A breakthrough that will *liberate* all the students."

Cody scratched his head. "You mean, set us free?"

"That's right. Free from the burden of bad behavior—forever."

Huh?

"Wait a minute." Cody backed away in his chair.

"It'll be a glorious day," Dr. Farley went on. "We'll celebrate! We'll invite your parents, there will be special guests, awards committees, and . . . *ahem*. I'm getting ahead of myself."

Dr. Farley smiled at Cody, showing his hideous teeth.

"Rest assured, Cody Mack," he added. "When that day comes, you'll be at the center of it. I knew when I first met you that you'd make a perfect specimen."

"Specimen?"

"Er, example." Farley coughed. "Your progress will be an example to all."

Cody stood, knocking over his chair. "I want to go to class. That's okay, right? I mean, this is a school, isn't it?"

Dr. Farley pressed the buzzer for Miss Threadbare. "It is. Nice job being committed to your studies. Here. Have a Swedish fish."

CHAPTER NINE

THE ASSIGNMENT

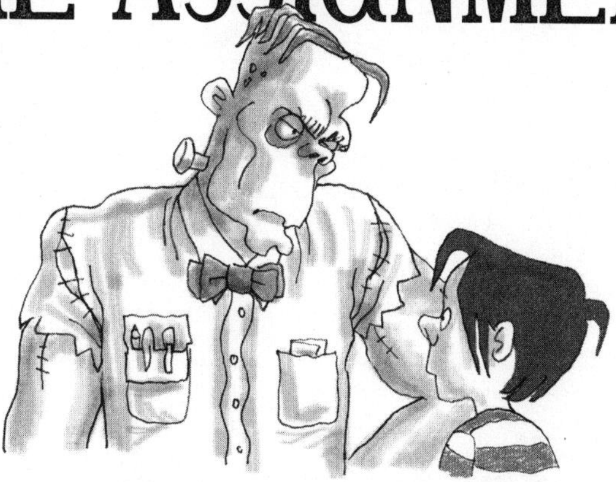

After lunch the next day, Cody returned to class to find Mr. Fronk sleeping at his desk. Cody burped. *Ugh*. Baloney stir-fry was bad enough the first time around.

Fronk opened one eye. "Homework essays due in ten minutes."

Uh-oh, Cody thought. *Forgot about that. "Why I Love Splurch Academy"? As if!*

Cody didn't generally do homework. But sometimes, to prevent certain teachers from going hysterical, Cody Mack The Poetic Genius saved the day. Teachers, Cody found, were suckers for poetry.

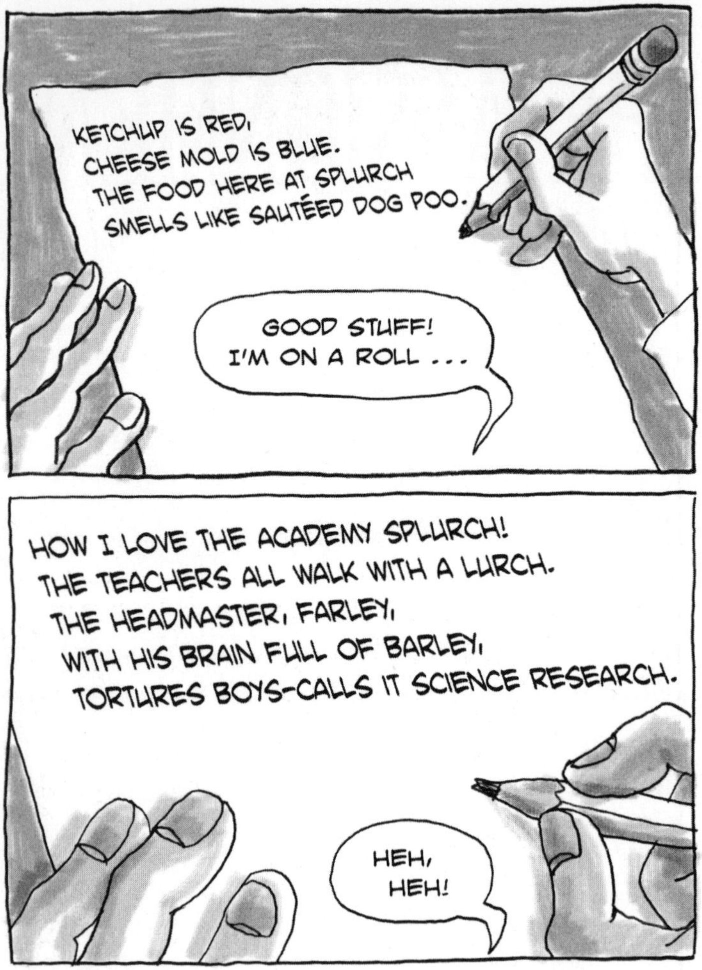
KETCHUP IS RED,
CHEESE MOLD IS BLUE.
THE FOOD HERE AT SPLURCH
SMELLS LIKE SAUTÉED DOG POO.
GOOD STUFF! I'M ON A ROLL . . .
HOW I LOVE THE ACADEMY SPLURCH!
THE TEACHERS ALL WALK WITH A LURCH.
THE HEADMASTER, FARLEY,
WITH HIS BRAIN FULL OF BARLEY,
TORTURES BOYS-CALLS IT SCIENCE RESEARCH.
HEH, HEH!

Not bad! An easy *C*, for sure. He dropped it in the homework basket on Fronk's desk and picked up his next assignment, a math packet. It made his eyes cross.

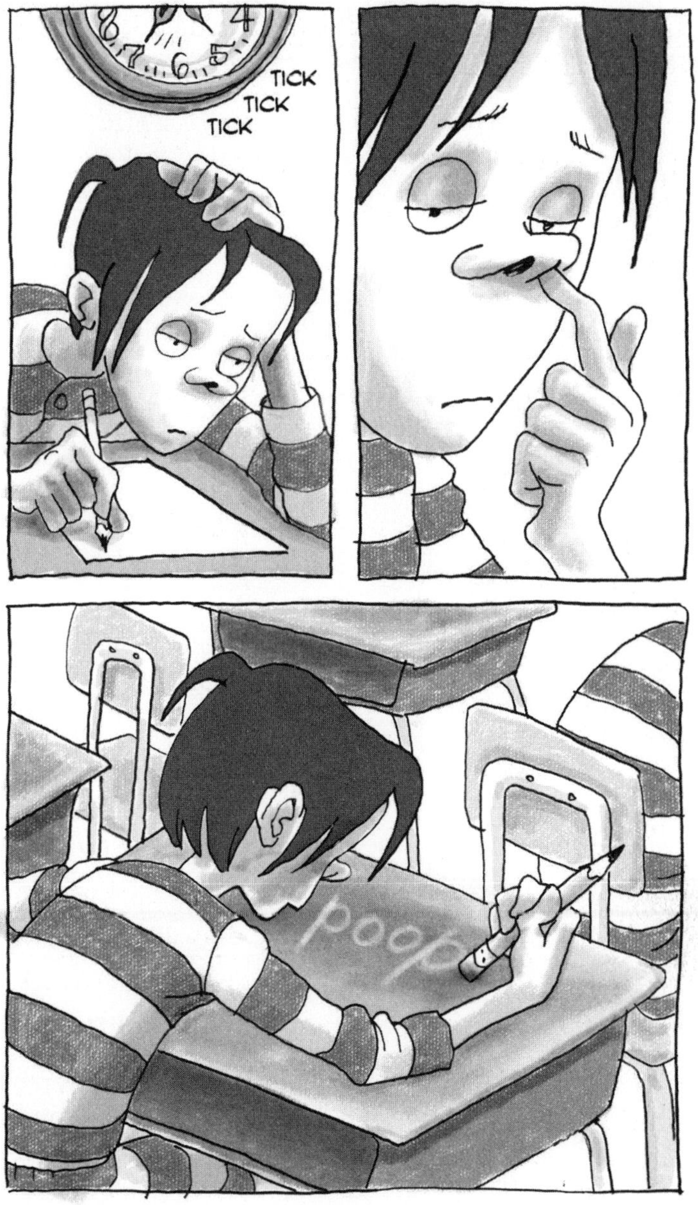
TICK
TICK
TICK
poop

Ten minutes before class ended, Mr. Fronk opened his eyes and started correcting the essays. Finally, the bell rang.

"Mr. Mack," Mr. Fronk said as the students filed out the door. "Up here."

Aw, man! He'd done *nothing* all day long, and he still got in trouble! Sheesh.

Cody approached the desk. Mr. Fronk shoved Cody's essay toward him.

Apparently Fronk wasn't a poetry fan.

He'd circled the line that read, "tortures boys, calls it science research."

"Well? What is it?" Cody asked.

"Care to tell me what you mean by this?" Mr. Fronk said.

"Uh . . ."

"We haven't been *snooping around the laboratory*, have we?"

"What *laboratory*?" Cody shook his head.

Fronk's voice rumbled. "Never mind. Don't look for trouble, new boy. It'll find you first." He slammed his folder shut with a bang. "You'll spend this evening in the library writing a real essay."

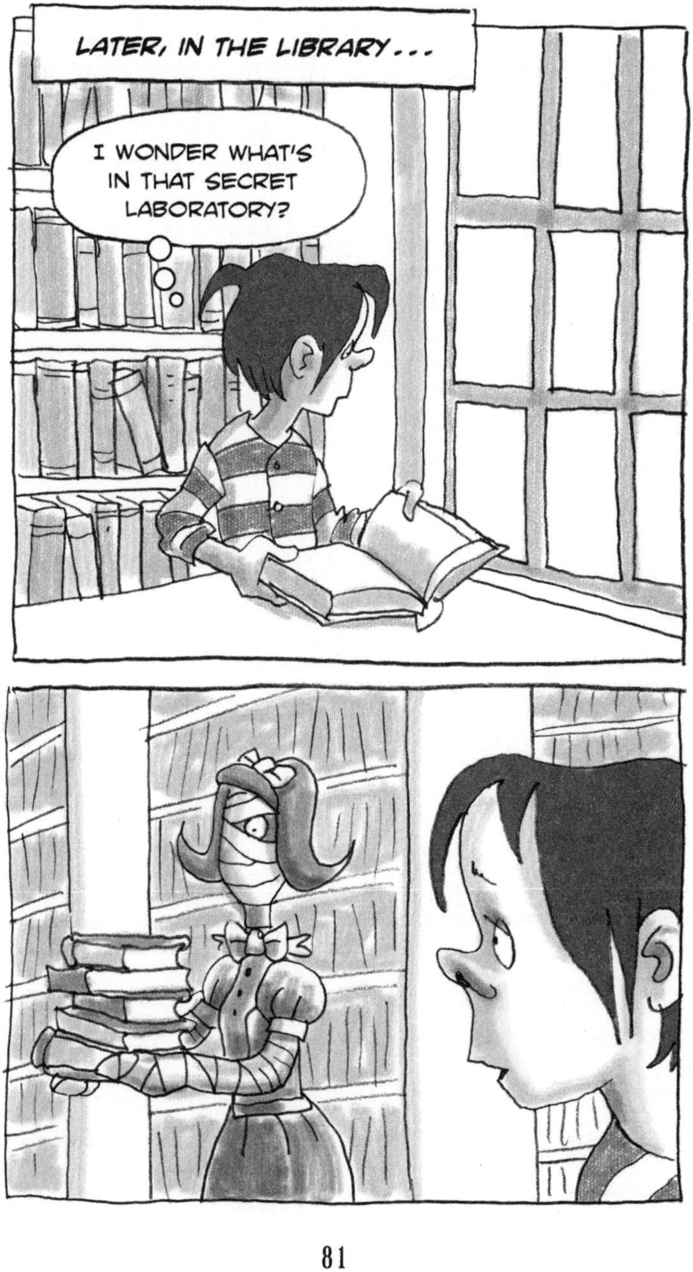
LATER, IN THE LIBRARY . . .
I WONDER WHAT'S IN THAT SECRET LABORATORY?

The librarian tottered by. Cody didn't like her bandagey face, but his mom always said to be nice to little old ladies and people with strange diseases.

So now he was supposed to write a real essay on why he loved Splurch Academy. Professor Fronk must be out of his mind.

Then again, from the looks of him, Cody wondered whether Fronk's mind was even his own. Probably not. At least, not originally.

Cody's gaze fell on the metal grate covering the air duct. It was pretty big. If only he could climb through the walls and find a way out . . . or maybe the laboratory would have something that he could use to escape.

Could he climb through walls?

Hmm. No harm in trying.

Unless, of course, this shaft led straight down to the heater.

Would he get sizzled to a crisp in the furnace?

Was that worse than staying here at Splurch Academy forevermore?

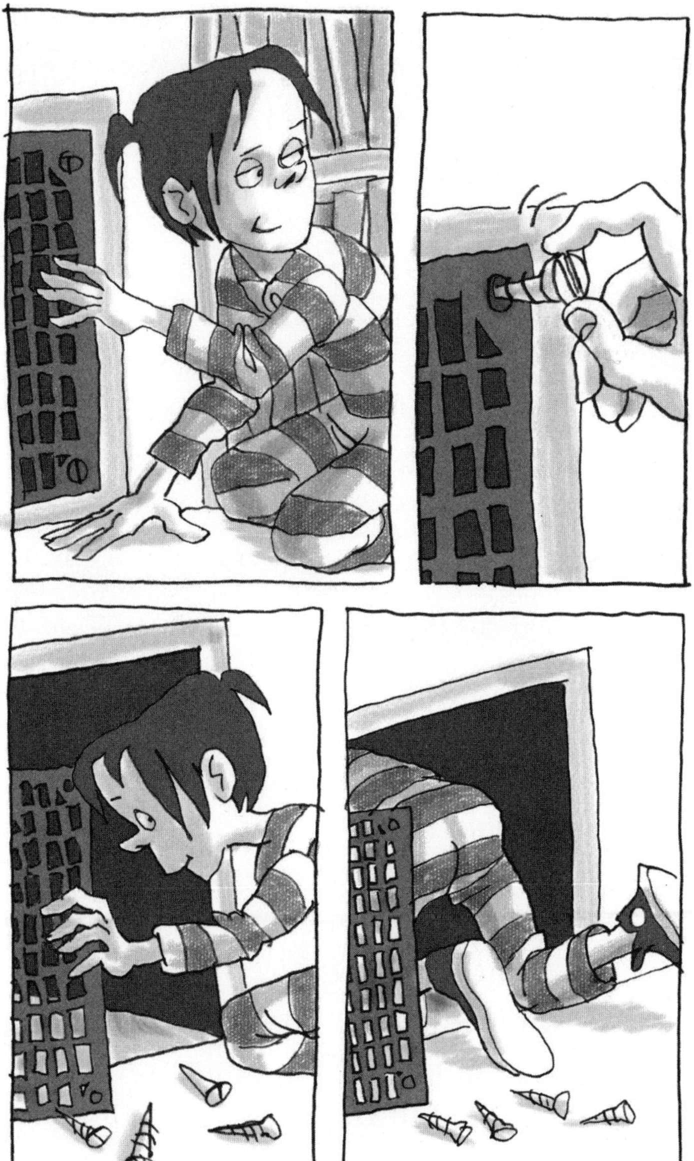

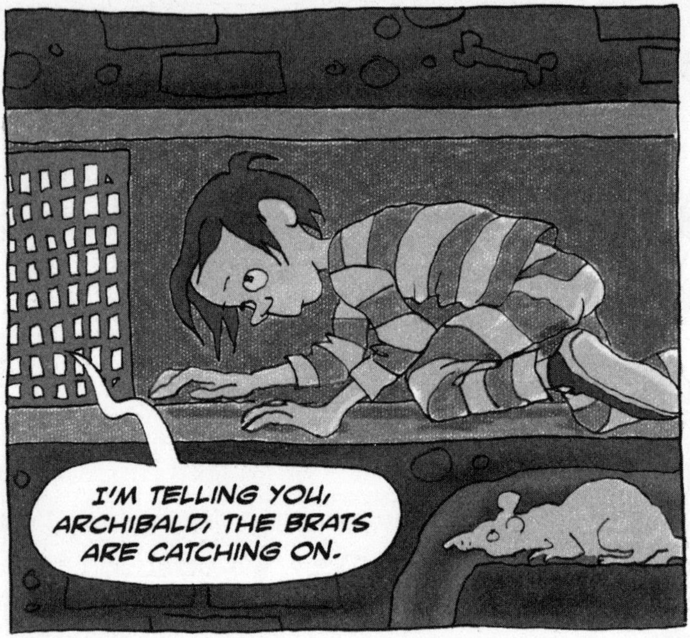
I'M TELLING YOU, ARCHIBALD, THE BRATS ARE CATCHING ON.

It was Fronk! Cody scooted closer.

"Cody Mack knows something."

Now *that* was something Cody'd never heard a teacher say.

"Calm yourself, Prometheus. I have Cody Mack well under control."

Oh you do, do you, Farley?

"How much longer do we wait? I'm sick of the nasty squids!" Nurse Bilgewater said.

Cody peeked through the vent.

"We're days away from testing the

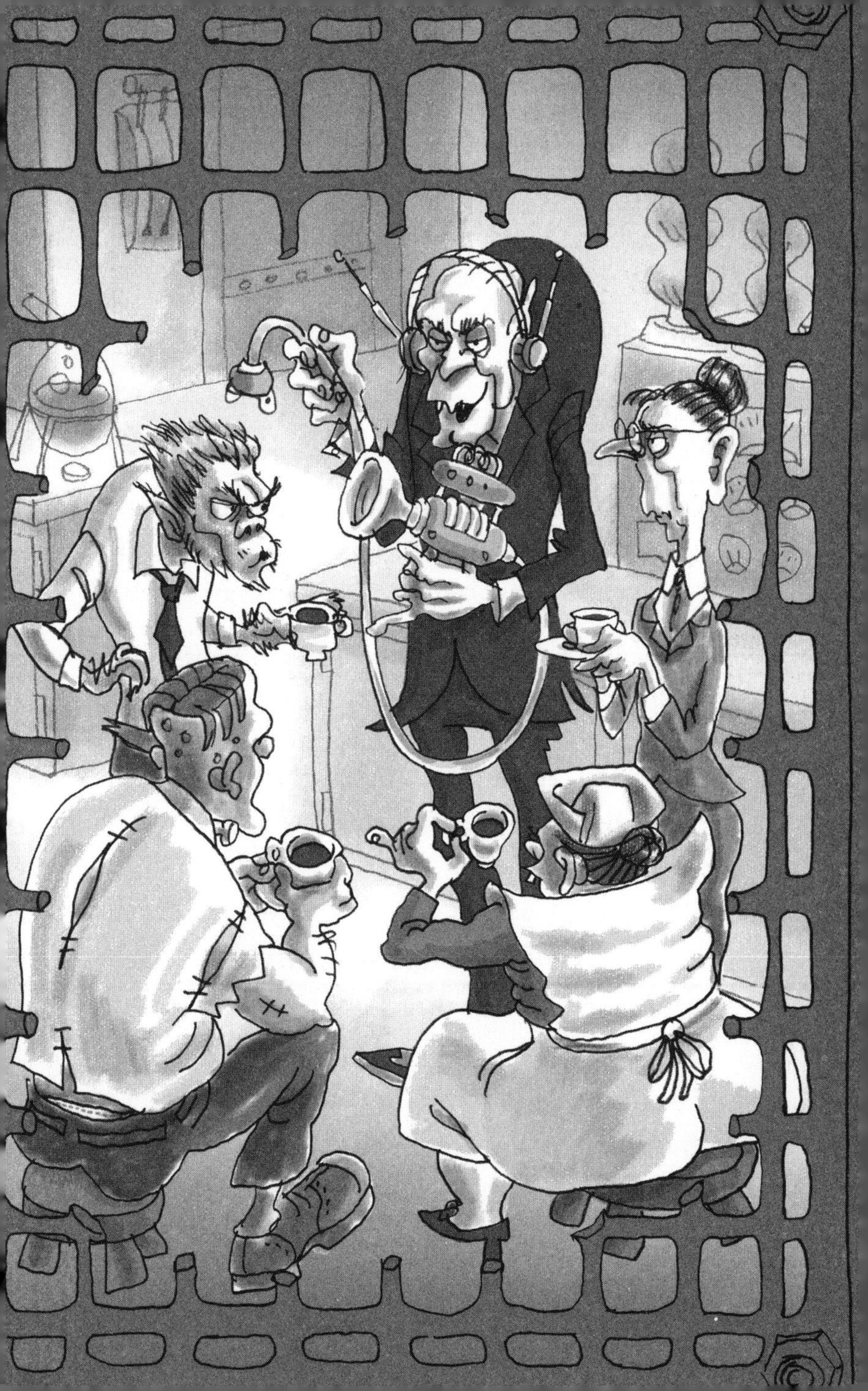

machine on actual specimens," Farley said. "A few refinements, and she's ready. I know just the boy to start with."

The teachers chuckled.

Cody gulped.

Nurse Bilgewater stuck out her lower lip. "Make it soon, will you, Archie?"

"As soon as we've taken care of Mr. Mack, Beulah, we'll swap all the students. With these," he tapped his earphones, "they'll do our bidding. The world will marvel at the revolutionary Farley Method for curing disruptive boys!"

Swap?!?! Huh?

"Getting dark out," Mr. Howell said, flexing his long arms. "Can we wrap this up?"

"One more thing," Fronk said. "I think inviting parents—and especially *her*—is a big mistake. Too risky. What if something goes wrong?"

"Nonsense, Prometheus," Farley said. "Where is your sense of adventure? The League of Reform Schools will be dazzled by our achievements! And we'll make a fortune. Celebrities and dictators worldwide will shower us with money to reform their rotten sons. We'll live like kings. And we'll never deal with another loathsome little boy. Ever! It's a brilliant solution."

"But will it work?" Mr. Fronk pressed. "Will it really satisfy the rules? We *can't* harm them."

"Inside the *school*," Nurse Bilgewater corrected him. "*Only* inside the school."

"We're not harming boys, we're fixing them," Farley said. "They'll be model citizens. Guaranteed!" Dr. Farley smiled his oily smile. "*This* is the loophole we've been looking for."

Mr. Howell rose, stretched, and threw open the double doors. "Enough of this chitter-chatter. Moonlight's wasting. Let's get moving. Chop-chop."

Howell threw open a large door, stepped outside, and sniffed the air, reaching for the moon. "Aaaahhh."

Cody crawled to the next vent for a better view. And just in time! Howell's body hunkered forward. Hair tufted from his hands and face. His shirt and pants split open as a giant wolf body emerged!

Pavlov barked and sprang off after Mr. Howell.

Nurse Bilgewater waddled across the threshold, pulling off her hairnet. Her dark hair waved like seaweed. Her legs dissolved into eight squelchy, dripping tentacles.

"Hurry up, Tessie," she gurgled.

Miss Threadbare stepped outside, tucked her spectacles into her pocket, then let out an earsplitting hawk's cry. She shook her head as a sharp beak replaced her nose. Her fingers became vicious talons. Bat wings popped from her shoulders. She leaped into the sky.

Mr. Fronk stripped off his jacket, unbuttoned his shirt, and lumbered outside. His skin went knobbly, his skull stretched, and the scars on his face turned into screws and stitches.

A Frankenstein!

"Hurry up, Archie," Miss Threadbare the bat-hawk screeched. "We're waiting!"

Dr. Farley nuzzled Rasputin, tucked him into his cage, then stowed his strange devices in a cabinet. He tossed his lab coat on the couch, then hopped out the door.

"He's a Dracula!" Cody whispered.

"Jolly hunting, my friends," Farley cried. "Tallyho!"

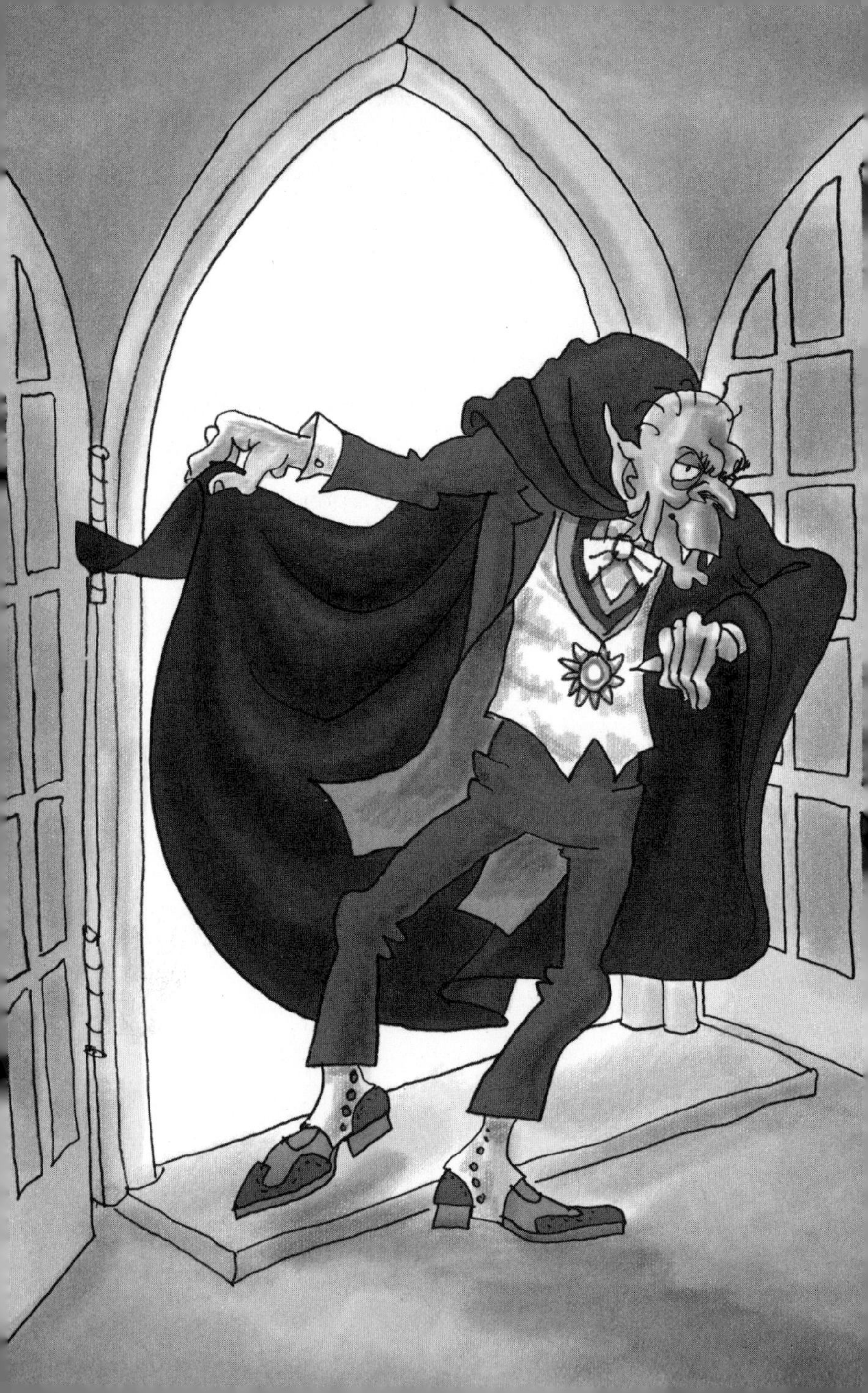

CHAPTER TEN
THE CADILLAC

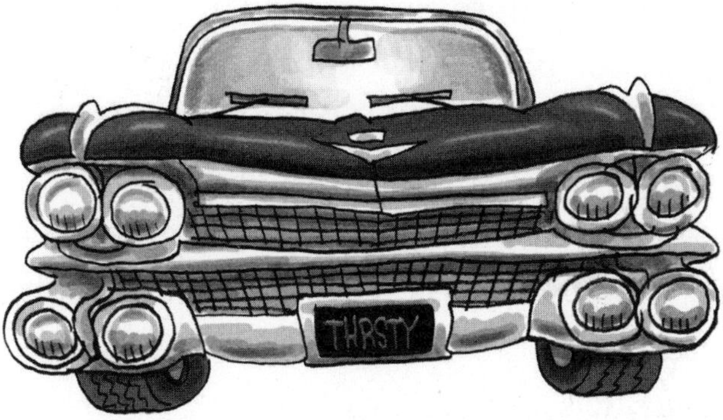
THRSTY

Splurch Academy's teachers slipped out into the night, wailing horrible monster cries. Their screams echoed until at last the sounds faded away.

Inside the dark, stuffy air ducts, Cody Mack shivered. And *not* because he was cold.

They were *monsters.*

Real monsters.

Real, live, rip-your-eyeballs-out-and-eat-them-with-ketchup monsters. The kind Cody thought only existed in comic books. If he hadn't seen it with his own eyes, he'd never have believed it.

On the other hand, deep down, hadn't he known from the moment he laid eyes on Farley?

But that didn't matter now. These Splurch Academy monsters had some kind of sinister plan to do something evil to the boys, and soon. Cody wasn't sure what, but he knew it wasn't anything good.

It was time to leave this looney bin. Quick, before Cody Mack became Midnight Snack.

But what about the other boys? They hadn't exactly bonded, but he didn't want their eyeballs eaten, either.

This might be the moment to run for it, while the teachers were outside. It might be the only chance they'd get.

He crawled backward through the air ducts until he reached another vent. He pushed through and tumbled into a dark room. Feeling along the walls, he discovered hanging tools, flashlights, keys, and finally a light switch. It was a garage, with Farley's old Cadillac parked inside. He ran out of the garage and up the stairs to the dorms.

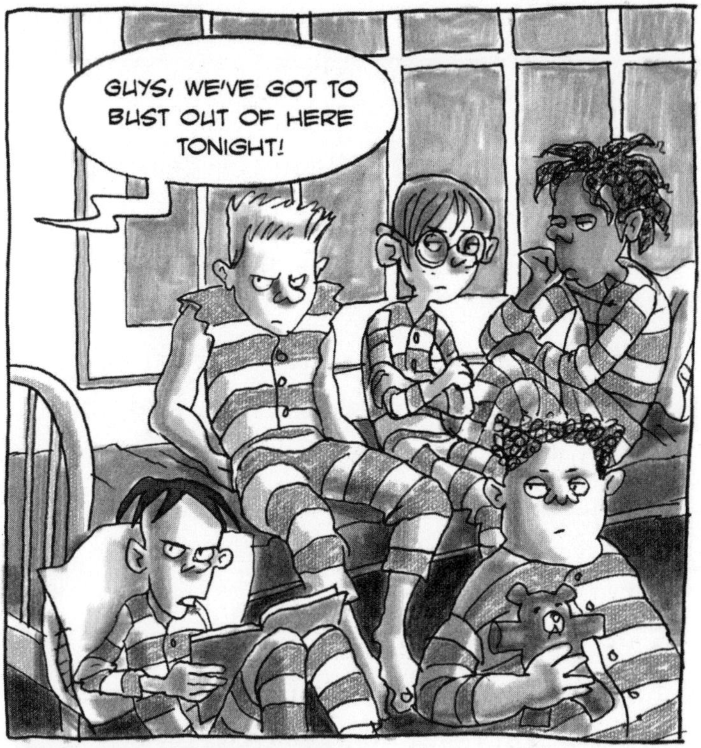
GUYS, WE'VE GOT TO BUST OUT OF HERE TONIGHT!

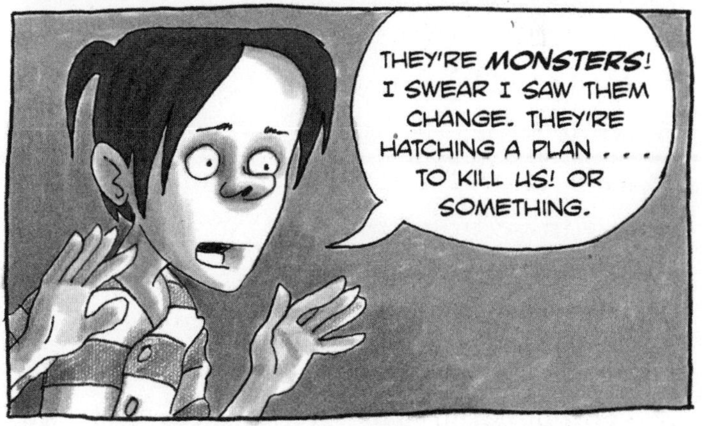
THEY'RE **MONSTERS**! I SWEAR I SAW THEM CHANGE. THEY'RE HATCHING A PLAN . . . TO KILL US! OR SOMETHING.

"Or something? How can it be: kill us or something?" Mugsy asked.

"Farley said, in a couple of days we'll be *swapped*, and they'll never deal with us again."

"Woo-hoo! They're sending us home!" Carlos said.

"They're retiring to Bermuda, and hiring pretty teachers!" Ratface added.

"Guys," Cody said. "They're not sending us home or retiring, I swear. You should've seen Farley's torture device. Like a plunger!"

"So Farley's fixing a toilet," Sully said. "Guys, meet the new Billy Whistler. Cody, nice knowing you. You're toast."

So much for saving lives! No time to waste. "Have it your way. Tomorrow morning I'll be eating Pop-Tarts and sausage and chocolate milk for breakfast. Have fun getting *swapped*."

He ran back down the stairs to the garage, felt along the wall for the keys, and climbed into the Cadillac.

Which pedal was "go" and which was

"stop"? He couldn't reach either. He cranked the front seat forward. Now what? Turn the key, and . . . think. Think! *You've watched your parents start cars billions of times!*

A tap at the window made him jump. It was Victor.

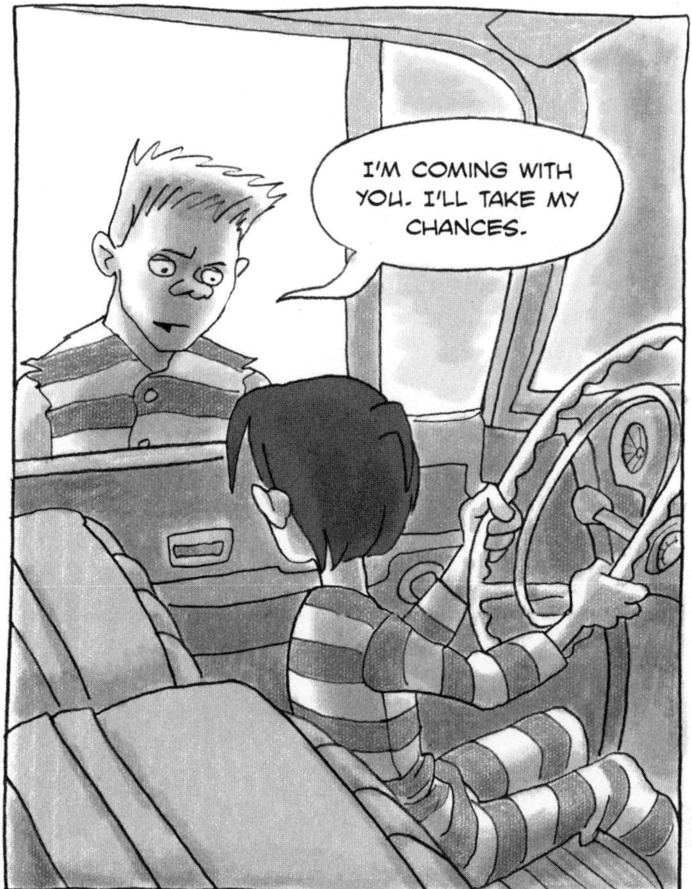
I'M COMING WITH YOU. I'LL TAKE MY CHANCES.

"Know anything about driving a car?"

"I'll do the pedals," Victor said. "Hey, Cody?"

"Hmm?"

"Instead of going to my house, can I, er, stay at yours?"

Cody looked at Victor. Victor looked away.

"Sure," Cody said. "Absolutely. So, is it key first and then shifter?"

Mugsy and Ratface squooshed their faces against the glass.

"Pop-Tarts and chocolate milk?" Mugsy said. They climbed in beside Victor.

"This had better work, Cody," Ratface said. "Otherwise we're dead."

"It'll work," Cody said. He wished he felt as sure as he sounded. "Ready, men? Home we go!"

There was a frantic knocking at the window. "Let us in!" Carlos and Sully climbed in. "Might as well die together," Carlos said.

"Ready?" Cody asked.

"Ready," Victor said.

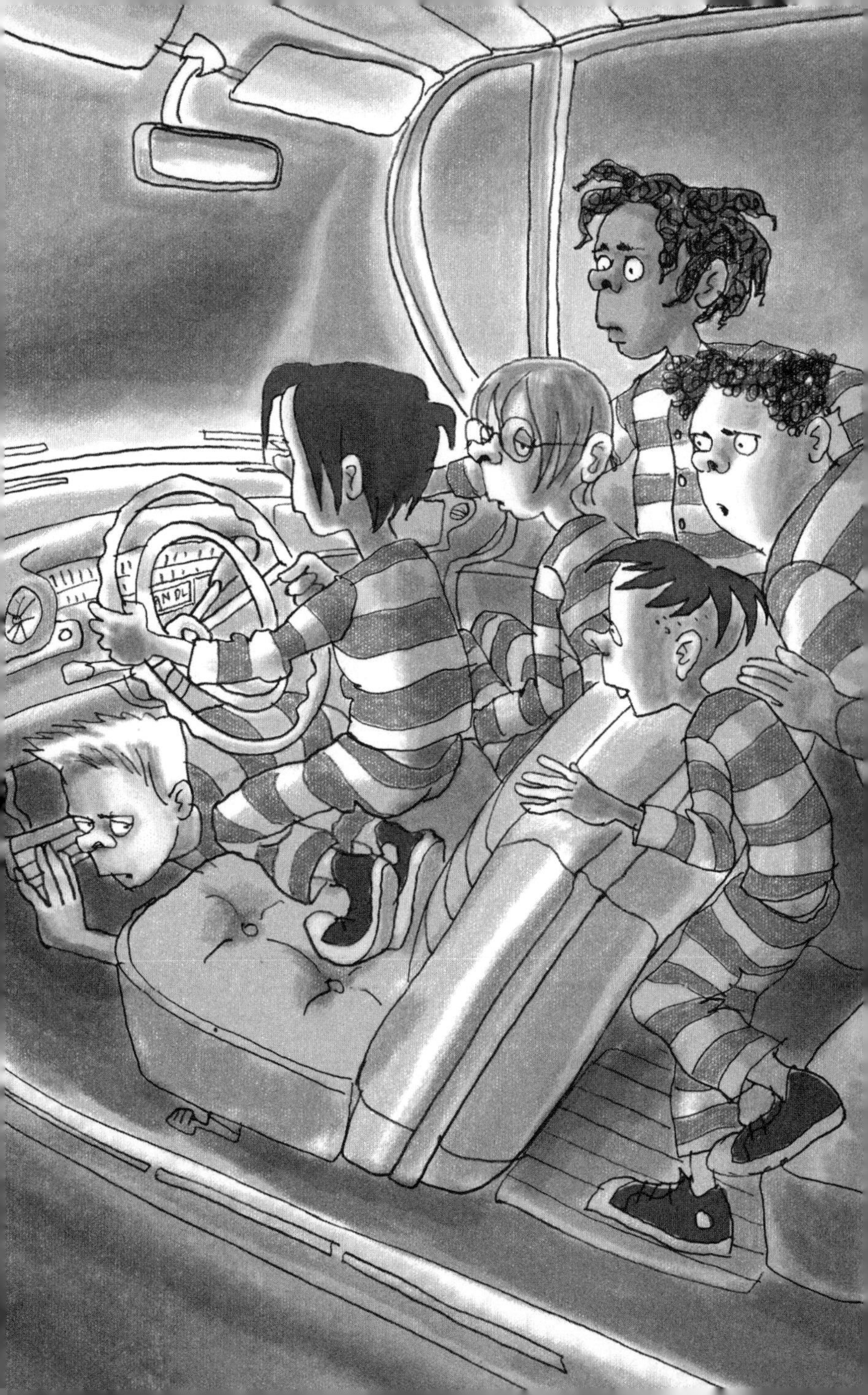

"You gonna open the garage door?" Carlos asked.

"When the car's running." Cody turned the key. The engine coughed to life. "Give it gas, Victor!"

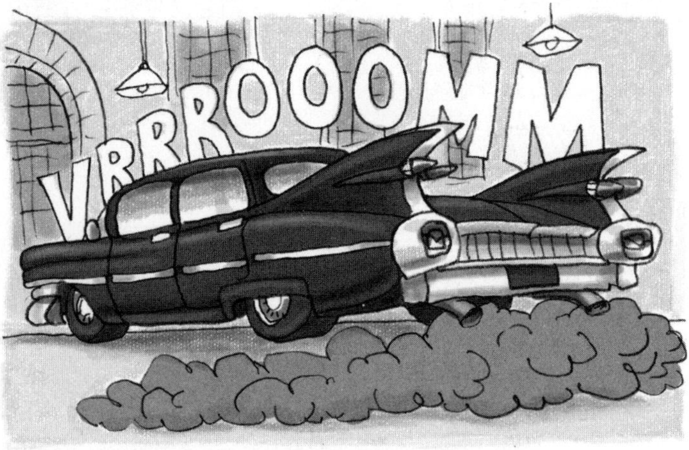
VRRROOOMM

The engine roared, but the car didn't budge. The huge roar reverberated off the garage walls. *If this were my dad's car, he'd kill me,* Cody thought.

"Why doesn't it go?" Cody asked.

"You've got to shift into gear," Sully said.

"Right," Cody said, embarrassed. "I knew that. Let off the gas, Vic."

"Use the brake," Sully said.

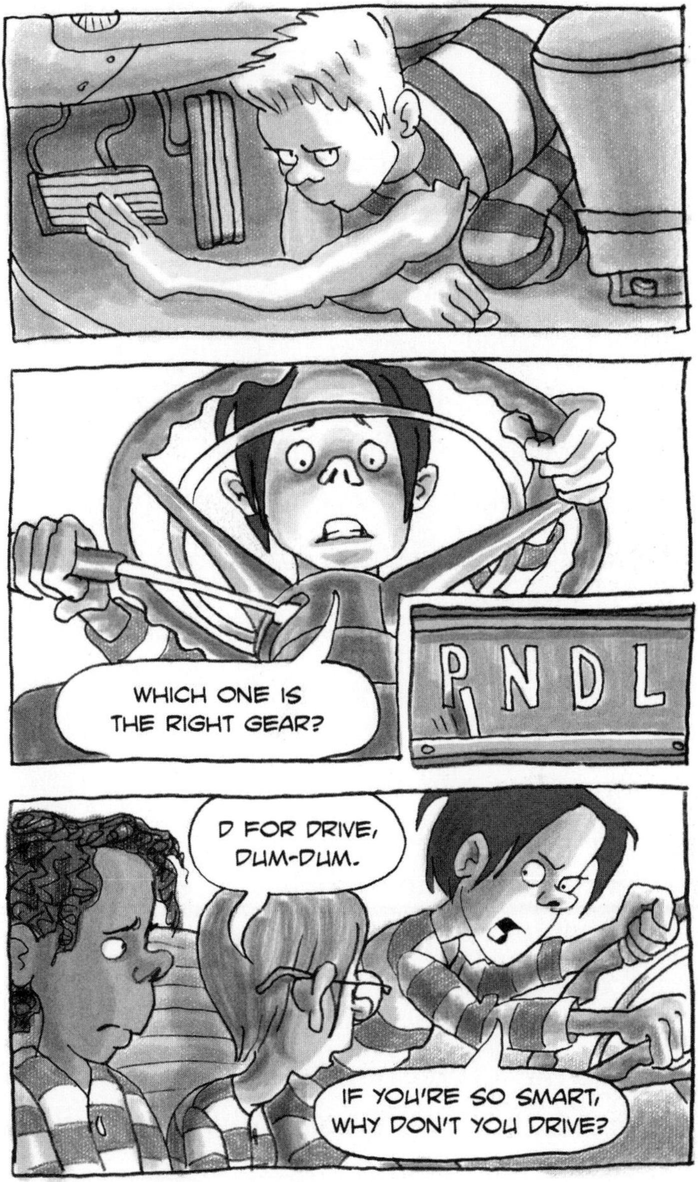
WHICH ONE IS THE RIGHT GEAR?
P N D L
D FOR DRIVE, DUM-DUM.
IF YOU'RE SO SMART, WHY DON'T YOU DRIVE?

Cody pressed the big button on the garage door opener. Nothing happened.

He pressed it over and over.

"My grandma's got one of those things," Mugsy said. "You're supposed to enter a code on the buttons."

"*What* code?" Ratface wailed.

"Try spelling 'EVIL,'" Carlos said.

"Are you kidding? We'll never crack Farley's code in time," Sully said.

Cody looked at his friends' anxious faces. It was now or never.

"Hit the gas, Victor," he said. "Hit it hard!"

"Wait . . . " Sully said. Victor pounded on the pedal.

Cody let go of the brake.

"We're dead meat!"

"I'm too young to die!"

"I can't see!" Cody said.

"Turn on the headlights," Sully said.

"Which one's the headlights?" Cody flipped the levers. Wipers swished, squirters squirted, the radio blared oldies, but still no lights. "I can't find them!"

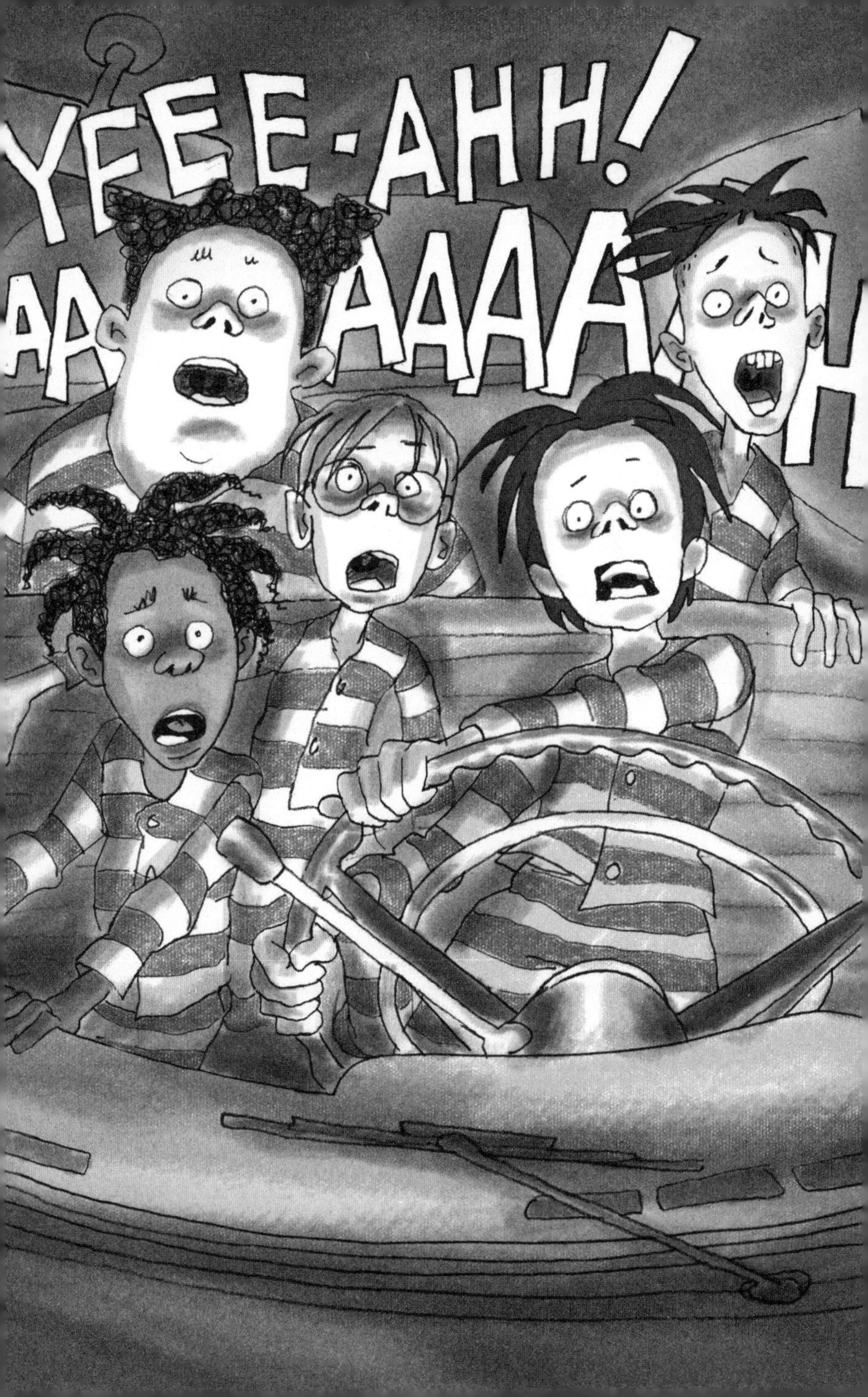
YEEE-AHH!
AAAAAAAH

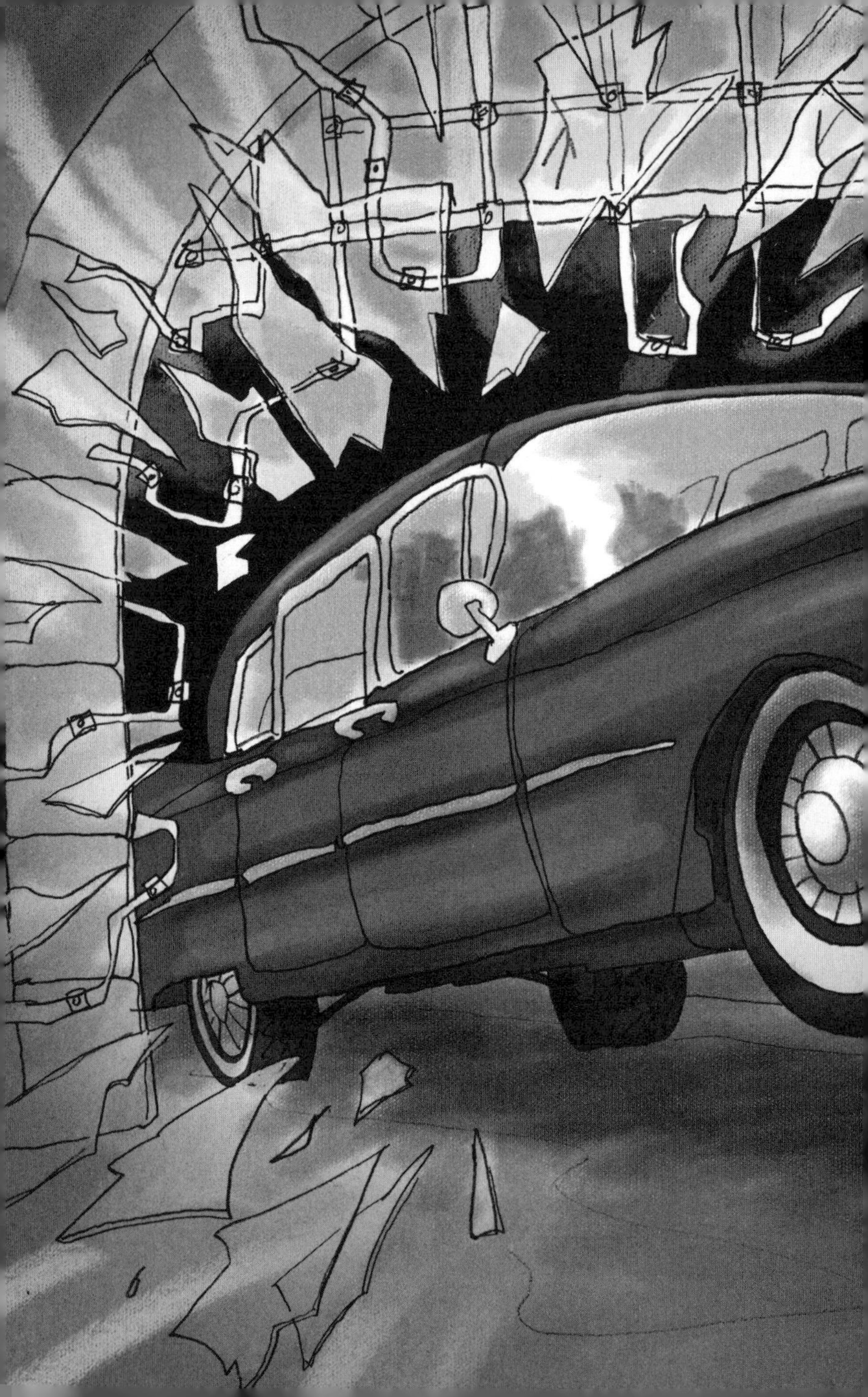

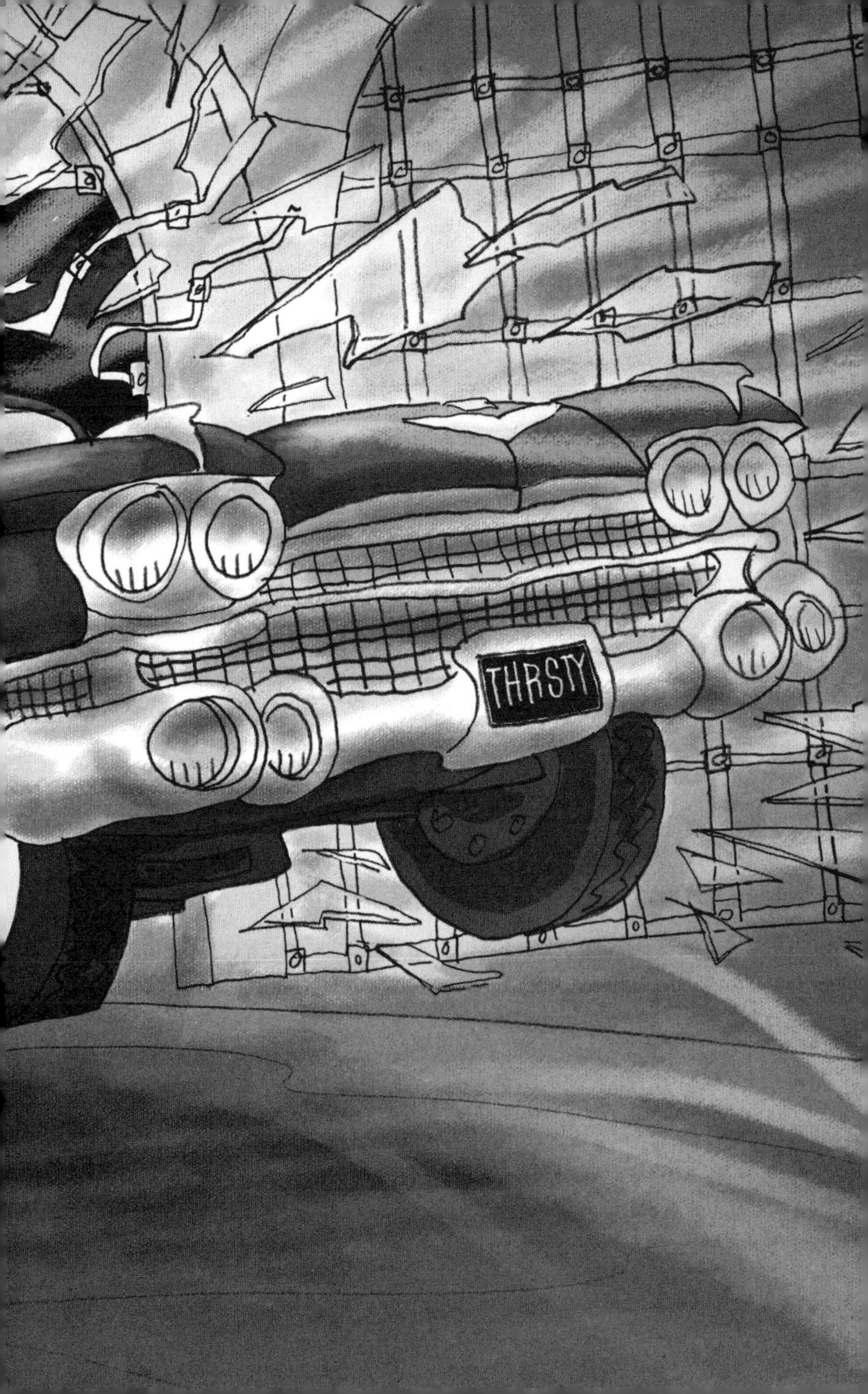
THRSTY

Cody spun the wheel. The car quickly swerved just before they crashed into a stone fountain.

"Quit the sightseeing," Sully said. "Let's vamoose!"

"What moose?" Mugsy said.

"Carlos, find the lights, " Cody yelled as the car veered again, this time just missing a bench.

They zigzagged across the grounds, the spinning wheels tearing up turf.

"Where's the gate?" Cody cried. "We're never going to get out if we can't find the . . ."

"Um . . ." Mugsy said. "Uh-uh-uh-ummm . . . Co-Cody?"

"Not now, Mugs!" Cody interrupted. "Carlos, find those lights!"

"Uh-uh-uh . . ." Mugsy's voice trailed off in a squeak.

"Quit whining!"

"C-c-company!" Mugsy sputtered.

"Found 'em!" Carlos cried, pulling out a knob.

The headlights burst on.

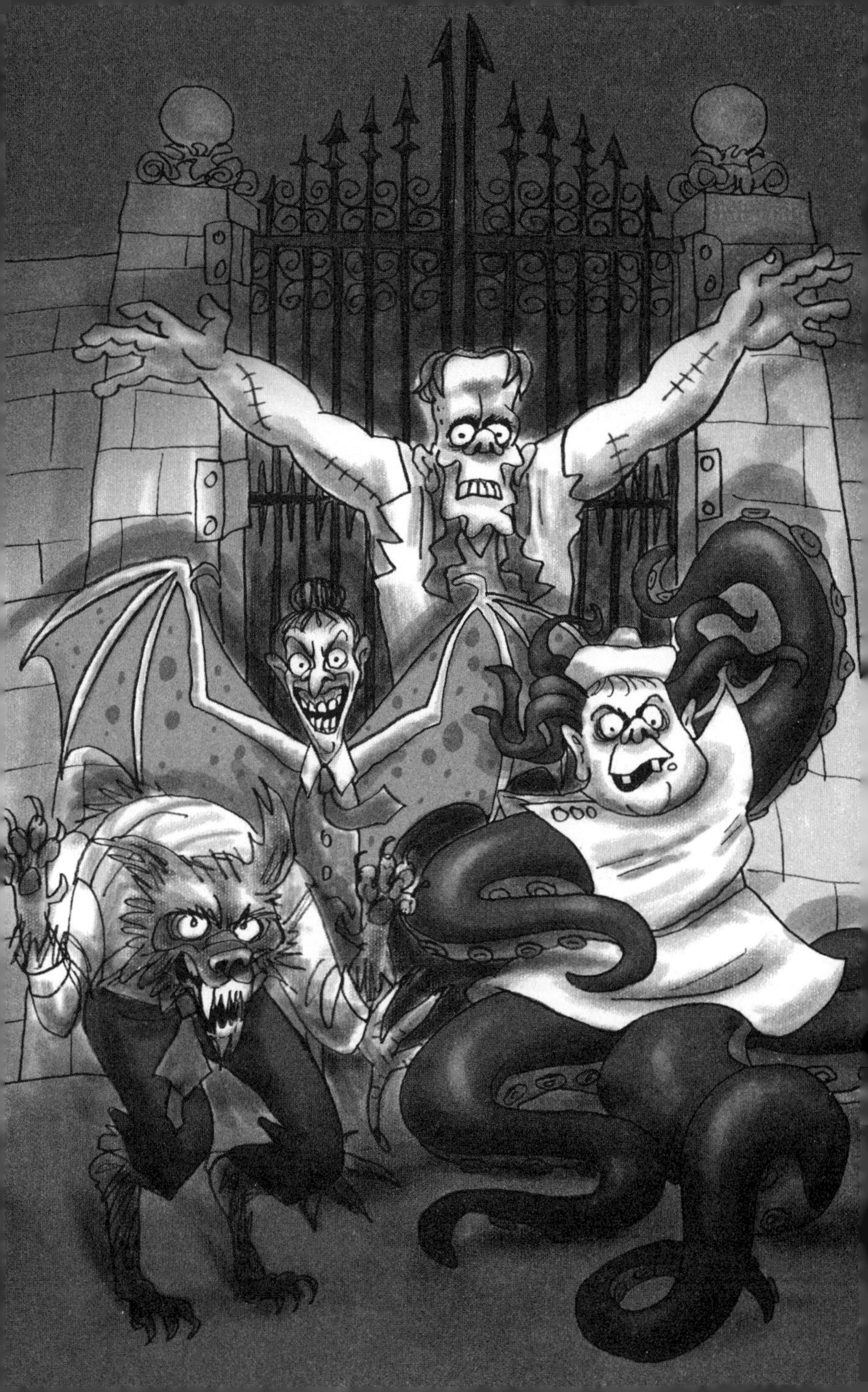

"Aaaaaaghhh!"

"BRAKES, VICTOR!" Cody cried.

"TURN AROUND!" Carlos yelled.

Cody spun the wheel. Victor mashed the gas pedal.

THUMP! The car roof caved. Fat tentacles probed the windows.

"Gas, Victor!" The car leaped forward. "Back to the garage!"

Monsters scattered like bowling pins. Howell, the werewolf, sprang for the driver's side, his jaw snapping.

"Lock the doors!" Cody yelled. Mugsy pounded the buttons.

The windows opened.

"Stop! Locks, not windows!"

Mugsy rolled the windows back up, pinching Bilgewater's tentacles as she reached inside. She screamed in rage.

The hawk-bat Miss Threadbare dived and slashed with her talons. One tire burst, and the car went wobbly. Mr. Fronk wrenched off the passenger door with a roar.

Dracula Farley suddenly appeared in the headlights, just before the garage.

Cody's hands shook with fear. Would they make it? Would they even be safe if they got back inside?

It was their only hope now. "Gas, Victor!"

Victor pressed the pedal all the way down. Cody steered hard to keep the car straight.

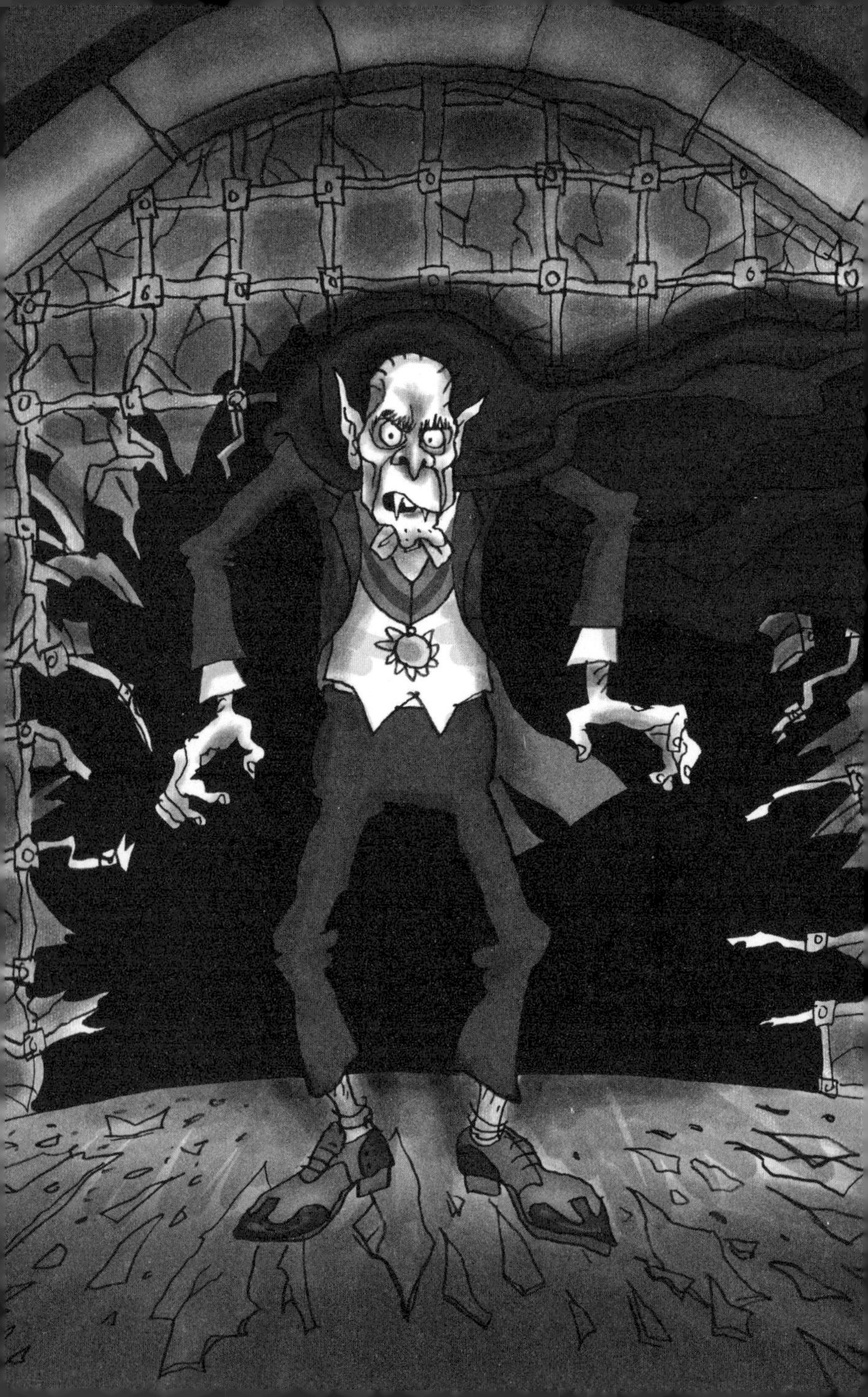

"You're gonna hit him!" Sully said.

Cody drove.

Farley vanished.

The Cadillac crunched into the garage's back wall.

Metal screamed and glass shattered. The boys shook themselves off and looked at one another. Slowly, they turned around.

Just outside the garage door, the teacher-monsters hissed and glared.

But they didn't come inside.

"L-lets g-go to bed," Cody stammered.

They climbed from the wreck, ran up to the dorms, and crawled into bed.

Cody waited for the insults and anger to begin. But nobody said a word. The silence was almost worse. They must hate his guts.

Then Cody heard a whimpering voice. He wasn't sure whose.

"They'll kill us in the morning."

CHAPTER ELEVEN

THE PHONE CALL

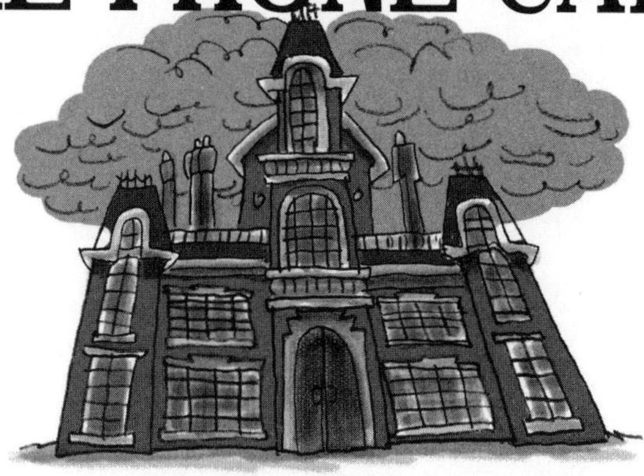

But the teachers didn't kill them in the morning.

The breakfast food didn't smell poisoned—no more so than normal. When they got to class, there was Mr. Fronk, just snoozing at his desk.

Cody's insides felt like a sackful of worms.

Outside, the skies were gray, thick with low-hanging clouds. It felt like a storm waiting to break. Not a blade of grass ruffled. Not a boy twitched.

The silence was so heavy that Cody

jumped when Miss Threadbare's voice came over the speaker. "Cody Mack to the headmaster's office."

Mr. Fronk cracked open an eyelid. Just enough to watch him leave.

Cody's shoes felt like they were full of lead. Was this how it felt to march to your doom?

Cody passed Ivanov in the hall.

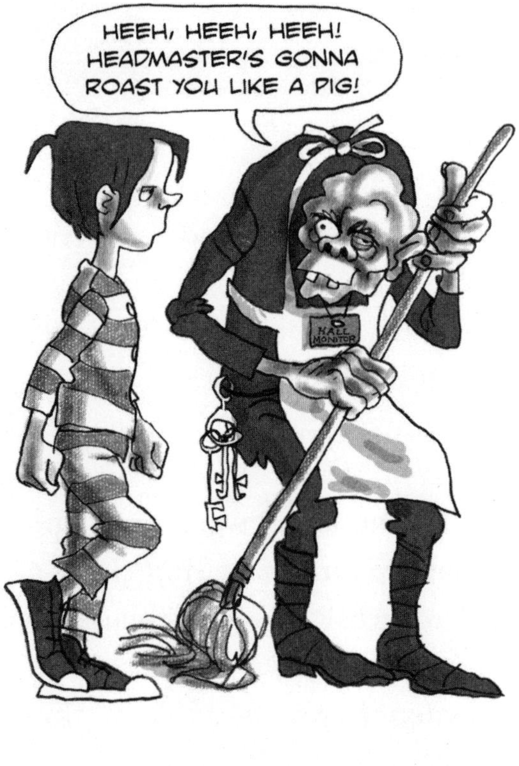
HEEH, HEEH, HEEH! HEADMASTER'S GONNA ROAST YOU LIKE A PIG!
HALL MONITOR

Cody's tongue felt like sandpaper. Did condemned kids get last requests? Was *he* the next Billy Whistler?

He took a deep breath and went inside.

Miss Threadbare stood at a filing cabinet. She peered at him, then buzzed Dr. Farley. "Mr. Mack is here."

"Show him in."

The headmaster sat behind his desk, smiling his phony baloney smile. Every muscle in Cody's body tensed. Would Farley invent some horrible punishment? Or just suck his blood right then and there?

"Mr. Mack," the headmaster said. "How are you this morning?"

Where's the trap? Cody waited for some net to fall.

"Come, come. I can't give you a Swedish fish if you don't answer." Farley's voice was as soft as a kitten's purr. "Is there anything you want to talk about?"

He's trying to catch me off guard.

"Well, then, I'll start the conversation. Isn't it a lovely day?" Dr. Farley steered Cody toward the window.

The clouds were nearly black, and a violent wind now buffeted the school. Crazy figure eights and deep-rutted brown grooves where Cody's driving had mangled the lawns stretched all the way to the faraway iron gate.

Dr. Farley took a toy car from his pocket— a replica of the one Cody had destroyed.

"Many boys are fond of automobiles," Dr. Farley said. "Do you like cars, Cody?"

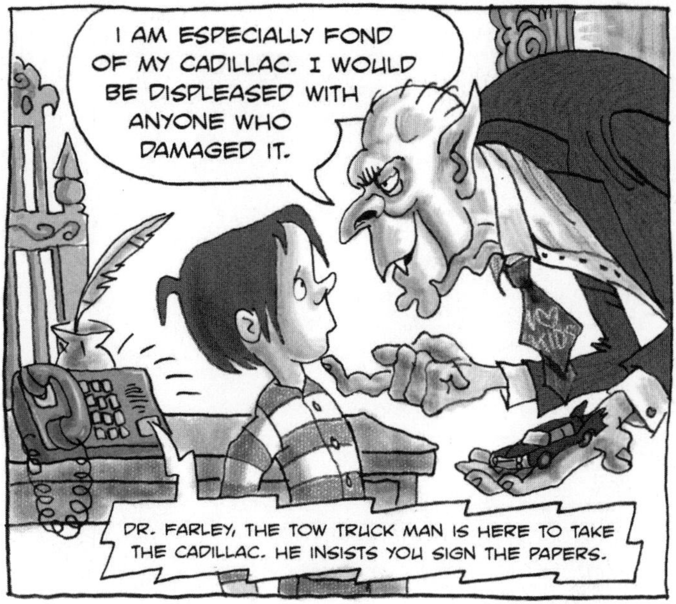
I AM ESPECIALLY FOND OF MY CADILLAC. I WOULD BE DISPLEASED WITH ANYONE WHO DAMAGED IT.
DR. FARLEY, THE TOW TRUCK MAN IS HERE TO TAKE THE CADILLAC. HE INSISTS YOU SIGN THE PAPERS.

At the word "Cadillac," Farley's left eye twitched. He stared at Cody while he spoke into the intercom.

"I'll be right there, Miss Threadbare." To Cody, he said, "Wait here." He turned and stalked out of his office.

Cody listened for the door to lock. Sure enough, there was the extra click.

Faraway thunder rumbled, and the lights in Farley's office flickered. Cody listened as Dr. Farley's footsteps grew fainter, then disappeared altogether.

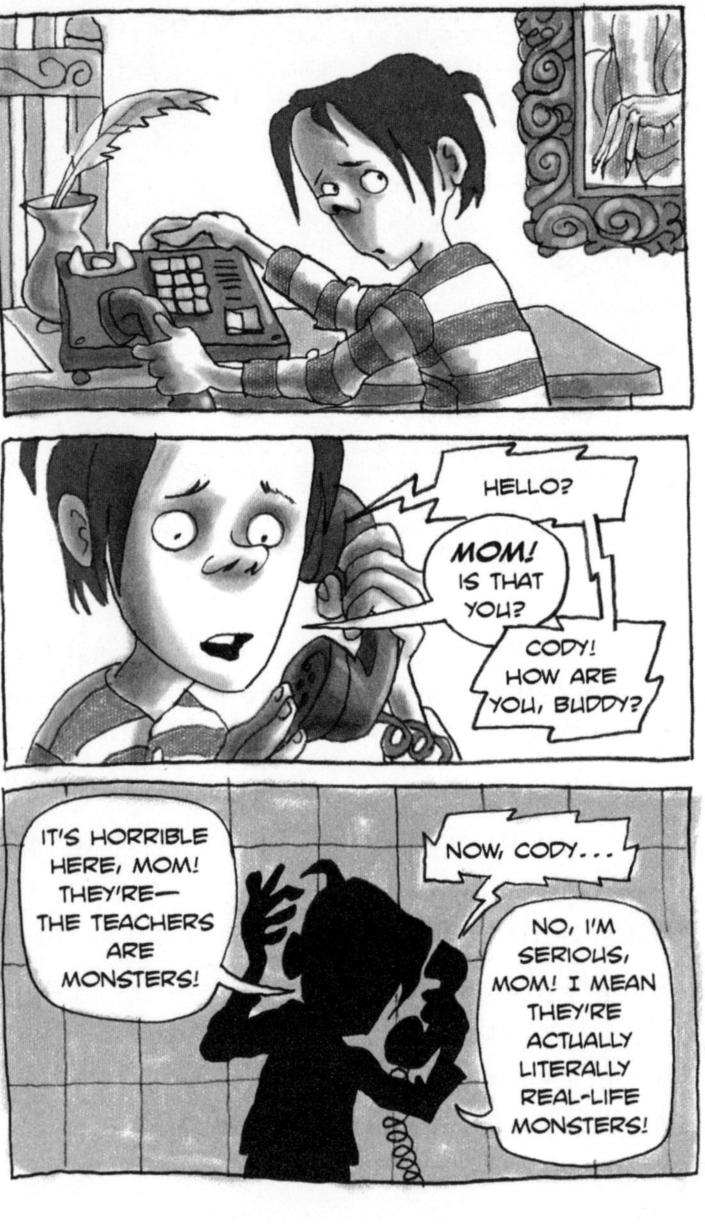
HELLO?
MOM! IS THAT YOU?
CODY! HOW ARE YOU, BUDDY?
IT'S HORRIBLE HERE, MOM! THEY'RE— THE TEACHERS ARE MONSTERS!
NOW, CODY...
NO, I'M SERIOUS, MOM! I MEAN THEY'RE ACTUALLY LITERALLY REAL-LIFE MONSTERS!

Cody's mom sighed. "I know it's hard adjusting. Discipline is no fun, but in the long run it'll help you . . ."

"Mom, they're gonna kill us! I swear! You need to come *now*, with police!"

"Cody. Be serious. They are *not* trying to kill you. It's a well-respected school!"

"By who, funeral parlors?" Cody shot back. "Mom, please! Take me home!"

"Is this like the time you said you'd climbed the school roof to save a wounded eagle, when really you cut class?"

Uh-oh.

Her voice got soft. "Oh, sweetheart. I know it's hard, but stick it out, okay?"

"Please, Mom. Please."

"We'll come visit you soon. I promise."

"They won't let you."

"Of course they will. Write me a letter and tell me everything."

"Good-bye, Mom. It's been nice knowing you."

"Oh, for heaven's sake, Co—"

Click.

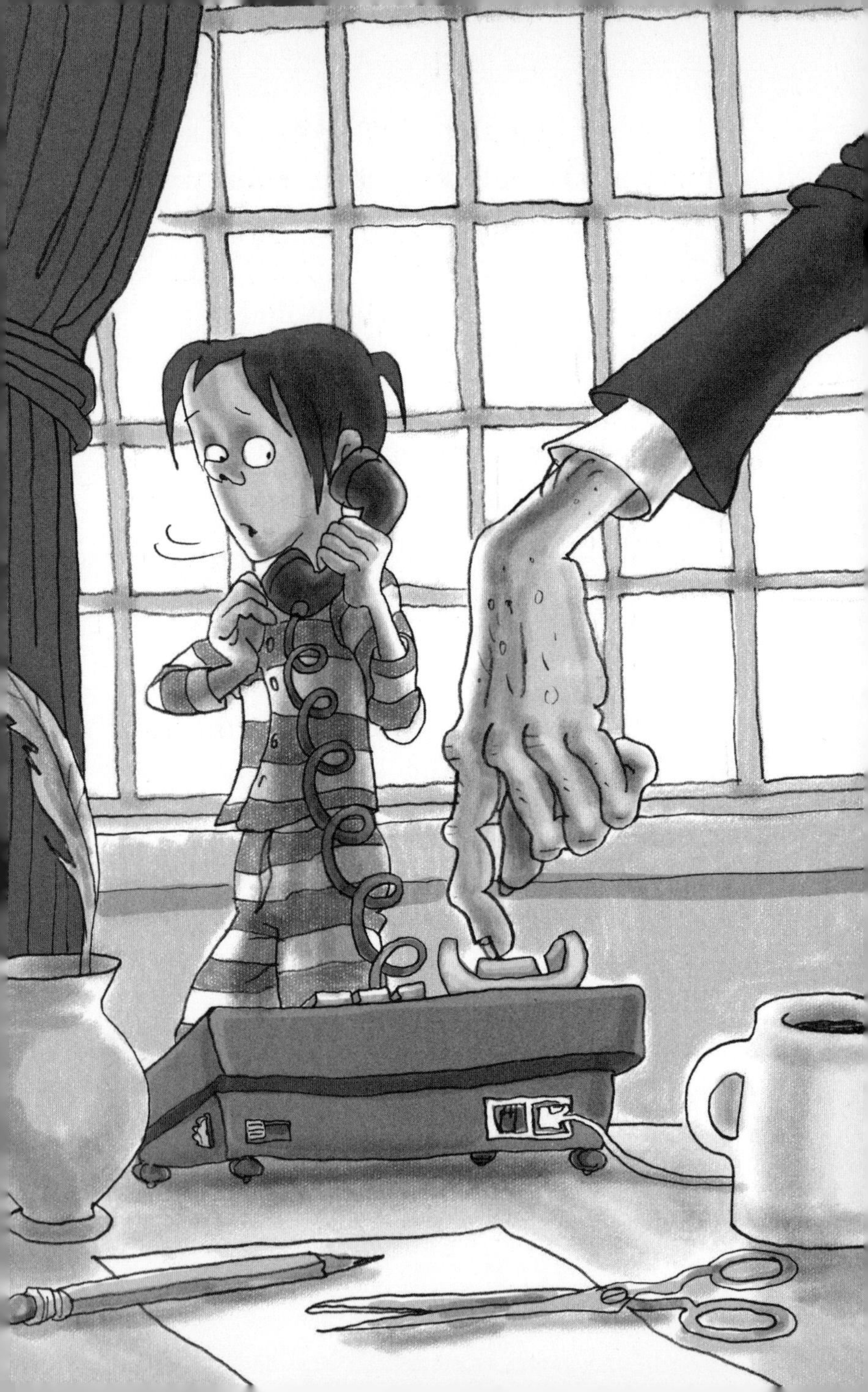

CHAPTER TWELVE
THE MACHINE

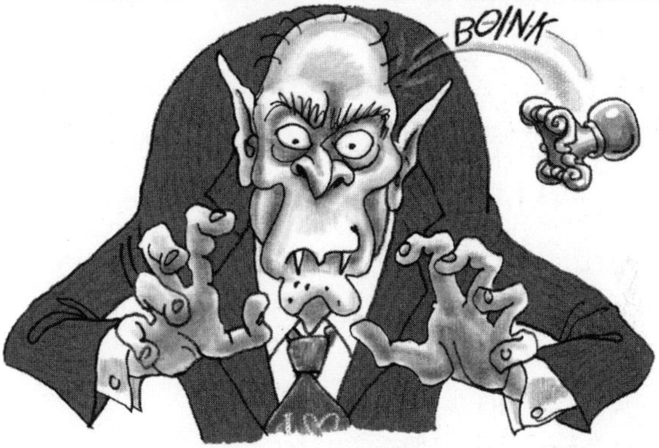
BOINK

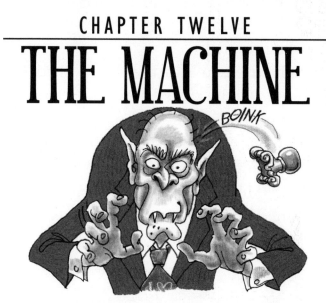

"A touching display of affection," Dr. Farley said. "It makes what I'm about to do a smidgeon harder."

Cody dropped the receiver and backed away from the desk.

"Your mother is a charming woman," Farley said. "A long, graceful neck, as I recall."

Cody whipped a paperweight at Farley. It bounced off his forehead. Farley didn't even flinch.

"Stay away from my mother!" Cody yelled. "Leave her neck alone!"

Farley advanced upon Cody. Outside, lightning flashed.

Cody tried to run but Farley had him cornered. Cody kicked his shins, and just about smashed his toes.

With an iron grip on his captive, Farley opened a door, revealing an ancient elevator. He prodded Cody inside, closed the gate, and flipped a squeaky lever. The floor dropped abruptly.

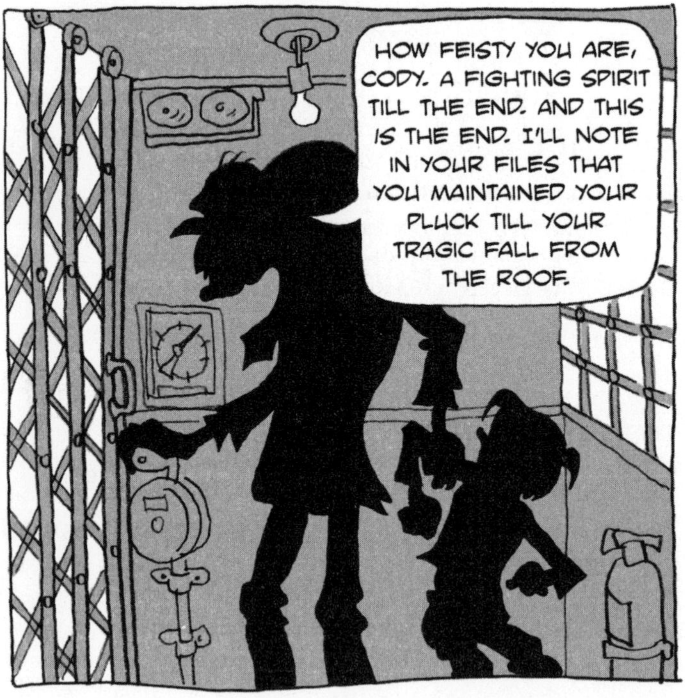
HOW FEISTY YOU ARE, CODY. A FIGHTING SPIRIT TILL THE END. AND THIS IS THE END. I'LL NOTE IN YOUR FILES THAT YOU MAINTAINED YOUR PLUCK TILL YOUR TRAGIC FALL FROM THE ROOF.

Shock hit Cody like cold water. Farley would kill him, and he'd already figured the story he'd tell Cody's parents. And they'd believe him.

They arrived in Farley's lab.

Farley forced Cody into a chair, then buckled straps over his arms, legs, and waist. There was no resisting his strength. He opened Rasputin's cage. The rat perched on his shoulder. Then the headmaster unlocked the cabinet with the plunger machine inside. He stroked the device.

"This, Cody, is my greatest invention," he said. "Its breakthrough technology will make me famous. *And* rich. Won't that be nice? That's why I can't afford to keep you around anymore. You're a danger to my plans."

"What'll you do, throw me off the roof?" Cody shouted.

"Oh mercy, no," Farley said. "What a waste of a perfectly good brain! A useful body, too. No, no. You, my boy, will not be killed. In fact, I'm bestowing a great honor on you. You will be the first student at

Splurch Academy to test . . . *the Rebellio-Rodent Recipronator*!"

A stab of lightning flooded the lab.

"Now hold very still, or it's bye-bye brain." He fastened Rasputin's head into a tiny helmet with a plunger.

Cody squirmed and fought for all he was worth. When that didn't work, he stalled for time. "What's a Rebellio—whatever you said?"

"Excellent question," Farley said as he attached a plunger over Cody's ear. "Tsk, tsk, I said hold still!"

He refastened Cody's plunger. "The rebellium cortex, or the part of the brain that makes you naughty, is located behind your ear. My invention, the Rebellio-Rodent Recipronator, sucks it out and swaps it with a rat's brain. No brain damage, no pain. At least, in theory."

"You sicko monster!" Cody screamed. "Why switch my brain with a *rat's*?"

"Not your entire brain," Farley corrected. "The part that makes you naughty."

"That's the part that makes me ME!"

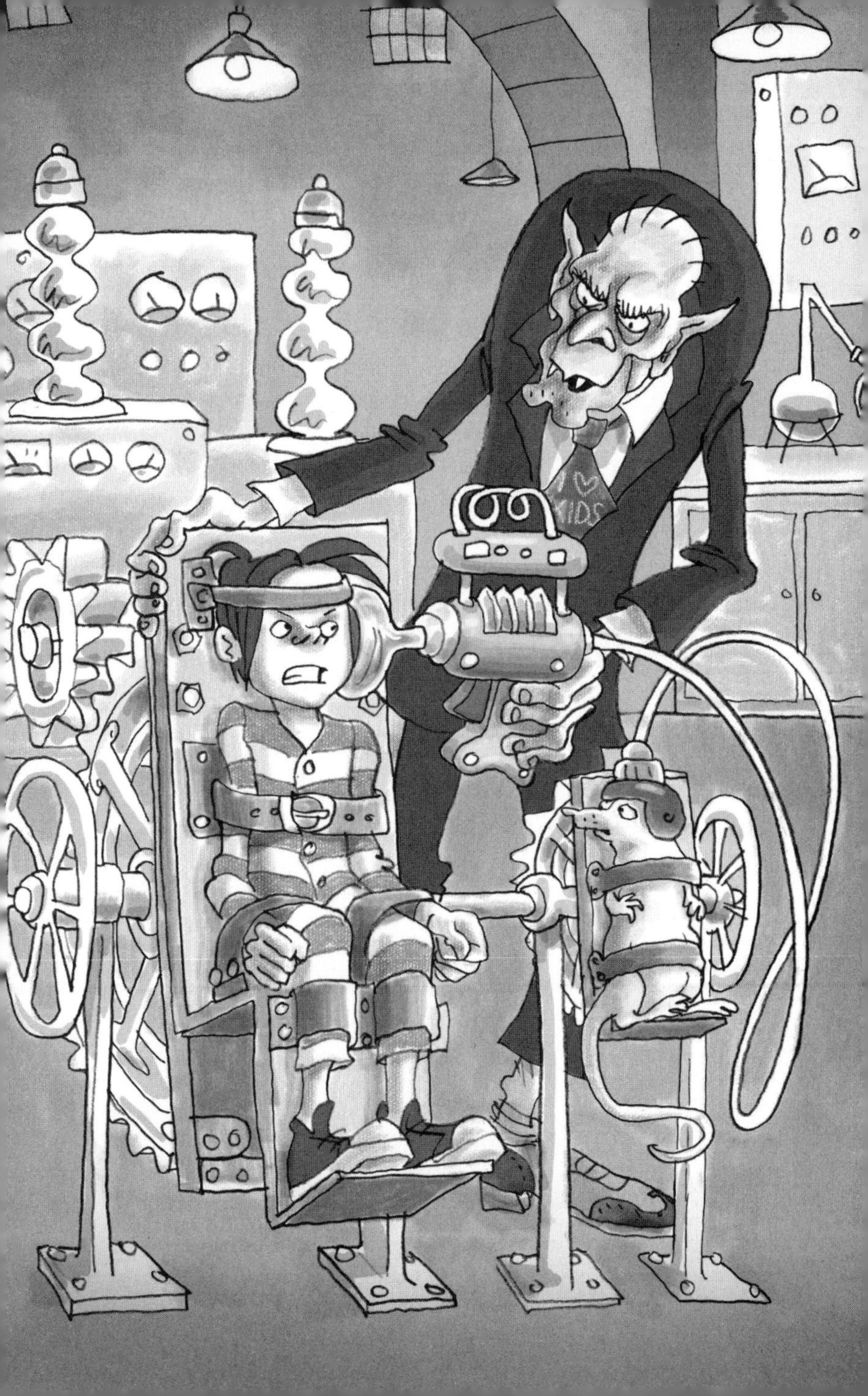
I ♥ KIDS

"Piffle. I'm replacing naughty parts with obedient brain tissue. When I'm done, you'll do everything I say. You'll be a model of obedience!" He chuckled. "At last, my lad, your parents will be delighted with you."

Could that be true? *Would* his parents like him better?

"Oh yeah?" Cody said, flailing in his chair. "What happens to the rat that's really me?"

"Hold STILL!" Dr. Farley calibrated buttons on his device. "Hmm, I hope this will work. I had planned on running a few more tests first. If the pneumatic-swap-o-tron isn't properly load-balanced . . ." He shrugged. "We'll find out soon, won't we?"

"What happens if it isn't?!" Cody squeaked. *"Then what?"*

Farley smiled and gave Cody a friendly pat on the shoulder. "Then, alas, your parents will receive a handwritten note from me, expressing my deep sorrow that you fell off the roof. I see in your files that you have a tendency to climb on roofs without permission."

Cody strained against his straps. Tears trickled down his cheeks. It was too late. Nothing could save him now. Farley had outfoxed him at every turn. He'd even figured out a story to tell his parents if things went wrong.

And his parents would believe Farley. Parents always believed the school over the kid.

"Ah, don't weep, young Cody," Farley said. "I know. It is a beautiful moment. The thrill of this historic occasion overwhelms you. You're sharing in an experiment that will forever alter science. The pinnacle of my career! The permanent solution to naughty boys! Aren't you lucky?"

Cody didn't even have the heart to answer. What difference would it make now?

Farley flipped a switch. The machine whirred. Cody held his breath. He felt suction pulling on his ear. More and more suction. And the machine's sinister sounds began thrumming in his ear. *Shoomp-thoomp*. *Shoomp-thoomp*, the hideous heartbeat of evil.

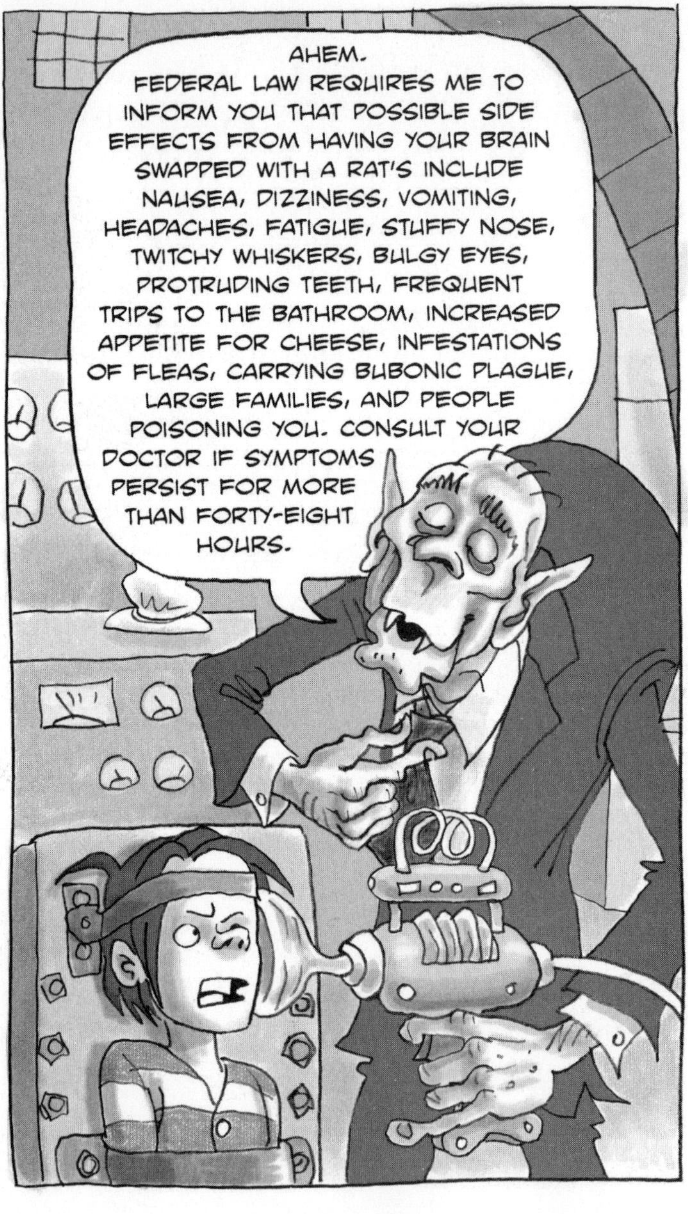
AHEM.
FEDERAL LAW REQUIRES ME TO INFORM YOU THAT POSSIBLE SIDE EFFECTS FROM HAVING YOUR BRAIN SWAPPED WITH A RAT'S INCLUDE NAUSEA, DIZZINESS, VOMITING, HEADACHES, FATIGUE, STUFFY NOSE, TWITCHY WHISKERS, BULGY EYES, PROTRUDING TEETH, FREQUENT TRIPS TO THE BATHROOM, INCREASED APPETITE FOR CHEESE, INFESTATIONS OF FLEAS, CARRYING BUBONIC PLAGUE, LARGE FAMILIES, AND PEOPLE POISONING YOU. CONSULT YOUR DOCTOR IF SYMPTOMS PERSIST FOR MORE THAN FORTY-EIGHT HOURS.

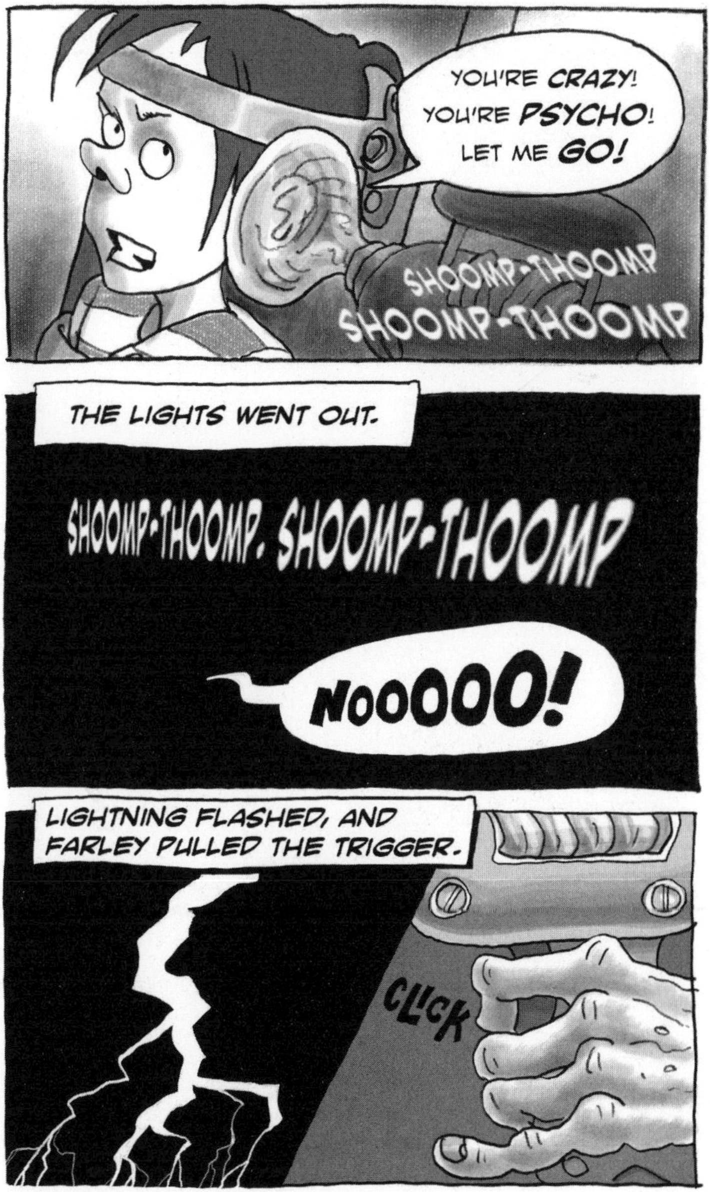
YOU'RE CRAZY! YOU'RE PSYCHO! LET ME GO!
SHOOMP-THOOMP
SHOOMP-THOOMP
THE LIGHTS WENT OUT.
SHOOMP-THOOMP. SHOOMP-THOOMP
NOOOOO!
LIGHTNING FLASHED, AND FARLEY PULLED THE TRIGGER.
CLICK

CHAPTER THIRTEEN
THE DREAM

They say when people are about to die, sometimes they feel they can step outside their bodies, and watch themselves from a corner of the room.

Cody was having a dream.

He dreamed he could see himself doing the strangest things.

He was watching himself from a corner of the room. All the teachers at Splurch Academy were seated on couches watching him, too. Dr. Farley told him, "Play dead!" And he, Cody Mack, clutched his hands at his throat, swiveled around on one heel, and fell to the floor.

The teachers clapped and yelled, "Bravo! Encore!"

Then Farley said to him, "Rise from the dead!" And Cody sat upright. He rose to his feet and stalked back and forth with his arms out like a zombie.

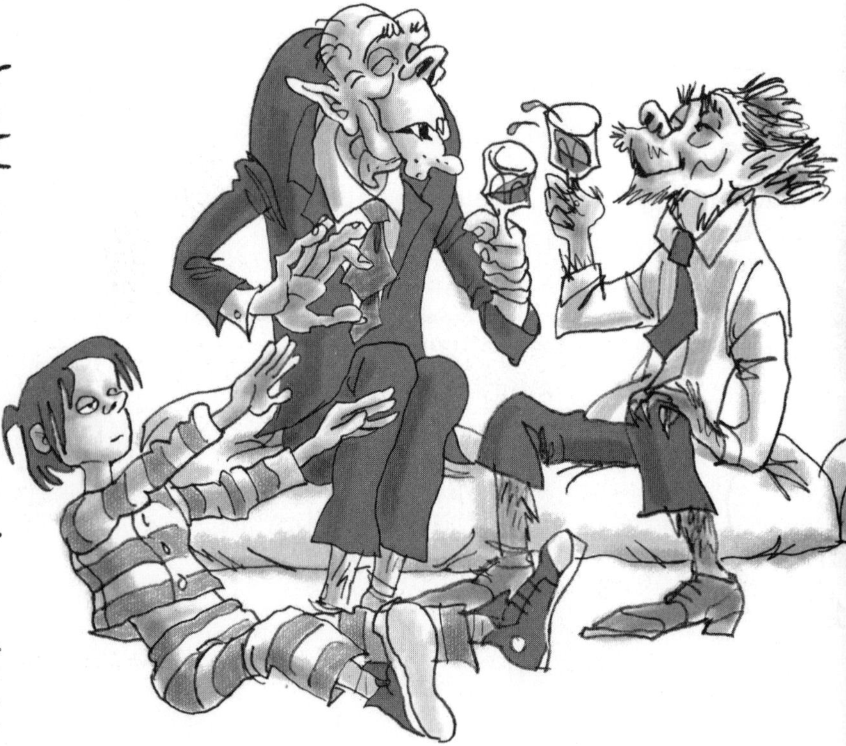

Mr. Fronk, saying something about having known it would work all along, pulled out glasses, and they all had a celebratory toast with Dr. Farley, patting him on the back and calling him a genius.

Was that *blood* in the glasses?

Cody hoped it was tomato juice.

Then, the strangest part of all, Farley put a set of headphones on and said, "Watch this, ladies and gents. With these headphones, I can control him with just my thoughts."

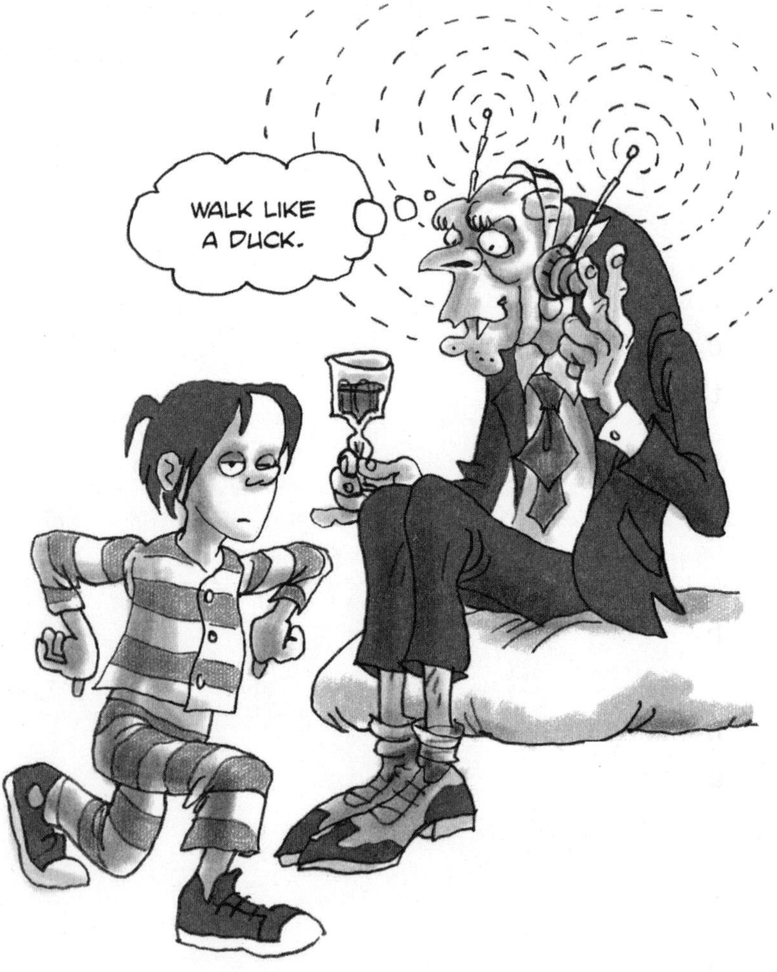
WALK LIKE
A DUCK.

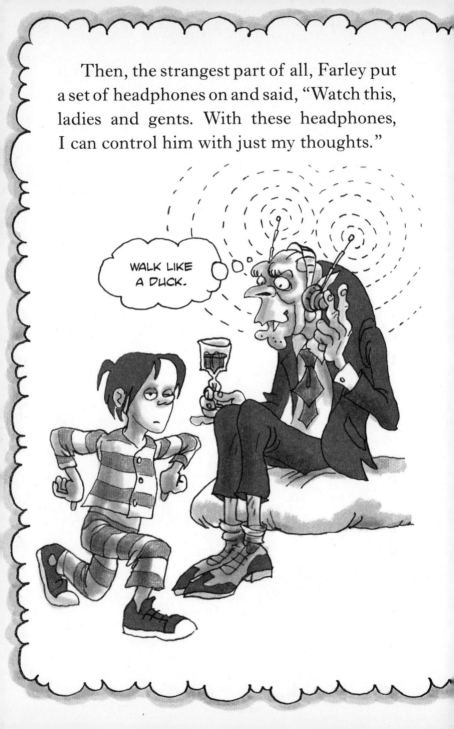

My rats are trained to receive thought-wave instructions from these headphones," he added. "Cody Mack will obey my every whim!"

Now, Farley didn't have to say a word in order to control Cody. The teachers howled with laughter.

"Hey, Archie," Nurse Bilgewater hooted. "You quack me up!"

"No, no, Beulah, check this one out," Miss Threadbare said, laughing so hard her eyes watered. "Why did the duck-boy cross the road?"

"Why?"

"To get to the other *side*!"

They all stared at her.

"You know," she said. "The other side of his brain?"

"That's the dumbest joke I've ever heard," Howell said. "It's not even a joke at all."

"Never mind that," Farley cried, his glass raised high. "Call the parents! Invite them to a special Open House! Tomorrow night, we show the world!"

Mr. Fronk clinked glasses with Farley. "The world, Arch?"

Dr. Farley took a big gulp. "Not only the world," he said. "I'll send a telegram to the Grand Inquisitrix of the League of Reform Schools. I'll extend her a personal invitation."

Several faculty looked alarmed.

"And she'll come," Farley said, swirling the drink in his glass, and grinning. "Oh yes. She'll come. This time, I'll dazzle her."

The dream faded.

Dreams are strange.

Cody rolled over.

He was asleep. Of course he was. He could tell. He felt that warm, muzzy, dozy, drowsy sleep feeling.

It was nothing more than a dream. Dreams never made sense.

Splurch Academy messed with your head so much, it could sure mess with your dreams.

Go back to sleep, he told himself. *It'll be better in the morning.*

CHAPTER FOURTEEN
THE TANK

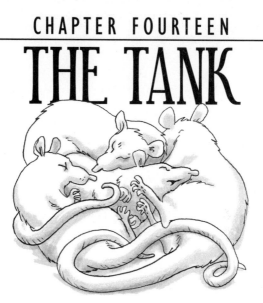

Cody woke up slowly. His eyelids felt heavy. His mouth tasted nasty.

He waddled over to the water bottle and licked the nozzle. It drizzled onto his tongue.

Something smelled interesting. Kibbles! His favorite! He shoved his snout in the bowl.

Wait a minute . . .

Cody spit kibble bits all over the tank's sawdust floor.

Kibbles? SNOUT?

He was a rat!

On one side of the tank, dozens of rats lay sleeping, piled in a heap. Were those the rest of the boys?

Cody ran around, panicking, looking for a way to escape. The exercise wheel pinched his tail. He squeaked, feeling pain in a place he'd never felt before.

He wandered back to the food dish and ate kibbles, trying to think. He was ravenous. He felt he'd slept for days. It had been—let's see—he counted on his teensy claws—Monday he came to Splurch Academy, Tuesday he tried to run but Mr. Howell caught him, Wednesday night he crashed the car, and Thursday morning, he got his brain swapped with a rat's. Or part of his brain. He wasn't sure which. It felt like all of his brain. Anyway, now the

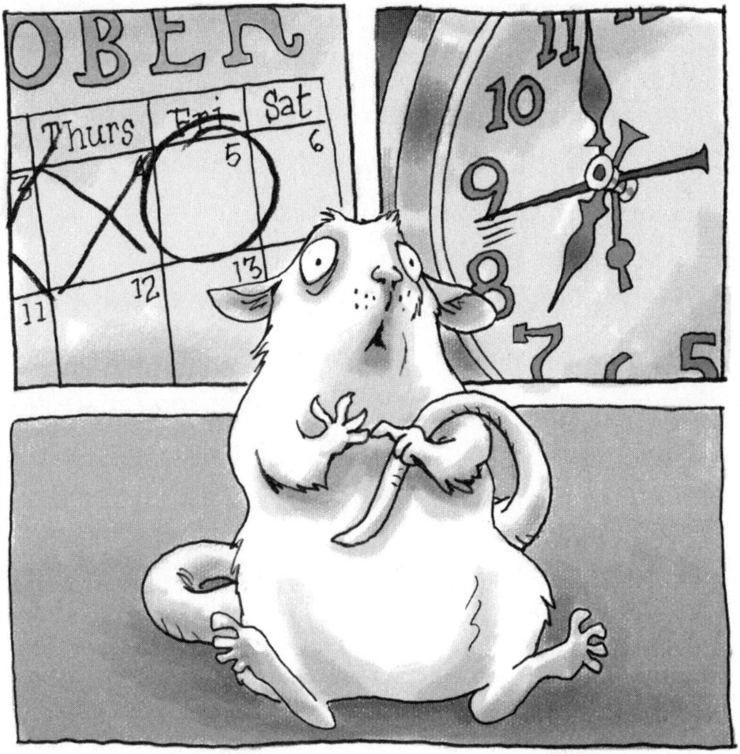
OBER
Thurs
Fri
Sat
5
6
11
12
13
10
9
8
7
5

calendar on the wall said it was Friday, and the clock said it was nearly seven at night.

What was it Farley had said?

Tomorrow night, we show the world!

Whatever Farley was planning, it was about to happen. Now.

Unless Cody did something to stop it.

But he was only a rat! How could one little rat-boy stop a fiend like Farley?

The door to the laboratory opened, and Dr. Farley walked inside, followed by Mr. Howell. Farley had dressed with special care tonight. There was a carnation in his jacket, ruffles running down his shirt, and he wore an Elvis toupee.

"The parents will be here any minute," Dr. Farley said, popping breath mints into his mouth. *Like they'd do any good*, Cody thought. "Are the headphones ready to go?"

"I'm workin' on it." Howell tinkered with Farley's headphones. "Stupid little gizmo, I can't get a good grip on the tiny parts."

"Well, try harder!" Farley said. "I need them to mind-control the boys!"

"When I was a kid, headphones were the size of hamburger buns," Howell said. "A guy could see what he was doing." He found another pair of headphones on the lab table. "There," he said. "Try the spare set."

Dr. Farley put the other headphones on, then adjusted his toupee. "Yes! It works." He straightened his tie. "You don't think these headphones are too obvious, do you?

No one will notice them, will they?"

"Uh . . ." Howell said.

"Oh, and Howell? Just one last thing."

"Yeah, Doc?"

"Call an exterminator, will you? We need to dispose of these rats tonight. They're too much trouble to keep around."

Howell nodded and slunk out.

Dr. Farley set the other headphones on the laboratory table. Then he rang his little bell. Pavlov's booming bark sounded. He galloped into the room.

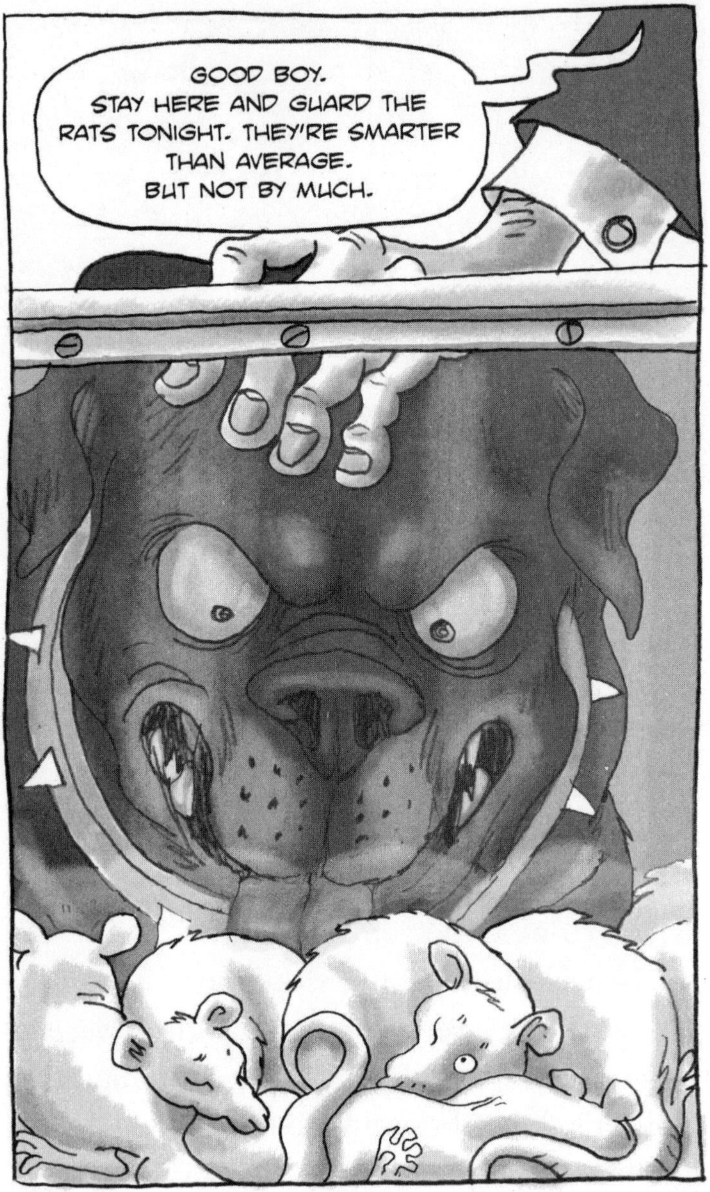
GOOD BOY.
STAY HERE AND GUARD THE RATS TONIGHT. THEY'RE SMARTER THAN AVERAGE.
BUT NOT BY MUCH.

Cody lay there, miserable, hearing sounds of commotion as the parents arrived. They would love the "progress" their sons had made. It made Cody sick thinking about it. There must be something he could do!

Maybe there wasn't much one rat could do. But a whole tank full of rats?

He jumped on the other rats' heads. "Wake up! Get up now! You big fat ratbrains!"

Whoa. He was speaking in *rat*! Would they understand him? His words came out as strange squeaks.

One rat lifted up his head. "Who're you calling Big Fat?" It had to be Mugsy.

The other rats understood him! And Cody understood them. Crazy!

"Get up, Mugsy," Cody said, tugging on his whiskers. "There's no time to lose. Get. Up. NOW!"

Mugsy climbed over the other rats. "Something's messed up. You're squeaking, and I understand you." He clutched at the fur on his rat chest. "I'm a rat!"

"I warned you guys," Cody said. "This is

what I was trying to tell you! Farley swapped your brain with a trained rat's brain. Well, not your whole brain . . . just a part of it. I don't know. Doesn't matter. We're us, and we're rats, and now our bodies will do whatever Farley tells them to."

"Yeah, but my brain doesn't know how to speak Rat," Mugsy protested.

A sleepy rat poked its nose out of the pile. "Young brains are highly adaptable," it squeaked. "Neurons form new pathways at astonishing speeds . . ." It was Sully.

"Get up," Cody said. "We've got to hurry to stop Farley if we ever want to get our bodies back."

Pavlov growled and pawed at the tank. That startled the rats awake and trembling.

"He's huge," one rat whispered.

"Which one are you?" Cody asked.

"Ratface," the rat replied.

"You sure are a rat-face," the rat that was Victor said. "Ha! Get it?"

"I'm Carlos," one of them said. "What's going on?"

Cody explained the Rebellio-Rodent

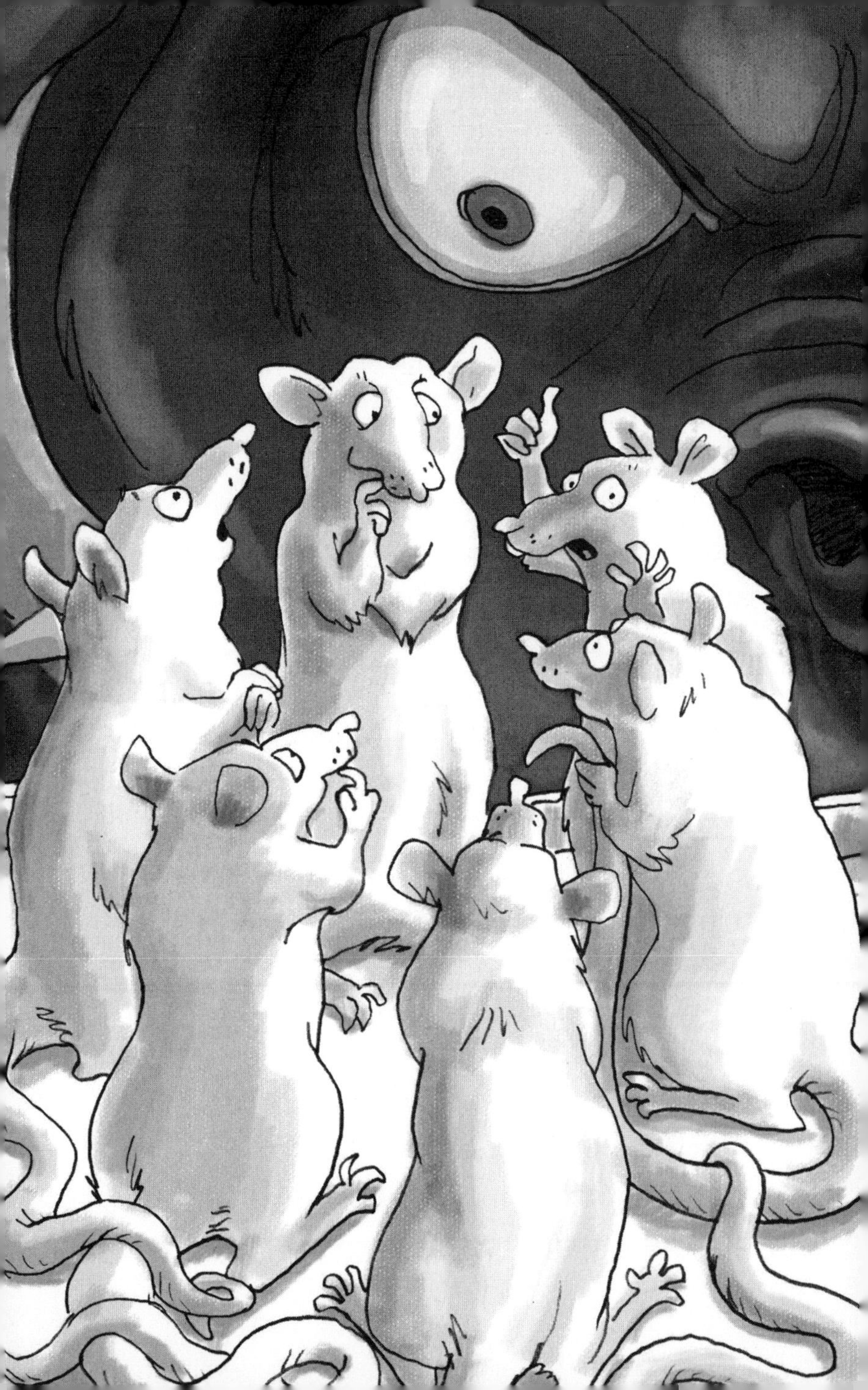

Recipronator, the mind-control headphones, the exterminator, and Farley's plan to show the world.

"Let's get him!" Victor the rat cried. "Let's rip Farley to pieces!"

"Yeah!" Ratface said. "Let's poop in his underwear drawer!"

They all stared at Ratface.

"We are fighting for our LIVES, people," Cody said. "Our parents are already here. There's no time to lose."

"Um, Cody?" Carlos said. "Aren't you forgetting something?"

Pavlov pawed at the tank. He was GINORMOUS! And, oh, did he smell of enemy dog.

"I don't want to feel my little bones go crunch!" Sully wailed. "I don't want to dissolve in dog stomach acid!"

"Will you can it a minute and let me think," Cody yelled.

Pavlov knocked off the top of the tank. The rat-boys shrank back.

The door to the laboratory opened. A head poked inside.

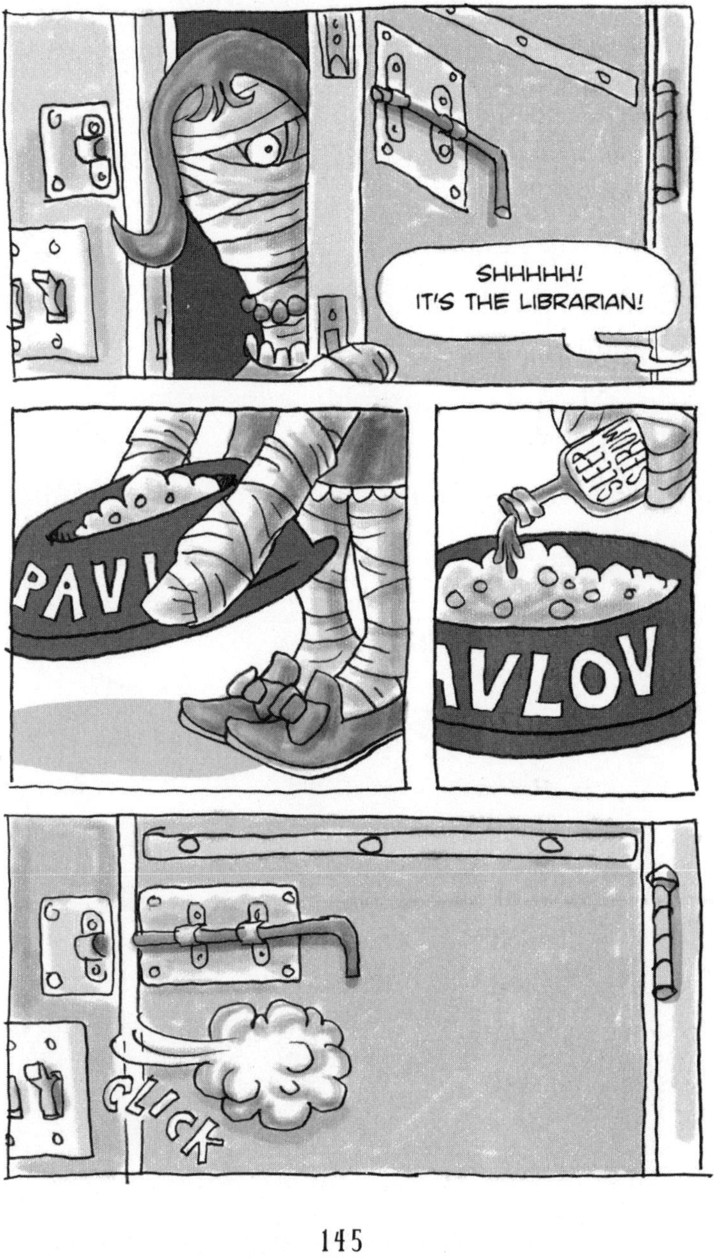
SHHHHH!
IT'S THE LIBRARIAN!
PAVL
AVLOV
CLICK

Pavlov cocked his head and trotted over. He attacked the bowl with noisy slurps.

The rat-boys stared at each other.

"What was that stuff?" Cody asked.

"Tapioca," Mugsy said.

"We had it for breakfast," Carlos said. "Mugsy put ketchup on his."

Pavlov licked his chops. Tapioca pearls quivered on his nose. His eyes rolled back in his head, and he tumbled to the ground.

"She drugged the dog," Carlos said. "But why?"

"Who cares!" Cody said. "This is our chance! Go, go, go!"

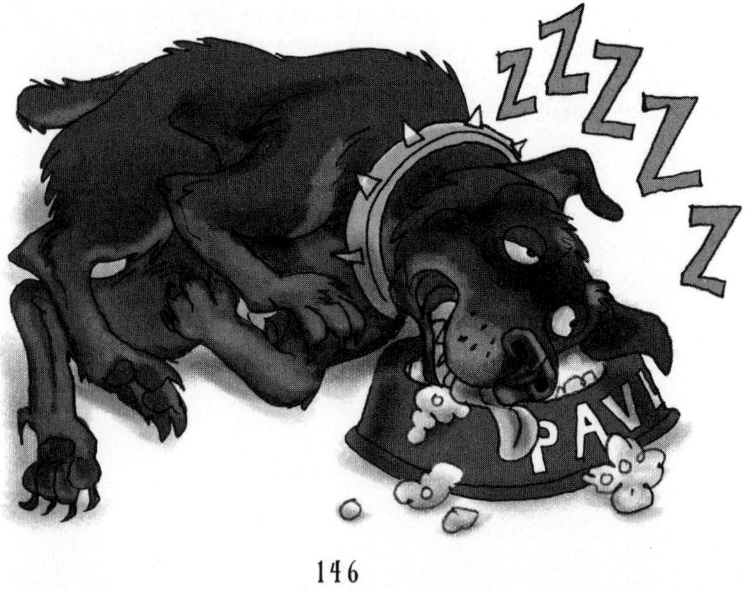
ZZZZZ
PAV

CHAPTER FIFTEEN
THE PRESENTATION

A team of rats crept into the back of the Splurch Academy auditorium, balancing the Rebellio-Rodent Recipronator over their heads. Sully and Carlos followed, carrying the brain-controlling headphones.

"We've reworked it to jam the signal from Farley's headphones," Carlos explained to Cody. "Now when he tries to control our bodies, *these* headphones will beat up his."

They hid behind the last row of seats and watched as Farley strode onto the stage to greet his guests.

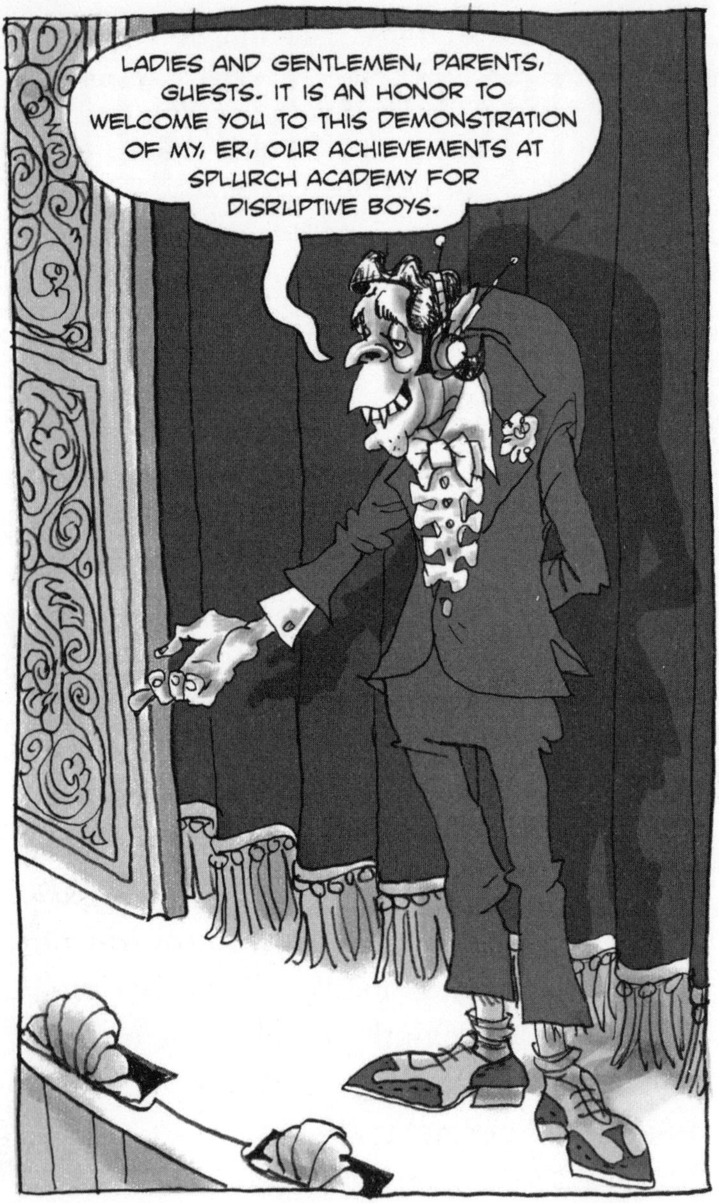
LADIES AND GENTLEMEN, PARENTS, GUESTS. IT IS AN HONOR TO WELCOME YOU TO THIS DEMONSTRATION OF MY, ER, OUR ACHIEVEMENTS AT SPLURCH ACADEMY FOR DISRUPTIVE BOYS.

"I see my mom!" Ratface squeaked, sitting on top of a tower of rats. *"Mommy!"*

"Quiet!" Cody hissed. "It's not time to make our move. *Yet*."

Farley cleared his throat. "First, I'd like to thank all the parents who were able to make it here tonight. I think you all will be pleased with the work that we've done with your children. I hardly think that you'll even recognize them."

"He's *such* a lamebrain!" Carlos said.

Farley adjusted his tie and wiped his forehead with a handkerchief. "And now it is my great honor to introduce, visiting all the way from Bucharest, the *illustrious*, the magnificent, the preeminent Grand Inquisitrix of the League of Reform Schools for Fiendish Children, Her Grace the Dowager Duchess of DeKay, Madame Desdemona Chartricia Sackville-Smack!"

A spotlight appeared on the stage. Trumpets sounded. Ivanov, in a tuxedo, rolled out a red carpet, and Miss Threadbare, who was trying to prance and failing, scattered rose petals.

Farley bent to kiss her hand, but she snatched it away. The pug dog in her lap growled at Farley.

"Archibald," she said. "Turn that spotlight off! Can't you see it's blinding me?"

Farley clapped his hands. "Ivanov! Lights!" He swallowed and slid a finger underneath his collar. "Ahem. Before we proceed with tonight's demonstration of the miracle that has taken place at this academy," Farley said, "a transformation that is entirely due to *my* groundbreaking efforts, I'd like to commemorate Madame Sackville-Smack . . ."

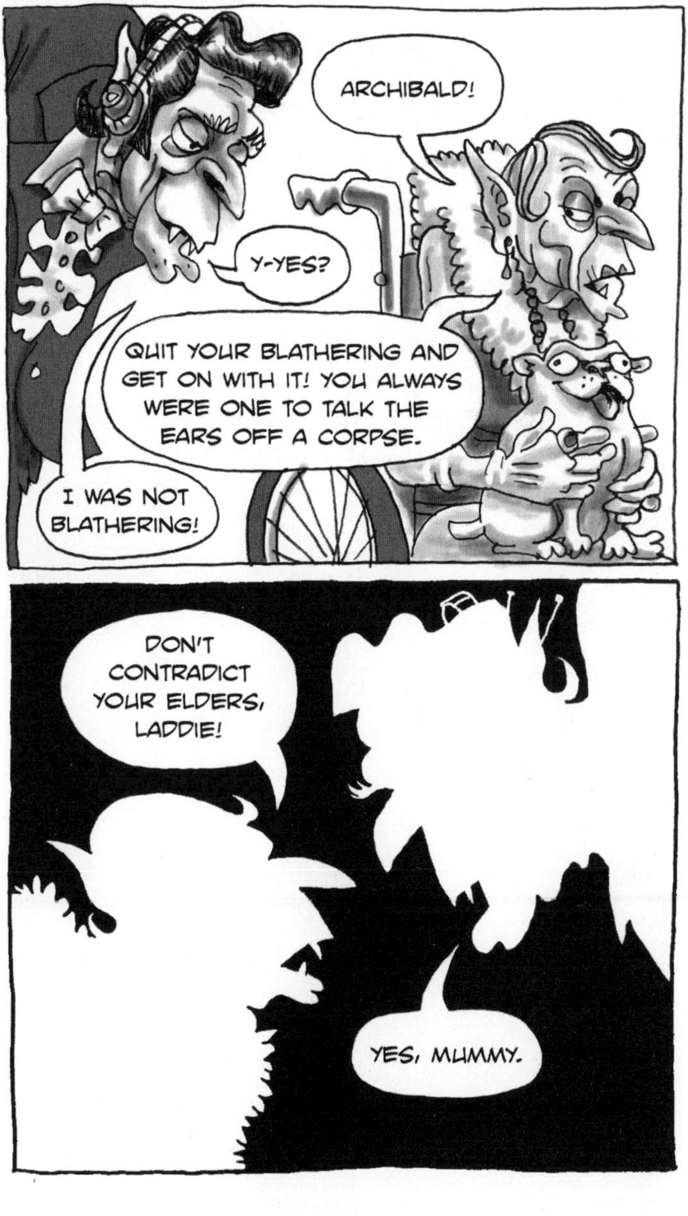
ARCHIBALD!
Y-YES?
QUIT YOUR BLATHERING AND GET ON WITH IT! YOU ALWAYS WERE ONE TO TALK THE EARS OFF A CORPSE.
I WAS NOT BLATHERING!
DON'T CONTRADICT YOUR ELDERS, LADDIE!
YES, MUMMY.

Mummy?

"She's his *mom*!"

Farley seized the microphone. "Our first exhibit is Cody Mack. When he arrived just days ago, his former principal said he was the worst case that he had ever seen. Ladies and gentlemen, feast your eyes"—there was a drumroll—"on *Cody Mack today*!"

Cody's mother gasped. "Isn't he darling? And so well-behaved! Dr. Farley, you're a marvel!"

"*That's my boy,*" Cody's dad said.

"Oh, man, where's my camera," Carlos said. "I wanna remember this."

"Shut your snout!" Cody hissed. "You're all next, you turkeys!"

Cody's body waltzed over to Madame Sackville-Smack, bowed, and kissed her hand.

"Oh, *gross*," Cody the rat moaned. "When I get my body back, I am boiling my lips in disinfectant for a week."

"It's the greatest honor of my pathetic young life to bask in your glory, Madame Sackville-Smack," Cody's body said. "I'll never wash this hand again."

"See that you do," the Grand Inquisitrix replied in a gravelly voice. "I loathe boys with germy hands."

"Farley's mind-controlling you," Carlos the rat said. "Look at him. He's making you sound like a dork, too. Aren't you going to try to stop him?"

Madame Sackville-Smack said, "Tell me, Cody, what do you like best about Splurch Academy for Disruptive Boys?"

"Jam his signal, Cody," Sully the rat whispered. "Do it now. You can't let Farley win. Send brain waves to tell your body to do something else. Something you'd do if you were inside your own skull."

Something else, Cody thought. *But what? What* would *I do if I were up there?*

He pressed his little rat ear against the squooshy earpiece and thought hard.

"What I like best about Splurch Academy," Cody's body said, "is the kind, caring, helpful . . ." He blinked. "Um . . ."

Dr. Farley frowned. Cody gripped the headphones. *Come on, come on . . .*

"Want me to recite a poem about it?" Cody's body asked.

Dr. Farley's eyebrows shot up. He fiddled with his earphones.

"Please do," said the Grand Inquisitrix.

Cody the rat concentrated with all his might on sending brain waves through the headphones. *C'mon, body, do your stuff!*

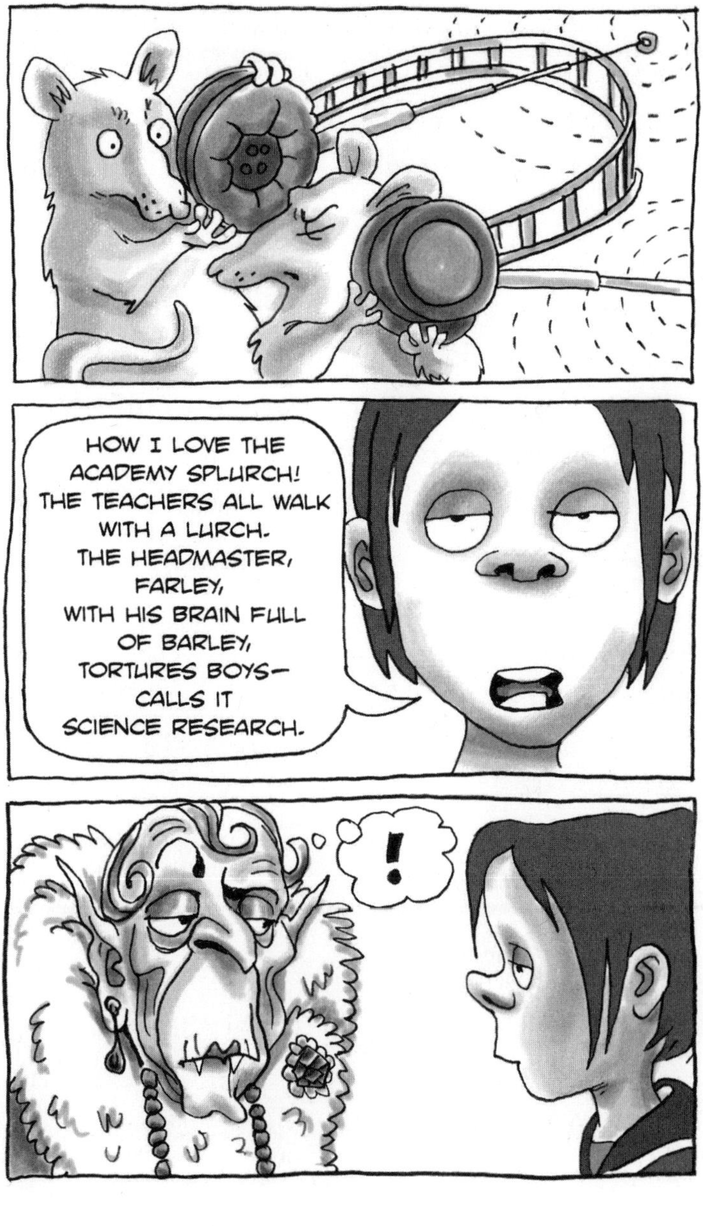
HOW I LOVE THE ACADEMY SPLURCH! THE TEACHERS ALL WALK WITH A LURCH. THE HEADMASTER, FARLEY, WITH HIS BRAIN FULL OF BARLEY, TORTURES BOYS— CALLS IT SCIENCE RESEARCH.
!

"What a refreshing sense of humor our Cody has," said Farley.

*"Ketchup is red,
cheese mold is blue.
The food here at Splurch
smells like sautéed dog poo!"*
shouted Cody's body.

"T-time for the little number the boys prepared," Dr. Farley stammered. Miss Threadbare hammered a tune on the piano. The boys' bodies marched out.

The brain scientists applauded.

The mothers gushed.

"Boo!" the rats cried.

Cody gathered the rats into a huddle. "Now's the time, men," Cody said. "You ready to crash this party?"

They nodded.

"It's now or never," Cody said. "Mess this up, the exterminator will take us away, and it's bye-bye brains."

They shook their rat fists in the air.

"Each man grab a fork from the refreshment table. You know what to do. Ready?" Cody said. "Disruptive boys forever! ATTACK!"

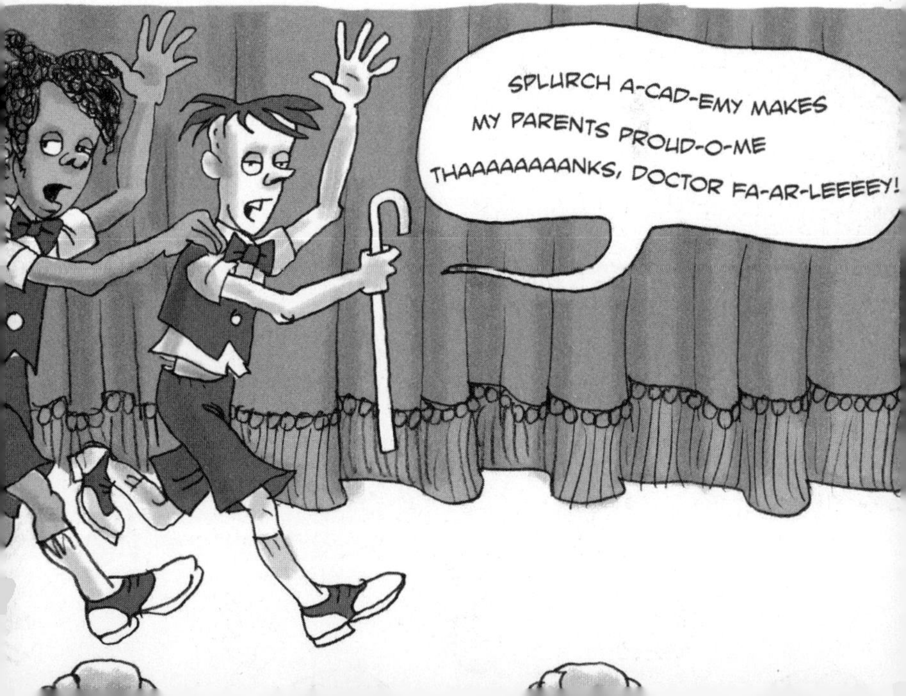
SPLURCH A-CAD-EMY MAKES
MY PARENTS PROUD-O-ME
THAAAAAAAANKS, DOCTOR FA-AR-LEEEEY!

CHAPTER SIXTEEN

THE ATTACK

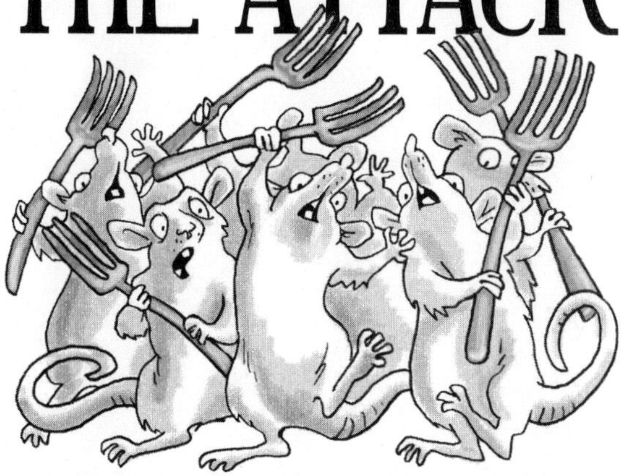

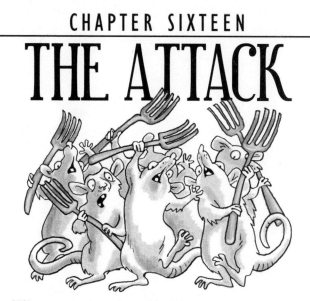

The rats took off like an angry mob, squeaking war squeaks, dragging the Rebellio-Rodent Recipronator with them, jabbing their forks like spears, and climbing over the visitors.

Guests rose, screaming. It's no fun having your parents try to squash you underfoot.

The rats stormed the stage and tripped up their own bodies. The boys' bodies nearly stomped their rat counterparts to death! But the rats dodged in and out, poking and nipping at their own ankles until their bodies fell.

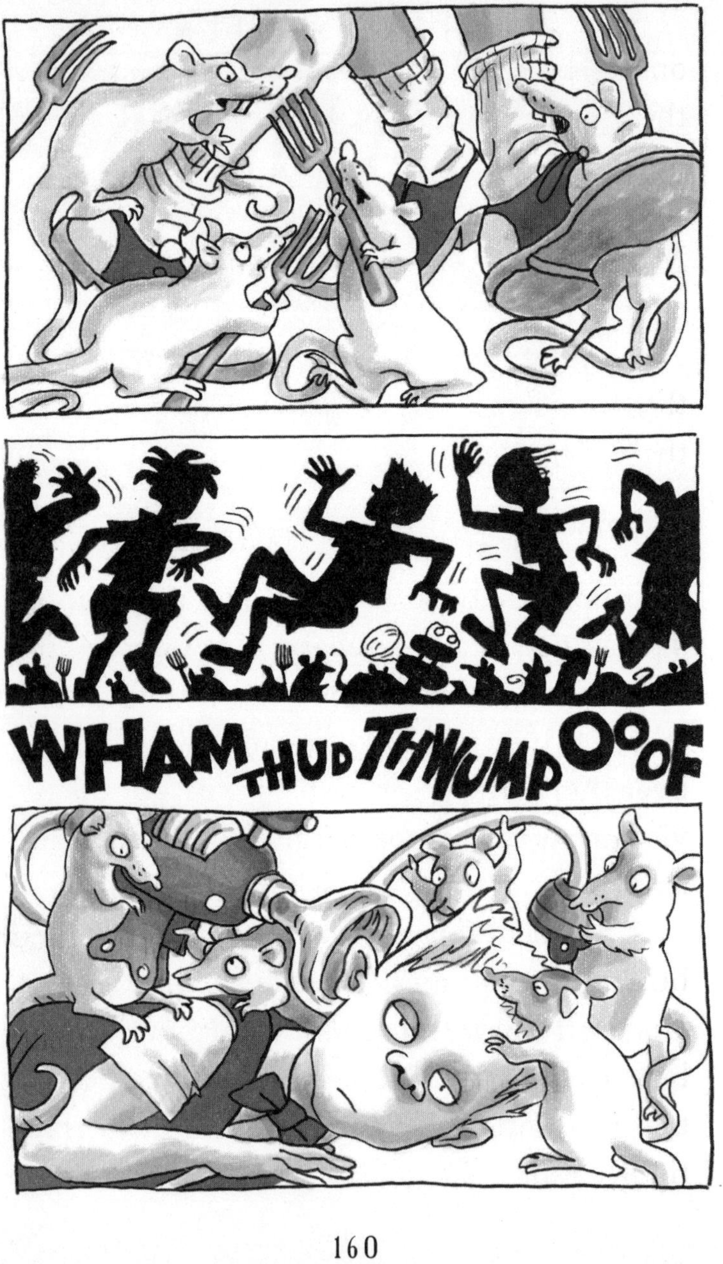
WHAM THUD THWUMP OOOF

The Recipronator rat team swooped in on the fallen Victor. Victor-the-rat pointed the device at his own ear, then swapped himself back.

Victor, as himself again, pinned Mugsy's body in a wrestling hold so they could swap him, too. And on it went.

"Ladies and gentlemen, I assure you that . . . uh . . ." Dr. Farley gave up. "Seize them!" he shouted. "Grab the nets!"

Guests ran shrieking from the auditorium. Several plowed into the table where Griselda stood serving appetizers. The punch bowl ended up over her head.

Mr. Fronk, Mr. Howell, and the other teachers wielded fishnets. Madame Sackville-Smack's pug jumped down, yipping like crazy. Dr. Farley tripped over it, and a pair of rats ran off with his toupee.

Cody sent brain waves to the remaining boys on the stage. *Get Farley. Get Farley. Hog-tie him and throw him in the dungeon!* A bunch of boys advanced on the headmaster, trying to tackle him. But he sprang from their grasp.

Cody ran up onto the stage and jumped onto his own feet. *Pick me up*, he told the rat brain inside his head. His own body picked him up and petted him gently, sniffing at him. *Sit down*. His body sat. Victor and Carlos, now back to normal, ran over with the Recipronator.

Shoomp-thoomp. Shoomp-thoomp. Cody's life flashed before his eyes . . . and suddenly his eyes were his own again! His head felt woozy-wobbly, but at least it was his. Rasputin curled up on his lap.

Someone's father yelled, "This is an outrage! What kind of institution are you running here, Farley?"

An angry horde of parents stormed the stage. Fathers yelled and mothers started beating Farley with their purses. "We're taking our boy home with us *this instant!*" one said. "We're reporting you to the state! This place is crawling with *vermin!*"

Farley fended off the blows. "Please, dear parents, don't be hasty! An unfortunate pest problem doesn't change the fact that we're achieving miracles here. I beg you!"

"Fraud!"

"Quack!"

"Montebank!"

"Lousy dresser!"

Madame Sackville-Smack rose to her feet. "Silence!" she cried. The room went strangely quiet.

She pulled a necklace out from under her dress. A small pouch was attached, and from it she shook a handful of powder.

"Come very close, so I can speak with you good people, who are naturally concerned about the welfare of your sons," she said in a soft, sinister voice. All the parents stepped closer.

She flung the powder down onto the ground. A puff of smoke rose in the air.

Her voice rippled like water. *"It's been a long day, and you have a long drive ahead of you, back to your homes."*

YOU ARE GETTING SLEEPY.

One by one, the parents stretched and yawned. Cody shook the other boys. "Look. What's she up to?"

"*Your boys are thriving at Splurch Academy. Just look at the handsome little fellows. When have they ever been so charming?*"

Mothers and fathers beamed at their boys.

"She's a hypnotist!" Carlos said.

"*Splurch Academy is perfectly safe. It's so thoughtful of Headmaster Farley to allow each boy to have a pet rat. It comforts them while they're away from home.*"

One mother picked up a rat that was crawling across her shoe, and stroked its fur.

"I think she might be worse than a hypnotist," Sully said.

"*You are very proud of what your boys are accomplishing at Splurch Academy,*" Madame Sackville-Smack purred. "*Go home now. Drive safely. Au revoir.*"

Like zombies, the parents gathered their things and headed for the door.

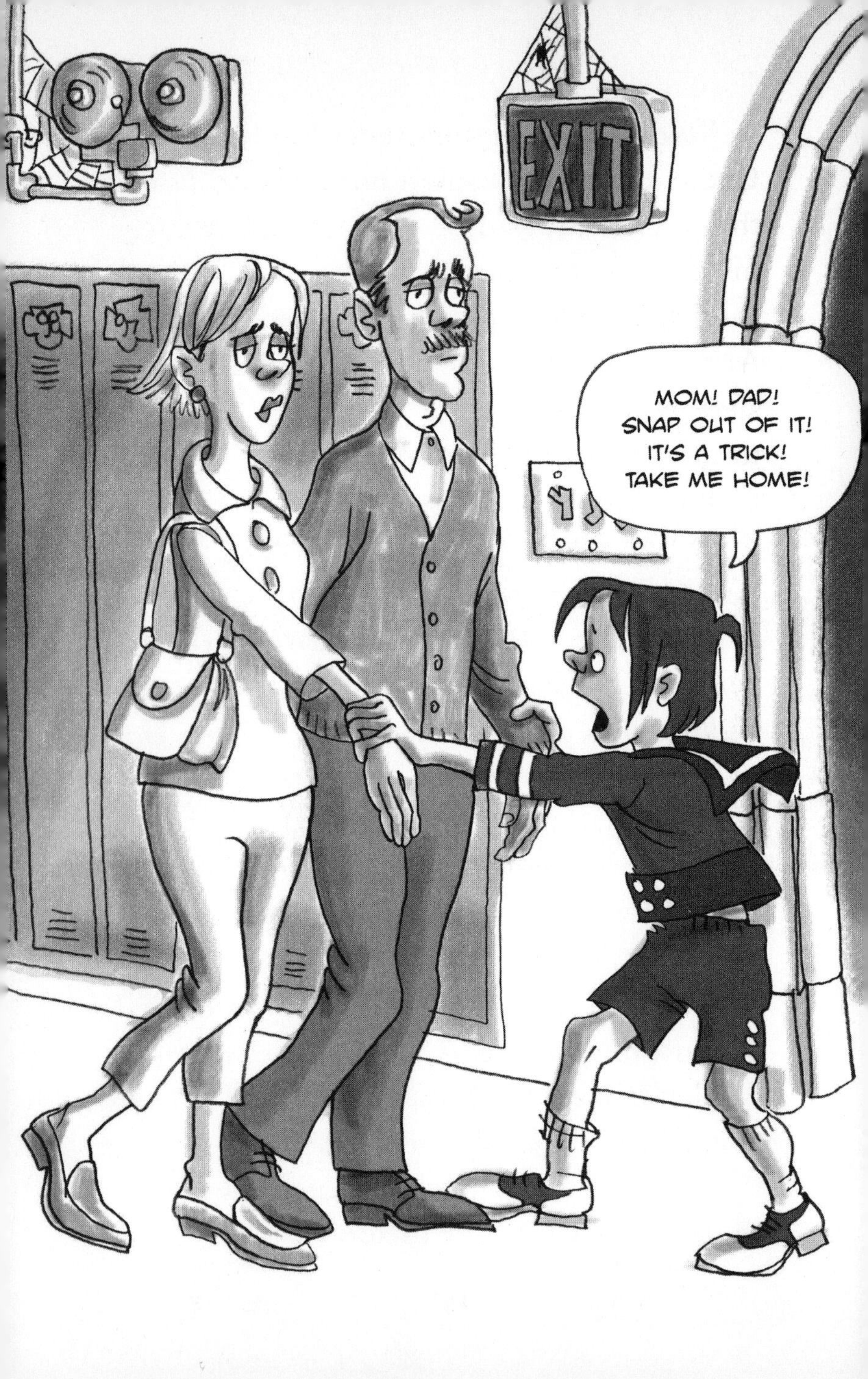
MOM! DAD! SNAP OUT OF IT! IT'S A TRICK! TAKE ME HOME!

The Grand Inquisitrix's dog sprang to Cody, and bit his ankle hard. By the time the boys had pried its jaws off Cody's leg, his parents were gone.

"Make sure the guests are all gone, Archibald," Madame Sackville-Smack said, sitting wearily down in her chair. "I get so tired of cleaning up after you."

Farley and the other faculty followed the parents out the door, and Cody and the boys followed, desperate to catch up to their parents. But when they got there, the last headlights were pulling out of the driveway and onto the road.

Farley watched them go. He clenched his fists.

He turned around and saw the boys on the patio.

He looked up at the moon.

He looked back at the boys, his eyes full of murder and rage.

He snapped his fingers . . .

. . . *and changed*.

CHAPTER SEVENTEEN

THE DOOR

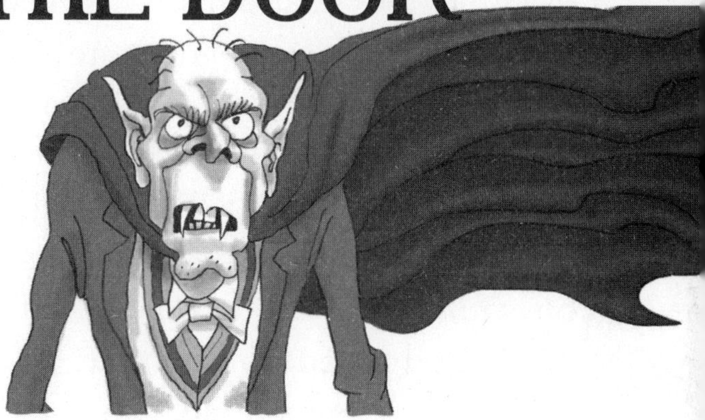

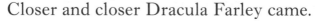

Closer and closer Dracula Farley came.

And the teacher-monsters, gnashing their fangs and flexing their claws.

"You worthless, odious boys," Farley snarled. "You ruined everything I've worked for all these years. You embarrassed me publicly. You . . . you . . . *you made a mockery of me before Mummy*!"

Cody's feet were riveted to the ground. *Run*, he told himself. *Go back inside*. But his feet didn't listen. Suddenly his legs were made of jelly.

Howell growled. Fronk's evening suit

ripped where his muscles bulged through the seams. Bilgewater's tentacles coiled.

"For eighty-two years I've been stuck teaching boys at this wretched school, and finally, I was going to have some rest. Twenty years I spent perfecting the Rebellio-Rodent Recipronator. Twenty years, I've waited for this day. The day when I would be done dealing with disgusting, naughty boys forever! What do you say to that?"

Cody backed toward the door. "Um, s-sorry?" he stammered.

"Sorry? *Sorry?*" Farley said. "Sorry. Is not. Good. Enough!"

And, with a horrible yell of murderous rage, he sprang for Cody.

The boys dragged Cody back into the school, just barely snatching him before Farley did. They slammed the door in Farley's face, and bolted it tight.

Cody sagged against the wall, panting. Safe inside! Right? They couldn't touch him here. Right? He hoped. On the other side of the door, ghoulish cries rose into the night.

"Get him!"

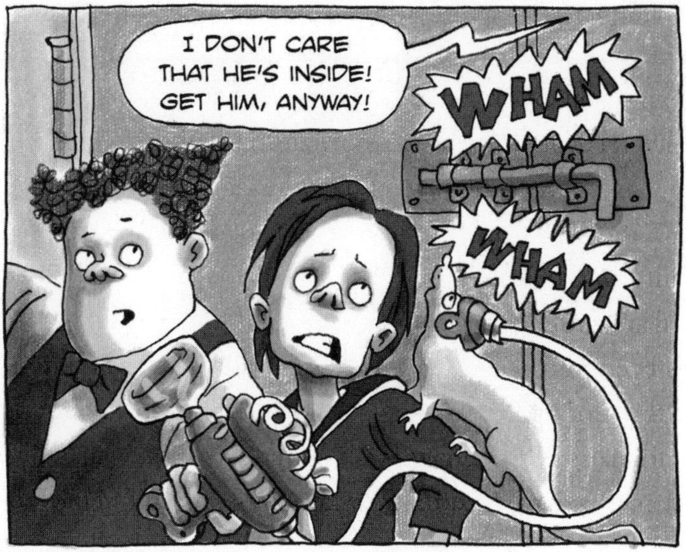
I DON'T CARE THAT HE'S INSIDE! GET HIM, ANYWAY!
WHAM
WHAM

The monsters were attacking the doors!

"I thought they had to stay out!" Carlos cried.

CRASH!

The shattered remains of the Splurch Academy door fell in a shower of dust. Monsters picked their way over the debris and stalked toward the boys.

"At last," Howell growled.

"I've dreamed of this moment," Nurse Bilgewater chortled.

"Push us too far, and even we break the rules," Frankenstein Fronk said.

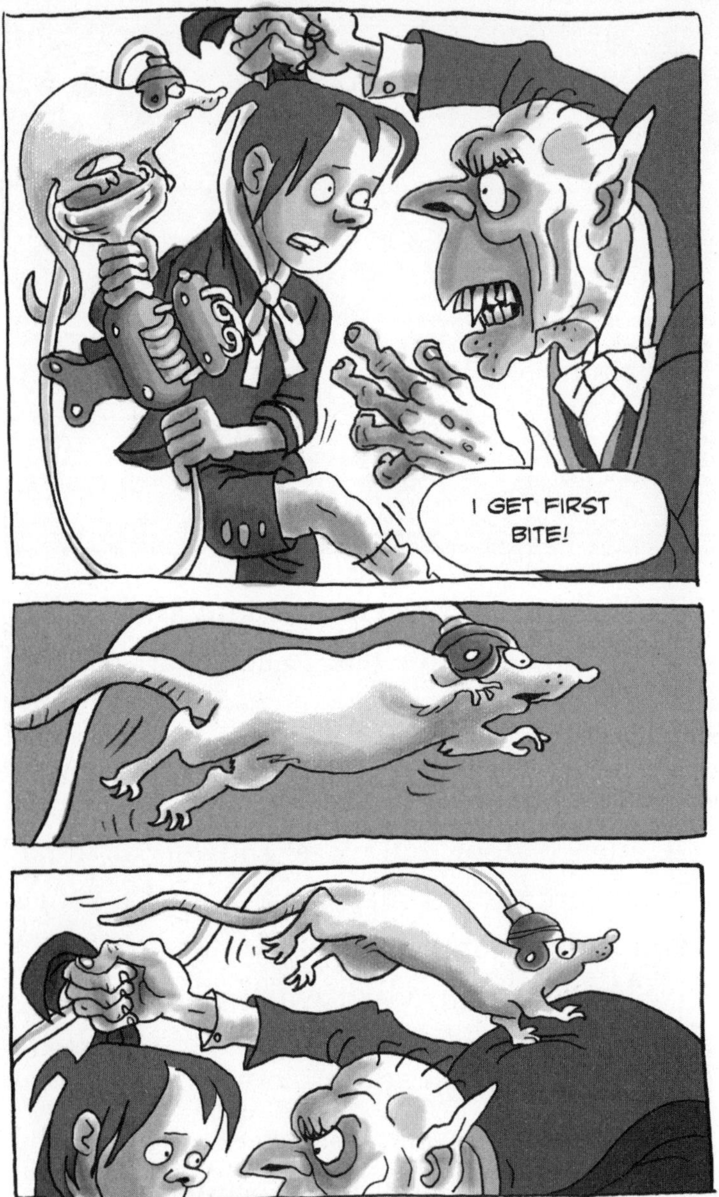
I GET FIRST BITE!

Dr. Dracula Farley pushed his way past the others and picked up Cody like he was a toy.

"I've lost more to Cody Mack than any of you," he hissed.

But then, the building shook and the windows rattled in their casings. Was it an earthquake? Even the faculty looked afraid.

A cloud of smoke came barreling like a sandstorm down the corridor. A voice from the cloud sounded like it came from the earth's core.

WHOOOOO *DARES* TO CROSSSSS MY THRESSSHHHOLD?

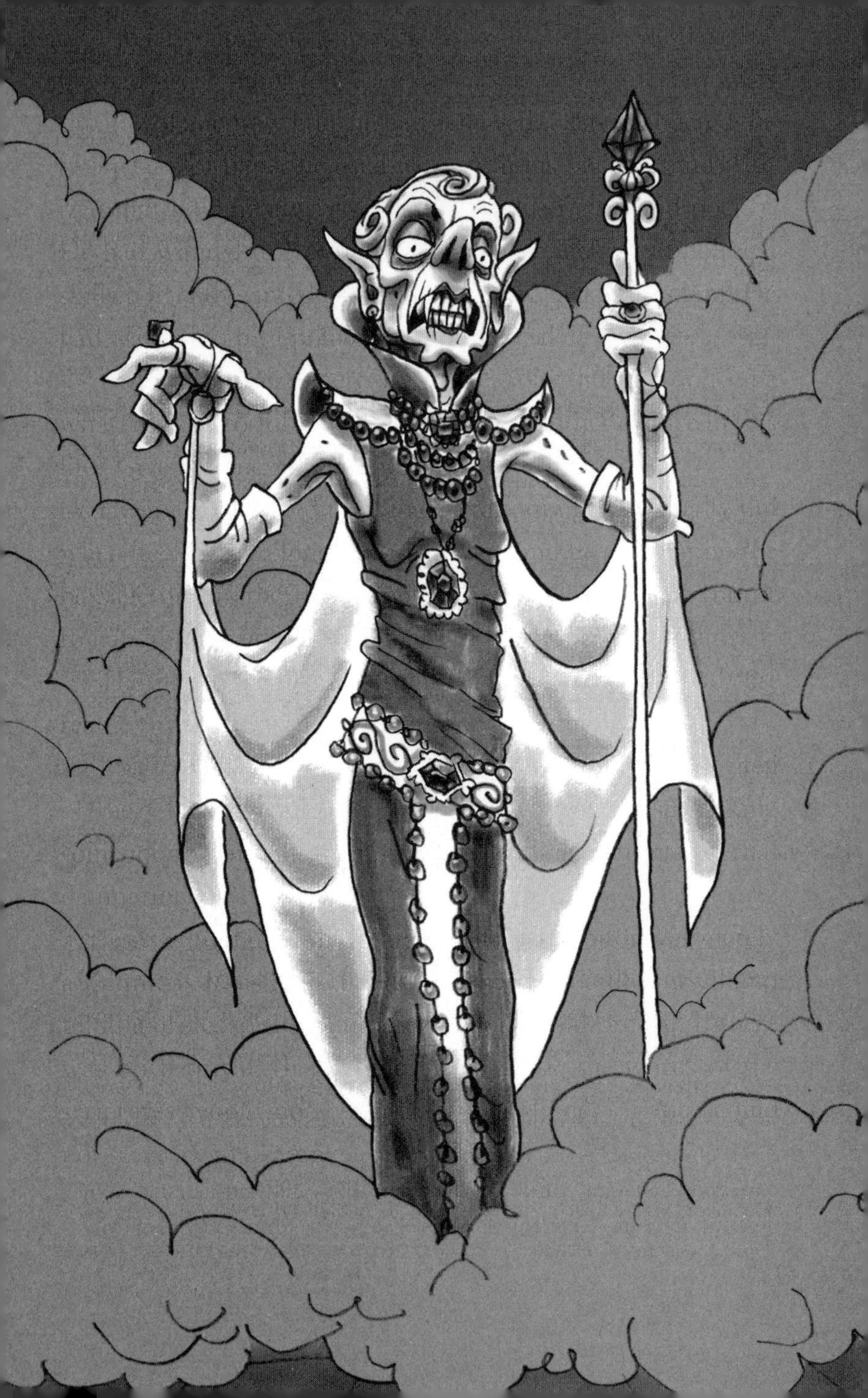

The monsters cringed. Mugsy tried to crawl away, but the vampiress plucked him up.

"My little dumplings," Madame Sackville-Smack crooned. "My helpless little naughty humans! I won't let anyone hurt you." She hissed like a cobra at the faculty. "BAD! Bad boys and girls. To scare my precious students! SHAME on you. *You know my rules.*"

Farley and the monsters quivered like Jell-O.

"I founded reform schools around the globe to *help* wayward children," Madame Sackville-Smack purred. "Not to feed them to teachers. My schools run like clockwork. Except this one. The one managed by *my own son!*" She sighed. "If only there'd been such schools when *he* was a boy."

Madame Sackville-Smack set Mugsy down on his feet and patted his head.

"P-please, m-madame," Cody said. His voice squeaked as if he was still a rat. "Can't we go home? You saw the kind of stuff Farley does. Can't you send us back to our parents?"

"Gracious, no," Madame Sackville-Smack crooned. "It's sweet of you to miss your parents. But we're not done reforming you. Oh no, mercy, no, you can't go home." She looked over at Farley, "Even if my son is a nincompoop."

Farley stuck out his lower lip. "I am *not* a nincompoop! It's all Cody's fault!"

Then, he spied the Recipronator in Cody's hands. "Give me that!"

Cody pulled it back. "No way. I'm not gonna let you swap me again!"

Farley yanked harder. "It's mine, you little cretin!"

"Boys," Madame Sackville-Smack said in a warning voice. "Stop bickering."

"But it's mine," Farley wailed, lunging for the Recipronator. "He stole it!"

"That's because you used it to steal our brains," Cody shouted.

"Give it BACK," Farley growled, straining to pull it from Cody's hands.

Rasputin squeaked in terror. The Recipronator slipped out of Cody's grip and revolved in the air.

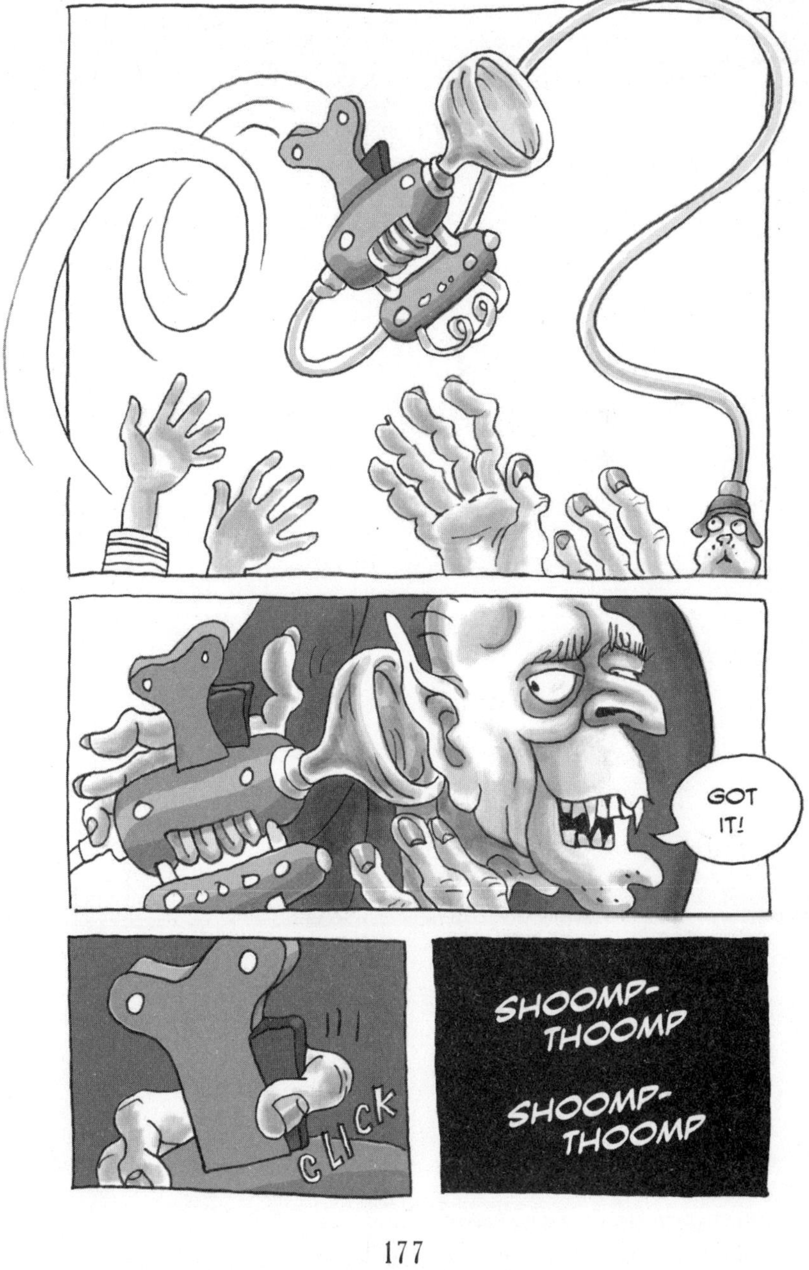
GOT IT!
CLICK
SHOOMP-THOOMP
SHOOMP-THOOMP

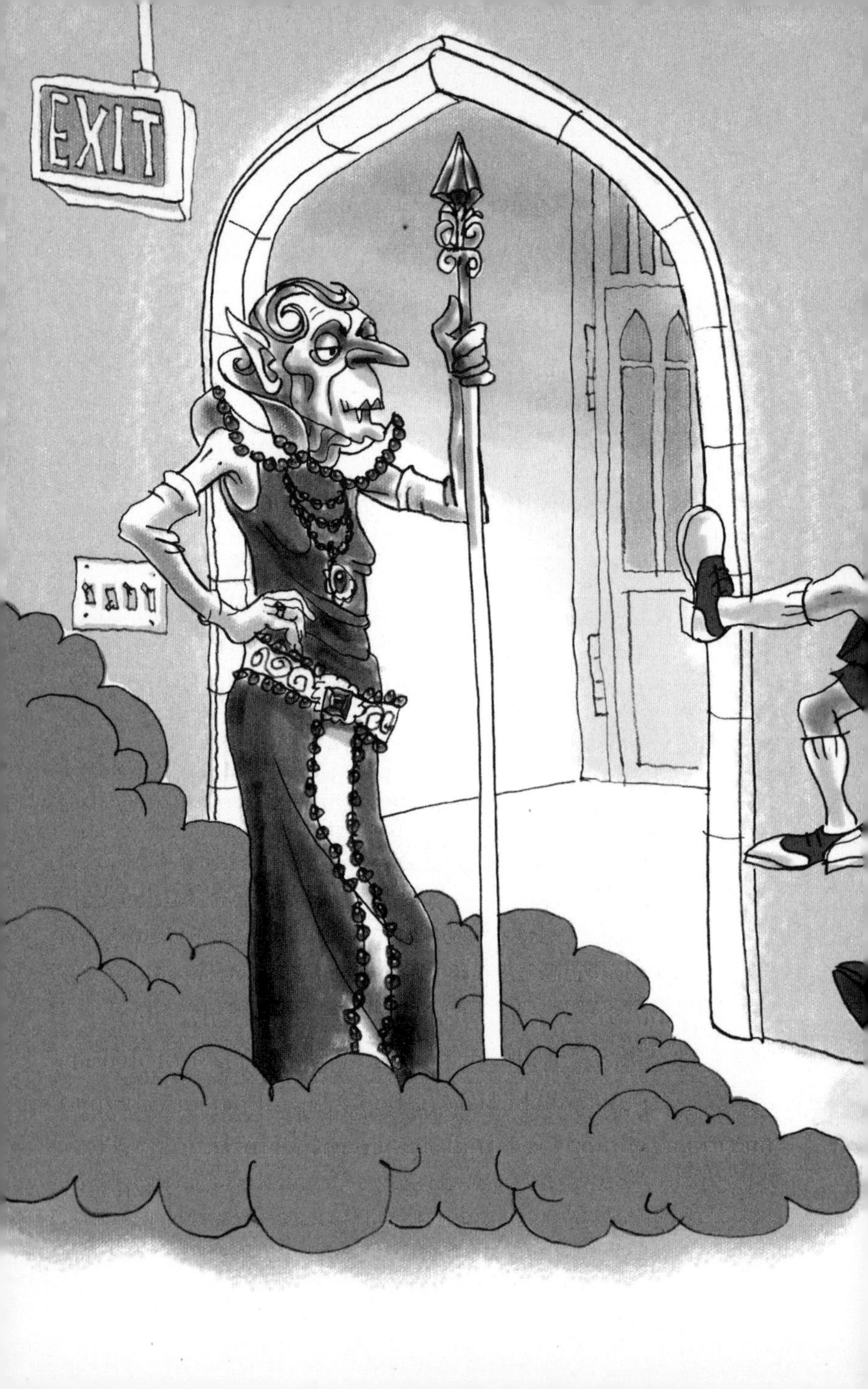
EXIT

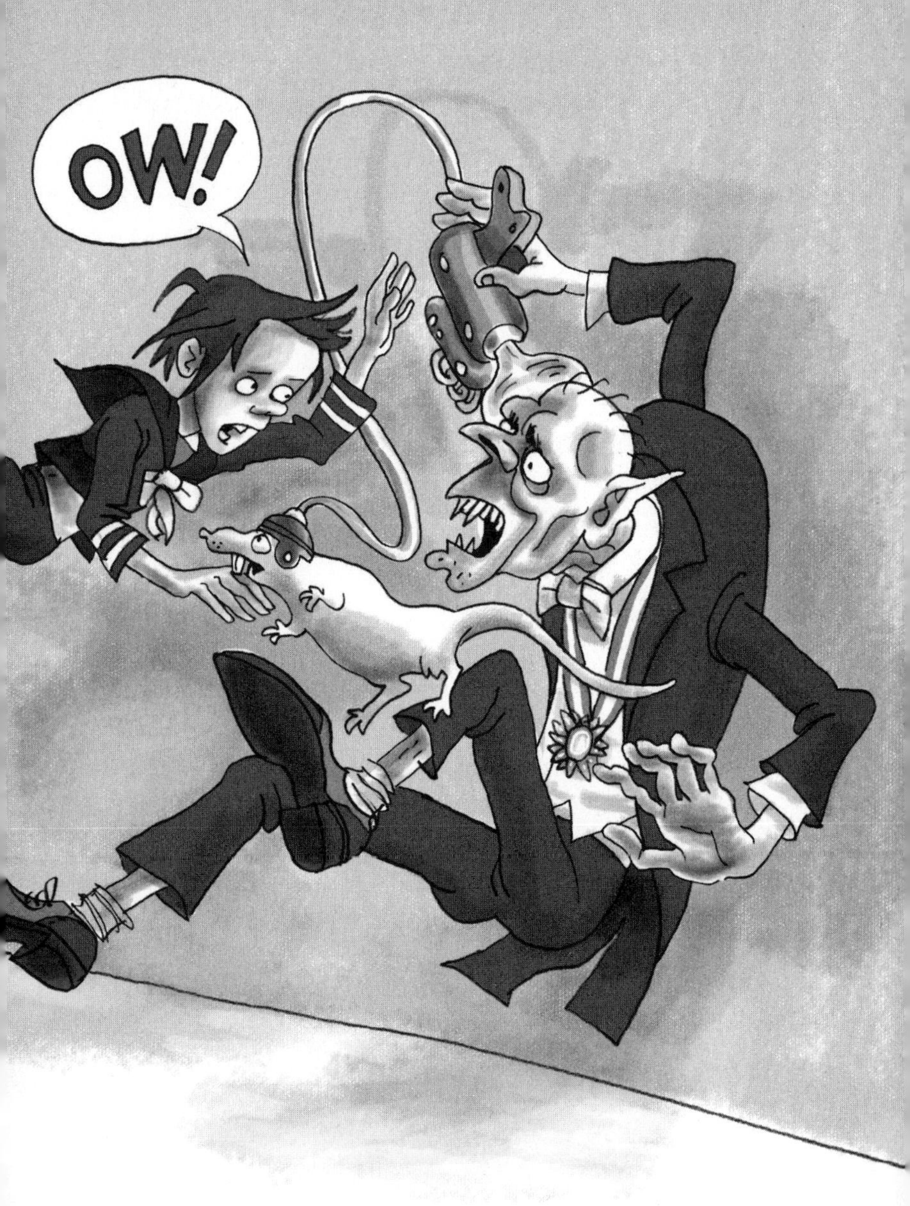
OW!

"Cease this tomfoolery, Archibald!" Madame Sackville-Smack snapped. "Now, march!"

Farley's face softened into a pleasant smile. Without a word, he marched back to where the other teachers stood, like an obedient soldier. Rasputin, still connected to the Recipronator, yanked his helmet off and scampered down from Farley's shoulder.

Madame Sackville-Smack approached the monster teachers. She glared at them with her evil eye until their knees knocked together. The monsters howled and moaned, except for Farley, who just smiled a vacant smile.

"You will each be punished for threatening innocent boys," Madame Sackville-Smack said.

"They weren't innocent!" Bilgewater wailed. "They were never innocent!"

The other monsters fell to their knees.

"Please, madame," Miss Threadbare screeched. "Farley made us do it. *He* wanted to eat Cody Mack. We tried to stop him!" The other monsters nodded frantically.

"Hmmm." Madame Sackville-Smack fingered her amulet. "This is an important point. If I punish you, then who will run the academy?"

"Why, how about us?" Fronk the Frankenstein said. "We practically do it now, anyway. Farley spends all his time in his laboratory, thinking up new ways to, um, be evil." He attempted a hearty laugh but it came off sounding about as lighthearted as a cement truck. "Somebody's got to take care of things while he's so busy. That's us!"

"Take care of things? That's what we do best!" Octopus Bilgewater gurgled.

Madame Sackville-Smack stroked the stray whiskers on her chin. "Why should I belive you?" she said. "Can I *trust* you to run the academy?"

The teachers all nodded furiously.

"You betcha!"

"We promise!"

"We're more trustworthy than . . . something that's really trustworthy!"

"If you fail," she said, "don't think for one minute that I won't find out. And, if you fail, have no doubt. I will come for you. Very well. And now to business." She flicked a finger toward her son. Farley's body hovered in the air. Magical chains bound him fast. "This one's going to time-out. A few years down there should set him straight. To the crypt with you, son!" She shook her head. "You always were a disappointment, Archie."

Rasputin scampered off with a terrified squeak.

Lady Desdemona Sackville-Smack turned her gaze upon the other teachers. "The rest of you, be off! Hunt while the moon keeps her eye upon you, and in the morning, back to your posts! *Remember!*"

The ground lurched once more as if a massive earthquake had struck. The boys toppled. Chunks of plaster fell from the ceiling. A yawning chasm opened in the ground, and Farley's chained body descended into the pit.

With a colossal groan, the hole closed. The floor looked as if it had never ripped in two.

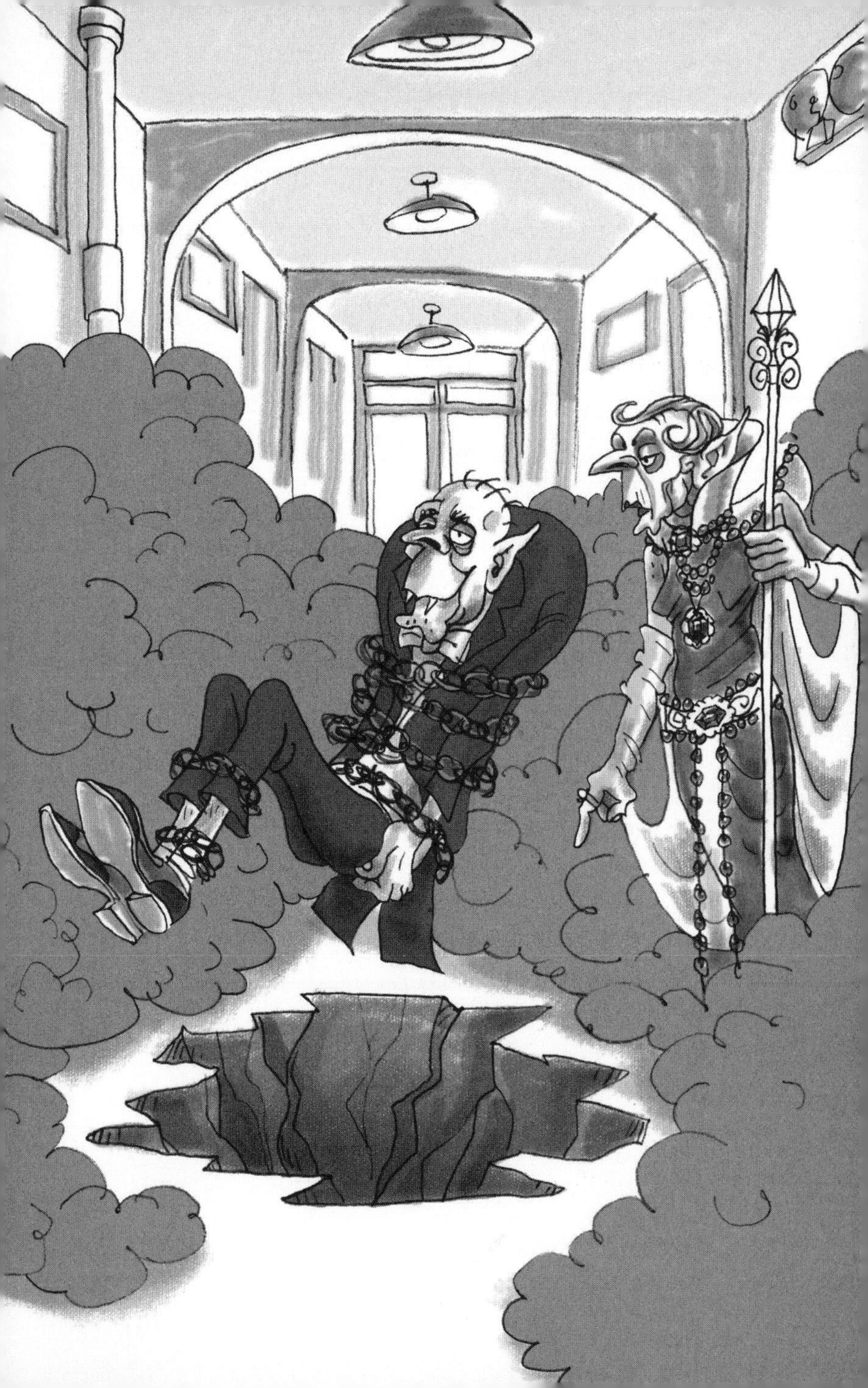

When the boys rose once more, Madame Sackville-Smack was gone. The Splurch Academy faculty's hunting cries echoed across the dark lawns.

The Grand Inquisitrix's servant pushed her empty wheelchair out the door, her pug dog perched on the seat cushion.

Cody looked at his friends. They stared back at him.

"Everybody got their brain back okay?" he said, finally.

They nodded.

He picked up the Recipronator and swung it against the stone wall. It crashed into a thousand pieces.

CHAPTER EIGHTEEN

THE END?

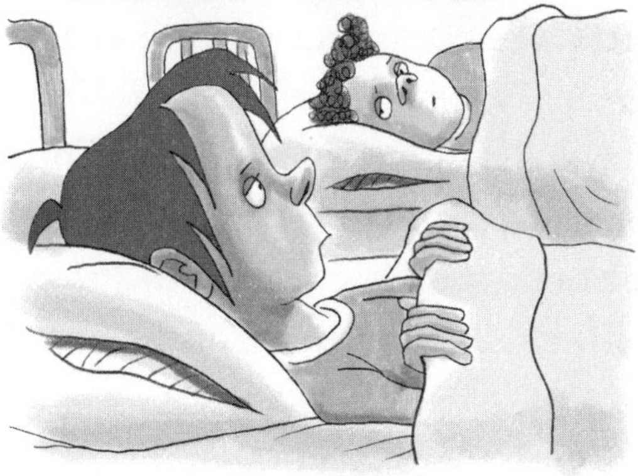

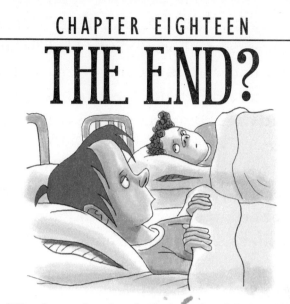

The boys lay in their bunks. Nobody said much.

The moon shone through the dormitory windows.

Outside, a wolf howled.

"I don't get it," Ratface said at last. "Did we win or did we lose?"

"We got our brains back," Cody said. "Would you rather still be a rat?"

"I dunno," Ratface said, scratching behind his ears. "It felt kinda natural. For me."

"We got rid of Farley," Carlos said.

"That's gotta be worth something."

"I want to go home!" Sully said. He hid his face under his pillow.

"Aw, what difference does it make?" Victor growled, punching his mattress. "What's the big deal about home, anyway?"

"Guys, listen," Mugsy said. "Tomorrow our parents will get us, for sure. That hocus-pocus Farley's mom did can't last. They'll wake up tomorrow and come to their senses."

"Doubt it," Sully said.

"Look at the bright side," Carlos said. "Farley's gone. We've got opposable thumbs again. Maybe things will get a lot better."

"*Ri-ight*," Mugsy said. "Just like maybe the classes'll get fun, and the food way better, and they'll buy us a huge entertainment system . . ."

"So, what'll happen now?" Ratface asked. "Who'll be in charge?"

"What I want to know is, is Farley really gone?" Victor said.

"And, do you think he could ever come back?" Sully added.

There was quiet in the dorms while they thought about *that*.

Cody rolled over in his bunk. "Let's get some sleep," he said. "I don't want to think about anything else tonight."

The boys' breathing drifted off to sleep. Cody lay awake thinking, until he, too, slept.

At midnight, Cody sat bolt upright. Something troubled him. A dream? Some sense of unfinished business? He groped in his mind for the answer.

It was something important. Urgent! Something he'd forgotten that changed everything. But what was it?

Nothing came. He lay back down.

Moonlight flickered through the dirty, old windows. Wind rattled the panes. Beams creaked, stones groaned. Splurch Academy felt alive, and restless.

Like the building itself was watching him.

Oh, for Pete's sake, Cody told himself. *You spend too much time here, you start imagining things. Go back to sleep.*

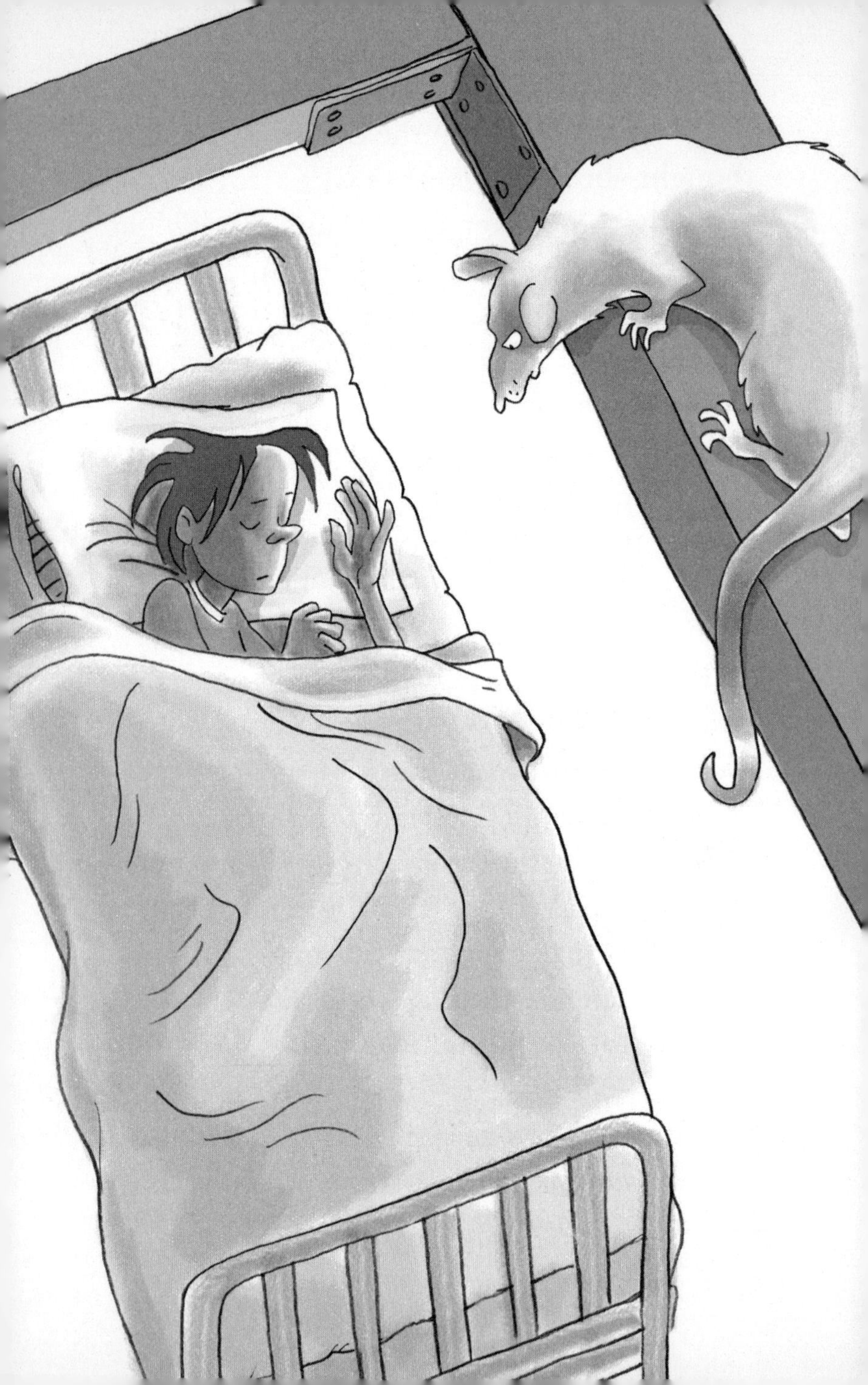

Available now:

SPLURCH ACADEMY
FOR DISRUPTIVE BOYS

#2 CURSE OF THE BIZARRO BEETLE

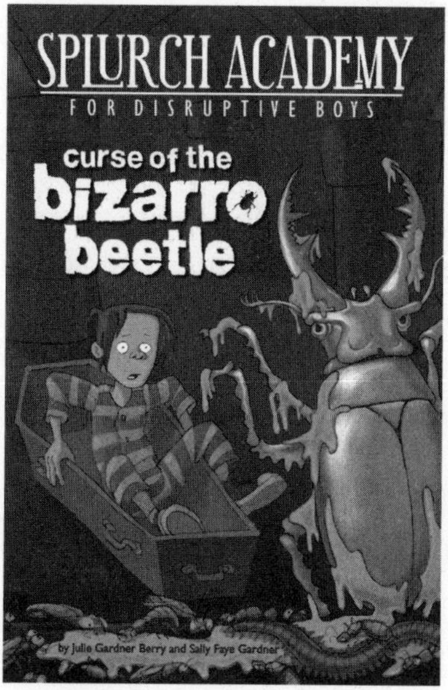
SPLURCH ACADEMY
FOR DISRUPTIVE BOYS
curse of the
bizarro
beetle
by Julie Gardner Berry and Sally Faye Gardner

CHAPTER ONE

THE COFFIN

A crescent moon hung low over the topmost towers of Splurch Academy. Across the windswept grounds, wolves howled and night birds moaned.

Inside the school, all was dark. Dozens of boys slept uncomfortably on their straw-filled mats stacked in bunks against the walls of the gloomy dormitories, dreaming of ice cream and swimming pools and life the way it was before they were sent to this nightmare school.

Cody Mack was one of them. But he wasn't alone.

Someone tapped his shoulder.

He sat up in his bunk, rubbing his eyes. He couldn't see anybody in the dark dormitory. But someone, he knew, was there.

A flash of lightning lit the room for an instant.

It was Headmaster Farley.

He lit a candle and gestured for Cody to follow. They walked down a dim corridor to an ancient elevator. Cody wanted to resist, to fight, to turn and run from his enemy, but some force prevented him. He had to do what Farley said.

The elevator began to descend. Second floor. First floor. Dungeon. Down, down, down it plunged, growing faster by the second. It opened into a room lit by a single torch. Inside were . . . coffins! Cody lifted their lids and found them full of dirt and old bones. He shuddered. Dr. Farley pointed to another coffin and, reluctantly, Cody threw back the lid.

Inside the coffin lay . . . Dr. Farley!

Cody took a step back. There were two of them! The Farley in the coffin looked asleep. His teeth gleamed in the candlelight. Clutched in his long fingers was a strange device that Cody knew all too well—the *Rebellio-Rodent Recipronator*, Farley's evil brain-swapping invention.

"But we broke the Recipronator!" Cody yelled. "We smashed it to smithereens!"

And that was true. But here was Farley—two Farleys—and a perfectly whole Recipronator. *Not good.*

Something moved near the sleeping Farley's shoulder. It was Rasputin, Farley's old pet rat. He scampered over to Cody and handed him a chunk of cheese.

"Thanks, Rasputin, old pal," Cody said, taking a big bite of cheese. Dee-licious.

The Farley in the coffin opened his eyes, and sat up. Both Farleys seized Cody and pinned the Recipronator nozzle against his ear, attaching the other nozzle to Vampire Farley's ear. A third nozzle appeared, attached to a helmet on Rasputin's little rat head. *Wait, there's not supposed to be three of them*, Cody thought.

They were going to suck his brain out one more time! Only instead of swapping him with a rat, they were going to swap him with . . . Farley? *And* Rasputin?

"Nooooo!" Cody screamed. He kicked and fought and thrashed.

The Farleys threw back their heads and laughed.

And then—they pulled the trigger.

CHAPTER TWO
THE RAID

Cody's eyes opened. It was dark. Pitch-dark. No torch, no candle.

And no Farley.

It was only a dream. He watched, weeks ago, when Madame Desdemona Sackville-Smack banished Farley to a crypt deep under the school. The ground opened up like an earthquake!

The dream faded. Rasputin, who had once had Cody's brain in his skull, was curled up on his pillow, warm and comforting. He'd been hanging around ever since Farley got banished. It was nice having a pet. Especially in a spooky, creepy place like this.

He closed his eyes and went back to sleep.

The next morning before the breakfast bell, Cody and his classmates tiptoed down the dark stairs leading to the cafeteria.

"This way," Ratface whispered. "We're almost there."

"Are you sure this is going to work?" Mugsy asked. "There had better be some good eats."

"Trust me," Ratface said. "I do this a lot. The pantry's loaded."

"If it isn't," Victor said, "I'm gonna bust your head."

"If Pavlov or Ivanov catch us stealing," Sully said, "the teachers will use our heads for bowling balls."

"This isn't stealing," Mugsy said. "It's survival. They're *supposed* to feed us. Real food, not cockroach Raisin Bran."

"So, Cody," Carlos said, "what're you gonna be for Halloween?"

"I already told you, Carlos," Sully said. "Halloween doesn't happen at Splurch Academy. Not for us. Forget it."

"Yeah, but *if* it did," Carlos said. "What would you dress up as?"

"A kid stuck in a prison school, I guess," Cody said. "I've already got the costume."

"I'm serious!" Carlos said. "Last year,

I was Lord Galactitron."

"My granny made my costume," Mugsy said. "I was a supersize order of fries. I squirted myself all over with real ketchup."

"Gross!" Ratface said.

"Yeah, Granny wasn't happy about that."

They reached the kitchen door. Ratface twisted the doorknob, listened, then stuck an unbent paperclip into the lock and listened some more. There was a click, and the door swung open.

"Bingo," he said. "We're in. Come on!"

They switched on their flashlights.

"Welcome to the best thing about this lousy school," Ratface said. "Griselda's pantry." He threw open the door to a skinny room full of shelves. The shelves were stocked with dusty, cobwebby cans and bottles labeled "insta-gruel" and "fortified beet stew" and "dehydrated cabbage nuggets." But on the other wall were . . .

"Doughnuts!" Carlos whimpered. "Doughnuts!"

"Not just doughnuts," Cody said. "*Store-*

bought Doopy Doughnuts!" He ripped into a box.

"And look!" Mugsy said. "Look at all these bottles of ketchup! Aren't they beautiful?"

"You'd better not put ketchup on that doughnut, man," Victor said.

Mugsy was offended. "These have powdered sugar. I only put ketchup on *plain* doughnuts."

Cody stared at all the shelves. "There's squirty cheese," he said. "And Garlic Smackems and Choco-fluffcakes and Cheddar Puffballs and Taco Twistitos." He took his doughnut and smacked it all over his face so the powdered sugar stuck to his skin.

"Cody's gone off the deep end," Sully said.

Victor smacked his face with his doughnut. "I'm the Splurch Academy ghost!"

Mugsy smacked his face with his doughnut. "I'm a marshmallow pie!"

Ratface smacked his face with his doughnut. "I'm a pair of tighty-whities!"

Sully took a bite of his doughnut. "One

of your *new* pairs, you mean."

Mugsy inhaled his doughnut. "I'm coming here every night from now on. To get a real meal."

Click.

"What was that?" Ratface whispered. "Everybody, hide!"

They ducked under the lowest pantry shelves.

"Only a moron wouldn't see us," Carlos whispered. They tried not to breathe.

The kitchen lights clicked on. Cody could see white shoes and thick, scaly ankles. Nurse Bilgewater! Acting as headmistress after Farley got banished to the crypt and, next to Farley, the creepiest grown-up at Splurch Academy.

"I smell thieves!" she cackled. "Grubby, stinking little boys with hands in the cookie jar!"

"Cookie jar?" Mugsy whispered. "I didn't see any—"

"Can it!" Victor hissed.

Nurse Bilgewater wrenched the pantry door open. "Aha!"

"I've been telling you, something's been stealing my food, Beulah," said Griselda, standing behind her. "You kept saying it was rats."

Nurse Bilgewater grabbed Cody by the collar. "Once a rat, always a rat," she said. "What's this on your face?"

She dabbed at Cody's face with one finger, then wiped it off on her uniform like it was hazardous waste. She sniffed the air. Her nostrils were huge.

Without warning, she wrenched Cody's mouth open and grabbed his tongue.

"Aaagggh!" Cody gagged.

"Do you see the contagious white boils all over their tongues?" Nurse Bilgewater said. "Their pale, ashy faces?"

Cody spit on the ground over and over. Bilgewater had touched his tongue! Infinite and eternal disgustingness!

"Looks like powdered sug—"

"Just as I feared," Nurse Bilgewater said. "These boys have a bad case of splagged gaskers."

Acknowledgments

Several highly disruptive people ooched
this project along, and we feel they
at least deserve a poke in the nose for it.

Alyssa Eisner Henkin first told us to
give it a whirl. Tim Wynne-Jones, Brent
Hartinger, Sergio Ruzzier, Joan Hilty, and
Jen Camper endured early drafts and art.
Rob Valois and Christina Quintero made
Splurch even Splurchier. Our great big
family and certain goofy friends fed us a
steady stream of both encouragement and
subject matter. Louise Sloan, Jennie
Livingston, Ginger Johnson, Jayme Lynes,
Hilary Lorenz, and Phil Berry, we mean
you. Our intrepid sister, Joanna Gardner,
came to Cody's rescue and saved our skins
as well. And our lying little sneak of a
mother, Shirley Gardner, who never
could resist a naughty critter, deserves any
embarrassment this project merits.

About the Authors

Sally Faye Gardner and Julie Gardner Berry are sisters, both originally from upstate New York. Sally, who now lives in New York City with a smallish black dog named Dottie, has, at various times, worked as a gas pumper, janitor, sign painter, meeting attendee, and e-mail sender. Julie, who now lives near Boston with her husband, four smallish sons, and tiger cat named Coco, has worked as a restaurant busboy, volleyball referee, cleaning lady, and seller of tight leather pants. Today she, too, attends meetings and sends e-mail. Julie is the author of *The Amaranth Enchantment* and *Secondhand Charm*, while this is Sally's first book.